The Vault of Kings

A Light in the Darkness

Book 1 in the Vault of Kings series

Matt Taylor

ISBN: 979-8-3492-4666-1

Illustrated By: Blake Davis
www.blakedart.com

Dedication

To my family and friends, for always believing in me.

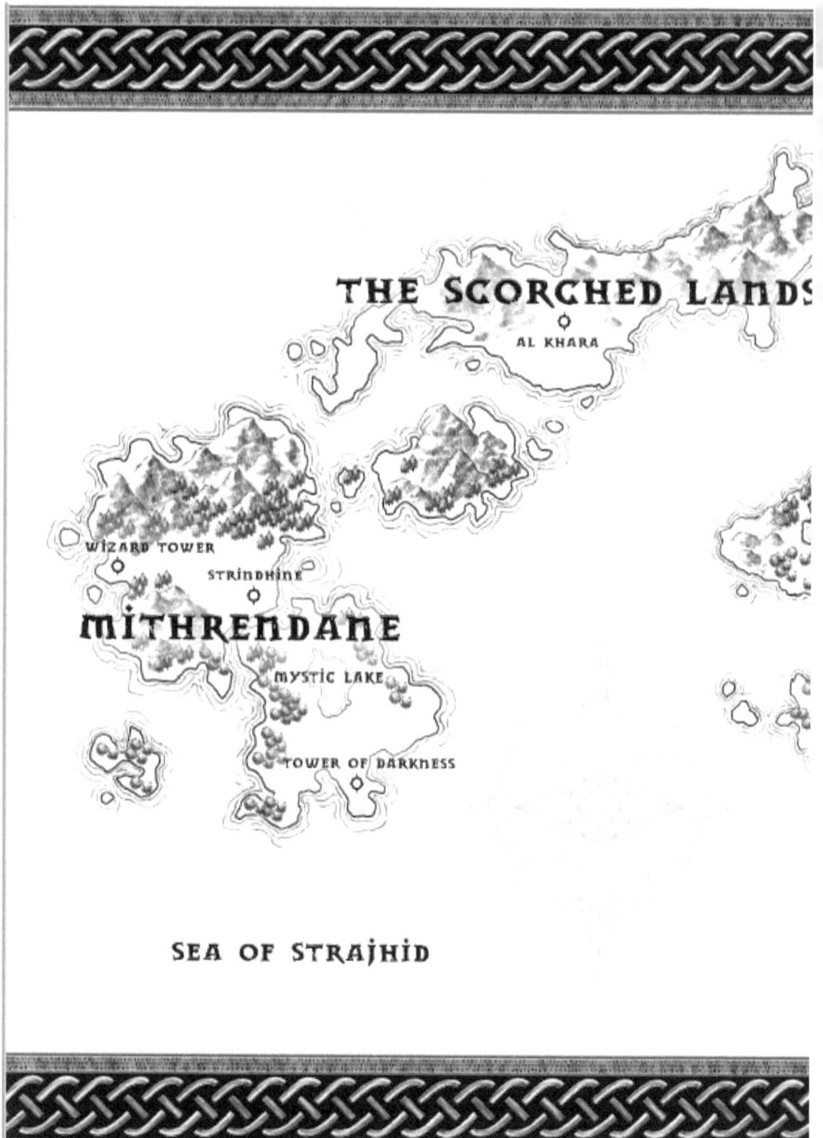

THE SCORCHED LANDS
AL KHARA
WIZARD TOWER
STRINDHINE
MITHRENDANE
MYSTIC LAKE
TOWER OF DARKNESS
SEA OF STRAJHID

NORTHERN SEA
AZRINDAL
AZUL
NORTHRINDE
KANDARIN MOUNTAINS
LAKETOWN
LAKE CRYSTALMERE
WYGRINDE
FROSTWIND BAY
EVENDREIL
GELENDOR
WINIJRITH
MERCHANT SEA
WHISPERING HILLS
LAKE OF TERROR
DUNWYR
TRINDJHIM
JHAST
FHAZID

CONTENTS

	Prologue	1
1	Desperate Times	5
2	The Ancient Crypt	24
3	The Council	44
4	The Second Mind	63
5	Lessons of Light	91
6	A Warning to Shilvrst	118
7	Dark Visions	135
8	Confrontations	163
9	Sky	190
10	Gelendor	219
11	Enchantments	250
12	Army of the Dead	282
13	Sindmyr	317

PROLOGUE

The lantern of souls glowed softly as it sat upon the desk in front of him. A gentle wail escaped as he tapped a finger against its smooth glass. Bright wispy lights swam slowly up and down their eternal cage, waiting for their release, begging to be used so that they could finally rest.

Maelos stood, turning away from one of the greatest creations he had ever made. They would get their chance... soon enough. Preparations would come to a close swiftly now that this final discovery had been made. Who knew that such awesome power could come from one element? Even if it was the most powerful element of them all.

He turned, looking towards the lantern of souls once more. If only he had found a way... A way to bring them back... Perhaps he would be a different person if he could just see them all again, tell them how sorry he was for all that he had done. It didn't matter now though; he had gone too far. He had waded into waters that were unforgivable.

Maelos shook the thoughts of weakness from his mind. He then walked towards a map hanging on the far wall of his quarters.

Gelendor, Winjjrith, and Sindmyr… The last standing cities that he had yet to conquer. Then Evendreil, and the entire world would truly be his. It angered him that they had not already fallen, but the capitals of Air, Nature, and especially Light had proven to be mighty foes.

He scanned the other continents stretched across the map. They had all fallen to his might, just as the last of the elemental capitals of Evendreil would in due time. His eyes then wandered towards Mithrendane.

Maelos stretched a hand towards the map and gently touched his finger to the depiction of Mystic Lake. The Darkness that swirled constantly within him like a raging whirlwind of raw, destructive power, softened for a moment. His mind went back to years past, of memories sweet, and companions unforgettable. Emotions swirled within him as his eyes slowly closed.

Taking in a breath of air, he forced the memories back into their hiding place. Deep, deep within the recesses of his mind, where they wouldn't cause him trouble.

Footsteps behind him helped to rid himself of the memories as well.

"My lord, the elites have returned from the Whispering Hills."

"And their report?" Maelos said without turning to look at the man.

"They… they were unsuccessful, my lord. Several of them perished in the attempt to find it. They said it was a miracle that any of them even made it back-"

"Captain," Maelos said, cutting the man off.

The man swallowed, "Y-yes, my lord?"

"The one and only chance for finding the Vault of Kings, for accomplishing our goals, is somewhere in those hills. It's not an overly expansive area. I'm having a hard time understanding what the problem is."

"M-my lord," the captain said shakily. "The creatures that wander those hills… they are quite fearsome-"

Maelos spun around, creating the symbol of Darkness with his hands. His eyes and hands started to glow with a deep purple, almost black glow. He held one hand outstretched towards the man as a shadowy purple mist began to flow around him.

"No! My lord, please!"

"Silence! You know not fearsome! Not until you have seen what I have… There is nothing in this world that can compare to the terror that lives where only I have walked."

The memories of Mithrendane returned, surging to the forefront of his mind. A spark of living flame almost seemed to float in front of him as his rage peaked. Tears filled his eyes, but he shoved them down, angrily banishing them back to the depths of his mind.

The purple mist swirled around the man and gently started lifting him in the air.

"Please! I will have them return. I'll personally accompany them! We won't fail you again!"

"No. You won't," Maelos replied. "Because I have a new use for your soul… in the front lines."

The man's eyes widened, a look of sheer terror spreading across his face.

"N… n… no- pl-ease," the man stammered, his fear so great that the words could hardly form.

Maelos squeezed his outstretched hand and pulled his fist in towards his body. The man let out a scream of terror that slowly faded as the light of his eyes dimmed. A bright white, wispy light slowly exited his chest. After the light had escaped his body completely, his lifeless corpse fell to the ground.

Maelos then pushed his closed fist outward and pointed towards the lantern of souls on the table in front of him. The wispy light floated gently towards the lantern, before being violently sucked in at the very last second.

The lantern glowed brighter as the soul entered into its grasp, its never-ending hunger satiated for a small moment.

"Welcome to the ranks, captain."

CHAPTER 1
DESPERATE TIMES

"What do you mean, potatoes are only five copper a sack?" Thren exclaimed. "Last year, it was fifteen a sack!"

"I'm sorry, Thren, that's the best that I can do. You're not the only one that's struggling, you know," the merchant Brandt replied.

Brandt was a tall, heavyset man with a thick black beard and deep brown eyes. He wore a pair of brown overalls and a long sleeve tan button-up shirt with his sleeves rolled up to the forearm.

"I need to make a living too. With things the way they are, I'll barely break even as it is. I know it isn't much, but it's all that I can offer."

Thren frowned. "I don't know if I'm going to have enough to make it through this winter if we don't get more… please, you have to make an exception!"

Brandt frowned, tapping his fingers on the wooden table in front of him, "I'm sorry, it's really the best I can do."

"Fine. I guess I'll take what I can get," Thren growled under his breath.

"I truly am sorry," Brandt said as he counted out the copper pieces. "One hundred and three small sacks, is that correct?"

"Yeah, that's right," Thren said with a sigh. "We lost a lot of crops this year. This was all I could manage to scrounge up."

Brandt finished counting out the copper coins and slid them across the wooden table. "Five hundred and fifteen is our total then. Five gold pieces and fifteen copper. Is that alright?"

Thren looked at the measly amount of money that sat on the table, mocking his year of hard work with their slight metallic shine.

"Yes," he finally said, scooping the coins off the table. The coins struck one another with a jingling sound as he placed them inside his pouch. A 'thank you' was all that he was able to mutter, wondering how he was going to break the bad news to his family. Brandt walked around to the other side of the table and put a hand on Thren's shoulder.

"I'm sorry, my friend. I wish that there was more that I could do, I really do. Maybe if I can get some good bargains when I'm in Trindjhim, I can come back and give you a bit more? Or perhaps trade-"

"No!" Thren spat, cutting him off. "No, it's okay…" he said, more softly this time. "You need to take care of your family too. I appreciate the offer, but we'll be okay. We'll figure something out."

Brandt gave Thren a pat on the shoulder. "Good luck, my friend." Brandt slowly returned to his side of the table, his eyes cast downward in shame.

Thren lingered for a moment, wanting to say something, anything that might get him more. Ultimately, his pride wouldn't allow himself to beg, so he turned around and left the trading tent. Grabbing his cart, he pulled his years' work towards a pile of goods that had already been traded off. He unloaded the sacks of potatoes one by one from his cart with a sigh. Leaving the market square, he passed several other people that were waiting in line, ready to sell what little produce they had been able to harvest. Their faces drooped with lost hope. From what Thren saw, he wasn't the only one that would be unsuccessful in the trades this year.

What am I going to tell Iriana? He thought to himself. The empty cart at his back somehow felt heavier now than it had before. *How are we going to survive this winter when all I have is five gold and fifteen copper?* He kicked a pebble out of the way in frustration. *Curse you, Maelos... Curse you!*

****

Sylas was sitting on an upside-down barrel just outside the front door of his family's house. Wood shavings fell gently to the ground as he whittled away at a stick with his knife. He was trying to carve an owl for his younger sister, but so far it looked more like a beaver or a mole than an owl.

Sylas had just turned fourteen. He still wasn't quite old enough to go with his father to the merchant trade, so he waited eagerly for him to return. He worried about what might happen this year. He'd heard from some friends that recent trades had been harsh. They had also lost a bunch of crops… which could mean bad news.

His thoughts were broken by the sound of footsteps. Sylas raised his eyes to see his father dropping off his empty cart and slowly making his way towards the house.

"Hey, Dad. How did it go?"

Looking at his son, all Thren was able to mutter was "Hey, bud" and gave Sylas a quick smile.

Sylas dropped his knife and owl that he had been carving and opened the door for his father. It crushed his heart to see him this way. He was a fighter, not a farmer! He used to be in the King of Shilvrst's royal guard before Maelos had taken over and put everyone under his rule. Sure, Shilvrst was really too small to have a king in the first place, but the royal guard was the real deal. His father didn't know much about the ancient art of Elemental Magick, but could hold his own better than almost anyone when it came to physical combat. After Maelos had taken over, it had reduced almost everyone in the town to simple farmers, including him.

"Dad's back," Sylas called out as he stepped into the door, trying to lighten the mood.

His Mother, Iriana, responded cheerfully as she descended the stairs. She was a short, skinny woman with almost white, blonde hair and light blue eyes. She always had a kind smile on her face, even if the world was falling apart around her.

"Hey Thren, how was it?" She asked hopefully.

Thren looked at her and then at Sylas before responding.

"Hey buddy, can you go find your sister and play with her outside for just a little bit? There are some things that I need to discuss with your mom."

His dad's words made a pit grow in Sylas's stomach. He did his best to keep his expression neutral as a plan began to form in his mind.

"Yeah, I can do that. Where is she?"

"I'm right here!" Arelia said, skipping up behind Sylas.

Arelia was ten years old and looked very much like Iriana. She had the same blue eyes and the same almost white, blonde hair. Even her personality was similar. She always seemed to be happy, even when days like this came around.

"Alright, Arelia, let's go outside. Come on, I'll show you the owl I've been carving."

"Yay!" she said, skipping her way to the door. After they were outside, Sylas picked up his owl from the ground and gave it to Arelia.

Sylas handed her his creation and her face twisted as though she had eaten something sour.

"This doesn't look like an owl at all…"

Sylas ignored the insult as he put away his knife. "Just, stay here for just a minute. I'll be right back."

"Hey! You were supposed to play with me!" She complained.

"I will- just give me a second," he shot back. "I just have to see something really quick, then I'll play with you."

Arelia gave him a doubtful look as he ran to the other side of the house and pressed his ear against the outside wall of his parent's room. He had done this many times before; his parents always talked about private matters in their room.

“I can’t believe he only offered you five copper per sack… how does he expect us to be able to survive this winter with so little?”

“I know. It seemed like he had no choice. Things are just bad everywhere.”

“I don’t know what we’re going to do, Thren. That’s only a third of what we were offered last year, and we had twice as much crop then too!”

Sylas heard his mom begin to cry, and he pulled away from the wall. *This isn’t good at all… We barely had enough food for everyone last winter, and that was with having leftover potatoes at almost every meal...*

“Sylas! Quit spying! You said you would play with me!” Arelia said, stomping around the corner.

“Okay, okay!” He said turning away from the wall. He led his sister away from the house, but his mind was elsewhere, desperately trying to think of something, anything that he could do to help his family.

****

That night, Sylas couldn’t sleep. He kept on thinking of the events that had happened just over ten years ago. He was only four at the time, but he still remembered parts of it very vividly.

Maelos, ‘The Dark Mage’ as most called him. He was said to be the most powerful user of Darkness Magick that had ever lived, besides the Original Kings of course. He had amassed an army of followers and overthrew the king of his own city, the capital of Darkness called Azrindal. He then moved to the northern continents of Northrinde and the Scorched Lands, forcing the knees of the people there to bend at his power. After that, he continued the battle across all of Evendreil with the goal of becoming the ultimate ruler of the entire world.

Unfortunately, Shilvrst was an easy target, and his town had also fallen to the tyrant. His father and the armies of the king of Shilvrst tried to stop Maelos, but his power was overwhelming. His mastery over the ancient elemental power of Darkness was terrifying. With it, he had easily taken over the small, yet growing town of Shilvrst, bringing its inhabitants to their knees and killing the king in the process.

Sylas shivered in bed as he remembered the vivid memory of actually seeing him in the flesh. He had been on the top floor of one of the town buildings when it all happened. He couldn't remember why he was there but remembered his mother telling him to get away from the window and not to look. He wished he had listened… The image of Maelos wearing black robes with a long hood that covered his head still haunted him at times. Although the hood made it difficult to see his face, Sylas remembered being able to see dark glowing eyes emanating from within his hood. His hands were glowing the same eerie purple color as he used Darkness to wreak havoc over the town.

It sent another tingle up his spine just thinking about it. After Maelos had killed the king and forced the armies of Shilvrst to surrender, he declared himself as the supreme ruler over all of Evendreil and placed a hefty tax over the people. He placed guards around all the major cities he had conquered so that no one could enter or leave without permission.

Sylas turned over in his bed as he tried to shake the memory from his mind. Forcing himself to change the subject, he thought about his most recent problem. *I need to do something to help my family survive the winter... but what?* He pondered the question for a moment longer, then the thought of the old crypt just outside of the town slithered into his mind.

He and his friends had already been there once before, it took some thinking and a cunning plan to distract the guards, but ultimately, they weren't caught. Memories of ancient artifacts, old trinkets, and other strange, lost, and forgotten objects of unknown worth filled his mind. A plan started slowly brewing in his mind at the memory. With the travelling merchants still in town for a few more days, there was a chance that he might be able to sell some of the more intact objects of the old crypt to one of them before they left.

Liking the idea, he decided that in the morning he would find Samara and Torren. They'd think it was a good idea too and go with him.

I'm sure that if we do find something of value, their families could use a little extra money too, he thought. And with that, he again tried to fall asleep without thinking of the soul penetrating image of Maelos.

****

He awoke the next morning a bit tired but determined. After completing his morning chores and eating one of the eggs that he had gathered from their chickens, Sylas asked his mother if he could go out, and assured her that he would be home in time for dinner. She agreed but didn't really seem to hear him. He could tell that the financial trouble that they were in weighed heavily on her mind.

I'll find something that will help us mother, I promise. With determination, he left his home and headed towards his best friend Torren's house.

He, Torren, and Samara had gone to the Ancient Crypt before. It had been Torren's idea. "What's the worst that could happen?" He remembered Torren saying. "They catch us and tell us to go home?"

He also remembered Samara telling them that being told to go home was definitely *not* the worst thing that could happen. She had heard stories of some kids who were caught trying to leave the town without permission and were flogged several times.

We'll make sure to be careful... Sylas thought to himself. His train of thought was then broken by a familiar voice.

"Sylas! What's going on, brother?" Torren said, walking towards him.

"Hey, Torren! What's up?"

Torren stretched his long arms upwards into the air as he yawned. His muscular arms caught the eyes of a group of girls their age walking past on the way to do their morning chores, sending them into a giggle fest. Torren laid the icing on the cake with a wink which sent them running away blushing.

Sylas watched the girls run away, trying to keep from letting his jealousy get the better of him. If there was *one* person he wished he could compete with when it came to catching the female eye, it was *definitely* his best friend.

Torren's father had been in the king's guard at the same time as Sylas's father. He might have even been his trainer at one point… Sylas couldn't remember. The two had become good friends and the friendship was passed down from fathers to sons. Torren and Sylas found themselves doing almost everything together.

"Yeah, I'm alright," Torren said with a smug smile, running a hand through his long hair. "Brandt ripped my father off at the trade yesterday though, and now we're worried about having enough money to get through this winter."

"Yeah," Sylas replied. "The same thing happened to my family too… That's why I wanted to come and see you. I have an idea about how we can make some more money for our families, to help them out."

Torren raised an eyebrow. "Oh yeah? And what is this *master* plan? I hope it's better than the plan you had that one time to spy on old man Uthren."

Sylas punched Torren in the arm.

"Hey, something is going on with that guy! I don't think he's just an old man like you say he is. Plus, how was I supposed to know that Samara would see that snake in the garden just as we were about to get into prime spying position?"

Torren rubbed his arm and laughed.

"Hey, take it easy. I'm only joking. All I'm saying is that you may need me to look over your plan and fine-tune it, or it might end in us having to repair a fence all summer long again. So, what is it?"

"We need to find Samara first, then I'll tell you," Sylas replied. "We have to keep it super-secret, so I want to wait until we're all together first."

Torren gave Sylas a wry smile, "Yep…I knew you liked her…"

Sylas punched him in the arm again, this time harder. "Shut up, no I don't!"

Torren grinned and cocked a taunting eyebrow, "Yeah okay, sure thing buddy… we can wait until we find Samara to, you know, just keep it more secret then." He finished his sentence with a wink, rubbing in the sarcasm that was already dripping from his words. Sylas wanted to hit him again but decided against it. Torren was a lot bigger than he was and didn't want to chance getting slugged back.

"Let's just go look for her," Sylas said, starting off in the direction of her house.

Torren gave a slight chuckle, put his hands in his pockets, and whistled a tune as he followed Sylas.

****

Samara cleared her mind and took in a deep breath.

"This time… this time for sure!" She said, looking at the illustration in her book one last time.

"Thumbs together, palms facing away from your body, index fingers together making a heart shape. Got it, now the rest of the fingers together at a diagonal, making a diamond shape at the top."

She closed her eyes, then reached deep, deeper than she had ever reached before. She could feel something this time- a small pool of energy deep within her core. Remembering the text of the book, she concentrated on bringing that pool of energy up into her arms. It tingled slightly as it rose from the middle of her stomach, through her arms and into her hands. A soft golden light met her gaze as she opened her eyes.

"I did it…" she said out loud, a smile forming on her face. The heart and diamond shapes that she made with her fingers glowed with a golden misty energy filling in where the air once was, the rest of her hands emanating a bright yellow aura. Ecstatic at her newfound success, she quickly looked at the book again to see what the next step was.

"Hey'a Samara!" a voice yelled out from behind her. Startled, Samara yelped and jumped forward, breaking the symbol she had made with her hands. The yellow light faded into the air as the tingling sensation slipped away. Spinning around to see the culprit of her distraction, her eyes met Torren and Sylas standing behind her.

"You idiot, Torren!" She yelled. "I was doing it! I had it that time!"

She stomped over to Torren, fists raised high ready to smack him. Torren quickly put up his hands in defense and took a few steps backward.

"Woah, woah! Hey, take it easy! I didn't do anything. What do you mean you were doing it? What were you even doing? It looked like you were just standing there."

She ignored his stream of questions and took several swings at him, which Torren easily parried aside. It was times like this that Torren was grateful that he had trained with his father in hand-to-hand combat ever since he was a little kid.

"Stop blocking me!" Samara angrily growled. "You broke my concentration. I finally conjured some Light Magick, then you ruined it!" She swung once more, aiming for his face, but Torren easily caught her hand in his.

"Wait, what?" He asked. "You mean you *actually* saw Light energy in your hands?"

"Yes!" She spat back at him. "And I was about to see if I could use it on that beetle over there!"

She pointed towards a book that sat on a table where she had been standing. A beetle that looked to have been accidentally stepped on laid on its back, moving its legs back and forth slowly as if trying to run away.

"I was going to heal him!"

Sylas walked over and examined the beetle more closely. Its attempt at escaping Samara's experiment didn't seem to be going very well. He then turned his attention towards the book on the table. It had definitely seen better days. Its leather cover was faded and cracking in places. Several pages also looked to be on the brink of falling out.

Sylas thumbed through several of the pages noticing that most of them had corners and edges that were torn or sections of words that were badly faded. Turning back to the page Samara was on, he looked at the diagram of the hands making a symbol of a heart and a diamond.

"Where did you get this, Samara?"

"I got it from old man Uthren a long time ago," she said, pulling her hand away from Torren. She walked over to Sylas and shut the book.

"He gave it to me as a gift after we fixed his fence last summer. He really is a nice guy if you just talk to him."

"What's the book about?" Torren asked.

"It looks like it's a book on Light Magick…" Sylas replied.

"Specifically," Samara said, swiping the book from his hands, "Light Magick and how to use it to heal."

"But why would old man Uthren have a book on Light Magick?" Torren asked, walking towards Samara. "I mean, he's just an old guy that tells a bunch of stories."

Samara sent him a look of disgust. "You know, you're really as dumb as you look."

Torren grinned, the insult not phasing him one bit.

"He used to be a great Light mage, so you know. He even tried to stand up to Maelos before he gained power over Evendreil."

"What? Nah, no way." Torren said, rolling his eyes.

"It's true! He was injured really bad during one of the battles, so he just doesn't do much anymore."

"Well if he's a great Light mage, why doesn't he just heal the injury?"

Samara twisted her face, "I don't know, Torren! Why don't *you* just go ask him? I believe what he says though. He told me a lot of stories of when he used to be in the Council of Light. He's done a lot of really cool things."

"That's awesome!" Sylas said to Samara, "I could definitely see that. I've always thought there was more to old man Uthren than meets the eye."

Torren looked at Sylas and gave him a wink and a little 'thumbs up' next to his hip. Sylas shot him a scowl but tried not to make it visible enough for Samara to see.

"Yeah, he's *way* more than just an old man," Samara continued. "I've learned a lot from him since last summer. And I *almost* had my first successful spell just a minute ago before you two showed up." She looked at Torren, giving him a death glare. He just shrugged his shoulders and gave a 'sorry but not really' look at her.

"Hey, Samara," Sylas continued. "I have an idea on how we could maybe make a little extra money for our families before winter. Did your family do well at the trade?"

Samara looked at the ground. "No, we didn't get much at all, actually. I don't like thinking about it." A doubtful expression crossed her face as she looked back up at Sylas. "So, what is this plan? It better not be something stupid."

Torren let a laugh escape his lips but quickly covered his mouth, faking a cough. Sylas glared at him then turned his attention back to Samara.

"It's not stupid, but we need to be sure that no one finds out about it. Let's go to the Black House, and I can explain."

The Black House was code for an old blacksmith shop that had gone abandoned ever since Maelos had taken over. It was their little place where they could get away from everyone and everything. It was on the side of town that had been almost completely burned to the ground by Maelos. In fact, the blacksmith shop was one of the only buildings that was still standing on that side of town, so not many people went over there.

They arrived at the blacksmith shop just as a cloud covered the sun, sending shadows dancing over the rubble that was spread across the ground. It really was a shame that none of them had seen this part of the town before Maelos had destroyed it. Remains of shops, places to eat, and other buildings that weren't intact enough to recognize their purpose lay scattered amongst the now deserted streets. They carefully entered the blacksmith shop, trying to avoid stepping on any hidden upturned nails, then lit the lone standing lantern that they had placed there when they had first discovered the building and shut the door.

"So, let's hear it," Torren started. "What's this amazing plan of yours?"

"Alright," Sylas explained. "I was thinking we could go visit the Ancient Crypt again-"

"You're joking, right?" Samara said, cutting him off. "We almost got caught last time! And I am NOT doing the distraction again!"

Torren and Sylas both laughed, the remembrance of what they had to do the last time they visited the crypt to distract the guards joyfully entering their minds. Samara was a gorgeous young woman, especially to Sylas. Her emerald-green eyes and dark brown hair packaged into her short, slim body hit all the right checkboxes for basically every boy in

Shilvrst. Sylas had convinced himself that there wasn't a girl alive more beautiful than she was.

Because of her good looks, the first time they went to the Ancient Crypt, they had Samara get into one of her swimming gowns and complain to the guards about not being able to go to the lake just outside the town. While she complained to them that it was 'so hot, she could barely even stand it,' they were able to sneak by. Funny enough, they actually let her through, and she was able to go to the crypt with the two of them.

"We won't make you do that again," Sylas replied with a smile. "Even though it was basically a flawless plan… No, this time, I have a *different* plan."

"Why do you even want to go in there again?" Torren asked. "And how is it going to help our families to get more money before winter comes?"

"You saw all of the old stuff that was down there," Sylas replied. "There has to be some stuff down there worth something to one of the merchants in town. We could see if we can trade it to one of them before they leave."

They all paused for a moment before Samara responded, "It does seem like a pretty good idea. There was a lot of really cool stuff down there last time we went. And some of it did look like it could be valuable."

Torren shrugged, "Meh, sounds fine to me, I guess. So, what do you propose we do this time instead of having Miss Sunshine over here flirt with the guards?"

Samara sent him a scowl but decided to say nothing.

"I was thinking about it last night... You know how the merchants are allowed to go in and out, basically as they please?"

Torren and Samara exchanged glances. "Yeah, so what?"

"So, what if we pretended to be merchants ourselves? Torren, you almost look like an adult you're so tall and broad. And Samara and I could hide in some barrels that we put in my dad's wagon. You could pull us right through!"

"Don't they check the contents of whatever you're carrying through? I mean, it would be stupid if they didn't," Samara responded doubtfully.

"I thought of that too. We have a bunch of old potatoes that went bad because we didn't have enough money to get fertilizer for all of the fields. We could get in the barrels, and then Torren could pour a bunch of the old rotten potatoes on top of us. They smell so bad that the guards wouldn't check very closely at all. Torren could say that he's taking them back to his hometown as pig slop or something."

"Eww, gross!" Samara complained, "I am *not* going to dump a bunch of nasty potatoes on my head!"

"You wouldn't be doing the dumping, I would! I like it!" Torren said, smiling.

"Yeah, of course, *you* would like it!" Samara shot back.

"Listen, it really wouldn't be that bad." Sylas continued. "If you want, you could put a couple of our empty potato sacks over your head first as a cover, then you wouldn't even get that dirty. It would just be a little hard to breathe… but just for a little bit is all.”

Samara frowned, “I still don’t like it… but it would be nice to be able to help my family out. And there really is a lot of stuff down there that we could probably sell.” She pondered for a moment longer before responding, “Alright, I’ll do it. But Torren, I swear if you aren’t careful when dumping those potatoes over my head…” She ended the sentence with a nasty look portraying the message loud and clear, to which Torren just smiled a slightly devious smile.

“It might be worth it…” He said quietly.

“What was that?” Samara shot back.

Torren chuckled, “Nothing, nothing. Come on guys, what are we waiting for? Let’s do this thing!”

CHAPTER 2
THE ANCIENT CRYPT

Sylas wheeled his father's cart to their meeting place. He and Torren were able to find a couple of empty barrels that were perfect for what they needed. Along with a few other miscellaneous items, as well as the potato sacks and old rotten potatoes, everything was set for the commencement of their grand plan.

"Remember Torren," Sylas said, "after you get past the guards, don't stop and let us out until you're far enough away that no one will see us."

"No, *really*? I was thinking I would just let you out after taking a couple of steps past the gate. *Whelp, looks like you can get out of those nasty barrels now fellas!*" Torren said sarcastically while pretending to act out the scene.

"I'm serious, Torren. We don't want to get caught. We would just be making things worse instead of helping."

"I know that Sylas, I'm not an idiot."

Samara gave a slight snort, just audible enough for Torren to hear.

Torren looked at her with a grin, “Hey now, remember I’m the one about to dump these potatoes on your head. You’d better show me some respect, or I might… slip a little.” He said, gesturing a motion of dumping clumsily.

“Alright, are we ready then?” Sylas asked.

Samara sighed, “I guess I’m as ready as I’ll ever be.”

Torren smiled “Oh yeah, I’m ready!”

“Good, I’ll get in the barrel first so Samara can see what I was thinking.”

Sylas climbed into one of the empty barrels on the cart. He took one of the empty potato sacks that he had been holding and placed it over his head and upper body.

“Then, just hold it. Like this!” He said, pressing his arms against the side of the barrel. The sack stretched tightly against the inside walls of the barrel, the idea to create a barrier between them and the potatoes. “Then hopefully, they won’t fall through. Alright, I think I’m ready, Torren.”

“Okay, here they come!” Torren said as he grabbed one of the buckets of small rotten potatoes and began slowly dumping them inside of Sylas’s barrel. Looking at Samara, he gave a devilish smile and raised his eyebrows several times. She raised a fist in his direction, which he ignored.

He stopped dumping once he had emptied most of the bucket’s contents into the barrel. “Alright, you’re pretty full. Want me to put the lid on?”

“Yeah, go ahead. Man, it smells bad in here!”

Torren placed the lid on the barrel and made sure that it was securely on.

"This way, my lady," he said, a sly smile curling up his lips.

Reluctantly, Samara climbed into her barrel and followed Sylas's example by placing the empty sack on her head and extending her arms as much as she could to try and prevent anything nasty from going where it shouldn't.

"Alright here it comes!" Torren said excitedly. He then slowly started dumping the potatoes on Samara.

Filling her barrel to the brim, Torren let her know that hers was full and gently placed the lid on top.

"Try and hurry past the guards, please!" Samara's muffled voice plead.

Torren put the empty buckets inside the cart and made sure everything looked convincing. Taking in a deep breath, he started pulling the now heavy cart towards the gate where the guards stood.

Stay focused... you need this to be convincing. He did his best to calm himself down and started whistling to try to make the scene look as natural as possible.

"Oye," one of the guards said as Torren reached the gate. "Where you think you're goin'?"

"Whelp, I'm just a headin' on home after getting all this garbage from the locals. Goin' to take some home to my pigs and probably burn the rest, ya hear?" It was just about the worst imitation of a twangy farmer voice Sylas had ever heard.

Sylas would have slapped his face with his palm if he weren't still holding the sacks to the edge of the barrel.

"Hmm..." one of the guards said, poking his sword at one of the barrels. "What ya got in 'ere? It reeks!"

"Those be some old rotten potatoes right there," Torren said, patting the top of Samara's lid. "Pigs love 'em, don't know why though... but hey, if they'll eat 'em' all the better for me because then I don't have to pay! Got these from a poor guy who lost a bunch'a of crops this year. You ever eaten a rotten potato? I can give you one to try if ya want?" Torren reached his fingers under Samara's lid and slowly pried it open.

No Torren you idiot, what are you doing? Samara thought.

"No, no," one of the guards said, interrupting him. "Get outa 'ere! I don't wanna have to smell you or those nasty things! Get outa my sight!"

Torren smiled, "Alrighty then. If you insist, I'll just be on my way."

The guards moved aside, a bit further aside than they normally do when letting people through. Torren started whistling again and pulled the cart down the dirt road and away from the town. He continued pulling them down the road until he'd put a good distance between them and the guards, then pulled the cart off the side of the road and into a grove of trees.

"Alright piggy piggies, you can come out now!" He said, tapping on the top of the barrels.

Both Sylas and Samara shot out of the barrels and gasped for air, ripping the sacks off their heads and spilling rotten potatoes on the cart and ground.

"I'm *not* doing that again!" Samara exclaimed. "I could hardly breathe! And what I could breathe was disgusting!" She clambered out of the barrel and took several deep breaths of fresh air.

Although he could still taste rotten potatoes in his mouth, Sylas was pleased that his plan worked. "You *really* outdid yourself there, Torren."

Torren gave him a thumbs up, "Yeah… I was pretty good, wasn't I?"

Sylas smiled and shook his head, "Alright, let's head to the crypt. I think I still remember the way."

They pushed their cart deeper into the grove of trees in hopes that no one would see them from the road. Grabbing a lantern, a few torches and their flintstones from the cart, they headed towards the crypt.

The Ancient Crypt was about an hour walking distance from the city of Shilvrst. They'd heard several stories about the crypt growing up from parents, friends, and other adults, but no one really knew what it was used for. No doubt several of the stories that they'd heard were a bit exaggerated, but one thing was certain, the Ancient Crypt had once been a place where a great evil lived.

From stories, they'd learned that the crypt had been built by an evil Darkness mage named Aracorn. Rumor had it that Aracorn was obsessed with learning many ancient, lost techniques of Darkness Magick. Stories told that he was working with Maelos and was one of his right-hand men.

His downfall came when rumor spread that he might be up to something nearby, and the Council of Light eventually found the crypt and were able to kill him before any of his plans came to fruition. The details of what he was up to in the crypt always varied wildly in the stories that were told.

Some said he was trying to figure out how to use Darkness Magick to have eternal life, others that he was working on a project for Maelos so that together they could create a world of never-ending night. Members of the Council of Light that had come to Shilvrst to stop him might have known his true intentions, but Sylas was pretty sure that they had all returned to Sindmyr after his death.

"I see it!" Samara shouted, "the opening is over here."

They had been in the general vicinity of the crypt for some time now but were having difficulty finding the small entrance. Even with the obvious signs of destruction from when the Council of Light had been here, the small opening was difficult to spot.

The entrance hid between several large rocks in a small ravine. A small opening in the ground connected the entrance to an old cave that led downward into the earth.

"Great job Samara," Sylas replied, lighting his torch. "Let's stick together. We don't want anyone getting lost or hurt."

"Or scared," Torren said, gesturing at Samara.

Samara just rolled her eyes, "Why don't you lead the way then, Torren?" She said, putting her hand out in front of her.

"Fine by me," he said, holding his torch out in front of him. He climbed over and around the large rocks that hid the entrance and then squeezed himself into the small hole. After helping Sylas and Samara down into the hole, they turned towards the long tunnel that led downward into the earth.

The tunnel started out small but gradually grew larger until eventually they could all walk without worry of smacking their heads. The air was musty and heavy, making it slightly hard to breathe. An audible *drip…drip…drip* could be heard from surrounding stalactites dripping water into pools beneath them. The cold air from the cave made Sylas shiver as he waved his torch in front of him.

"It's colder than I remember," Samara said out loud, her voice echoing slightly off the cavern walls.

The smooth stone floor was somewhat damp and made the air around them feel more humid than outside. The humidity seemed to amplify the cold that the lack of sunlight brought to the cave.

Holding the torches above their heads, the three continued their way down the cave. Each step brought a deeper cold and additional worries to Sylas. Was he *really* doing the right thing coming here?

Eventually a forked path caused them to stop. Remembering that the cave continued to the right, but the actual crypt itself was located to the left, they headed that direction.

Small crystals embedded in the cold stone of the cave caught the light that danced off their torches, almost seeming to absorb it and radiate the light as its own.

"This really is kind of a cool place." Torren said to the others, "I wish it weren't so far outside of town, then we could come here more often."

"Yeah, and if the guards would actually let you through without having to go through so much trouble," Sylas added.

Shadows of a broken doorway grew at the end of their vision as they finally approached the opening of the crypt. A large wooden door, broken and soaked with moisture, hung on only one hinge against the stone carved entrance. An eerie skull was painted on the outside of the door. Strange runic markings that were carved into the wood at the top of the door dripped with condensed water. A white bone handle curved out towards them, offering its help for passage.

Choosing to ignore the creepy door handle, Torren turned sideways and was able to squeeze through the door and into the crypt. Sylas and Samara followed and found themselves standing in a large open room.

Piles of bones were scattered across the ground. Most of them looked human, though there were some that Sylas could not identify. Books with torn pages laid strewn about the floor, along with all sorts of strange-looking tools and other items of unknown uses.

"Why did the Council of Light not clean this place up after they killed Aracorn?" Torren asked.

"Would *you* want to stay in this creepy room any longer than you had to?" Samara replied. "I wouldn't want to have anything to do with the evil Darkness Magick Aaracorn had been messing with. They probably just did what needed to be done, then got out of here."

"We'd better get started," Sylas said, then began looking for things that might catch the eye of a travelling merchant. Almost everything he found gave off a creepy vibe that only a twisted mind would appreciate. A couple of candlesticks that looked like they might be made of silver caught his attention, so he placed them inside one of the empty potato sacks he'd brought with him. The main room branched into several smaller rooms, each with their own varying degrees of creepiness. Following no particular method of approach, he stumbled upon a heavy bookcase that looked to have something shiny glinting behind it.

"Hey, I think I see something," Sylas called to the others.

He tried to reach his hand behind the bookcase, but the object was just out of reach. He placed his hand on his chin, then began searching for something long and skinny. A corner that somehow seemed darker than everything else caught his attention.

Walking towards the corner, Sylas saw what appeared to be a broken sword stuck inside of a skull made of deep black stone. Curious, he examined the sword. The sword's blade immediately caught his attention, sharp and black as night. With squinted eyes, the color of the blade blended into the surrounding darkness so well that it almost looked like its rusted steel hilt was hovering in mid-air. A stone, the same midnight black of the blade, sat in its pommel.

Sylas rubbed the black stone with his finger, his mind caught upon the mysterious presence that the sword seemed to emit. The stone beneath his finger was smooth and cold, much colder than he expected.

His curiosity was fully engaged now. Carefully, he began running his hand along the side of the blade. Just as the stone, the blade of the sword felt colder than it should have, like it had been dipped in an icy river and left to freeze. He continued examining the metal blade until he came to the skull it had been stabbed into. The skull looked surprisingly real, despite it being made of stone. The only thing that made it look different from a real skull was a dark black gem that sat right in the center of the forehead. His eyes met the gem, gripping his gaze. Like a magnetic pull, he found himself strangely fixated upon the deep black mystery that emanated from it. He almost thought he heard a string of whispers tickle his ear as he slowly reached his hand towards it.

His finger caressed the smooth surface of the precious stone, and the entire room went pitch black. Somehow, he was no longer holding his torch. Everything in the room had seemingly disappeared, all light had been extinguished. He stepped backward in surprise and fell over, landing upon a completely unseen floor. His eyes tried to focus on something, anything around him, but there was nothing but pure darkness surrounding him. Strangely, he felt as though he could still *see,* just that there was nothing *to* see. It was almost like being in a cave with no light, except that everything was visible, just not there. The sensation was tough for him to wrap his mind around.

He stood up and looked around, seeing nothing but blackness. His heart began to race, the cold chill of fear beginning to crawl up his back. Cautiously, he started walking in the direction he thought Samara and Torren were the last time he'd seen them.

"Torren! Samara! Are you there?"

Silence.

"What's going on?" Sylas said out loud. "Where am I?"

A strange thought, like a moment of pure instinct told him that even though he knew he was still inside of the cave, he was no longer in Evendreil. He felt as if he had traveled to a new world. Pausing, he noticed that his hand was icy cold, enough that it was beginning to hurt. Lifting his hand towards his face, he saw that he was holding the black gem that he had touched moments before. No… this was *not* the same stone. A strange, wispy-like purple substance that seemed to swirl in irregular patterns deep within stone glowed with mystical power, making it look almost alive. His first instinct was to throw it, to get far away from it, yet something *pulled* at him, drawing his eyes into the strange power.

Curiously he began rolling the stone around in his hand. It was perfectly round and smooth, the purple light within swimming and moving like a dancing shadow. It had a strange beauty to it, an eerie and mystical beauty, but beauty, nonetheless.

He continued looking into the stone, mesmerized by its strange beauty, when suddenly he heard a faint whisper coming from behind him. Startled, Sylas spun around. Through the blackness, he thought he saw a faint image of something circular in the distance. Against his better judgement, he started walking towards it. Whispers entered his mind again, louder, but still not clear enough to decipher.

What am I doing? He thought to himself. *What am I doing?* Yet despite the better judgement of his mind, his body continued to walk closer.

The whispers beckoned to him once more, its soft hush gliding through the darkness to his ears. Sylas continued walking towards the object. The whisper came again, but this time he was able to decipher what it was saying.

"Sy-lass…"

Sylas froze in horror. A primal instinct triggering in his body, freezing him in place.

"Sylas…" It continued again.

He wanted to run; he didn't want to be anywhere near here! But he couldn't move. It was as if he was being held by whatever this thing was. To his surprise, after a moment of standing there in absolute terror, he felt his legs soften, and he was able to move again. Then to his dismay, he found himself walking *towards* the object once again.

As he approached it, he saw that it looked like a silver amulet. It was suspended in the air and bounced up and down slightly as if it was bobbing in an invisible column of water. The amulet was about the size of his closed fist, with six circular indents that looked as if you could place something small inside of them. There was one slightly larger indent right in the center, surrounded by a darker metal ring that swirled outward and around the other smaller indents. In between each of the outer indents were engravings that Sylas didn't recognize. A long silver chain connected itself to the top of the amulet, making it appear to be hanging upon some invisible force.

"Sylas…" The voice continued.

Not knowing from whence the strength and courage came, Sylas reached out his hand and grabbed the amulet.

Suddenly, images flashed through his mind faster than he could comprehend. An ear-piercing screech rang through his ears. His entire body seemed to be engulfed in a darkness so suffocating, he thought he would drown in it. The images kept scrolling faster and faster through his mind, each one relentlessly overwhelming his senses with information. He felt as though he was about to perish, that the darkness was about to consume him, and his brain would explode from information overload. For an amount of time completely unknown to him he continued to suffer this strange fate. Then, as quicky as it began, everything once more fell into silent darkness.

Slowly, he opened his eyes and saw through blurred vision that he was lying on the floor inside of the crypt. Samara and Torren were kneeling beside him, trying to talk to him through ringing ears. Gradually his blurred vision cleared, and the ringing subsided.

"Sylas! Are you okay? Speak to us! What happened?" He heard them both saying in unison. Sylas sat up, his body still aching from pain.

"I- I think I'm okay. What happened…" A cold, burning sensation continued to chill his hand. Looking down, he noticed the strange silver amulet gripped tightly in his fingers. He screamed and threw it across the room. The amulet clanked and dinged as it bounced across the stone floor.

"Hey, what was that?" Torren asked, turning towards the thrown object.

Sylas didn't speak, his mind racing, trying to put reality back into his senses. Torren stood, walking towards the amulet he'd thrown.

"Don't touch it!" Sylas yelled to him.

Torren ignored him and picked the amulet up then rotated it in his hand slowly.

"Why not?" Torren asked. "It's really cool. Where did you find it?"

"Torren, this is no time to be looking at stupid trinkets. Sylas are you okay? You completely disappeared for a minute!" Samara exclaimed.

"I- what?" Sylas responded in confusion.

"You were standing right over there by that sword, I saw you. I was just about to come over and see what you were looking at when all of a sudden, you were gone!" Samara wrapped her arms around him. "I was so worried, I didn't know what happened to you, I thought you were gone forever!"

Sylas blushed, "I- I really have no idea. I'm a little freaked out at the moment." He shook his head, then did his best to recount to both Samara and Torren the strange world of darkness, the whispers, and everything else he could remember.

"But when the images were shooting through my head, it felt like it was going on for hours. You say I was only gone for just a minute?"

"If I had to guess," Torren chimed in, "I would say maybe two and a half minutes or so? Give or take just a little bit. I didn't see you disappear, but I definitely saw you re-appear. I didn't believe Samara when she said you touched the skull and disappeared, so I went over and touched the same skull, but nothing happened to me." He stuck out a hand and helped Sylas to his feet.

"Torren," Sylas said wide eyed. "Torren, look at the amulet! It has the stone *inside!*"

The same dark purple, almost black stone with the strange wispy purple light in the center was embedded right in the center indent of the amulet. Its eerie purple light swirled slowly in its irregular pattern as it sat firmly fused to the center of the amulet.

"Yeah, that's how it was when you threw it," Torren explained. "It wasn't like this when you found it?"

Sylas shook his head. "No… no, they were separated."

"What do you think this means?" Samara asked.

Just as Sylas was about to respond, they heard a low voice coming from behind them.

"What are you kids doing down here?"

All three of them screamed, jumping into each other's arms and falling down on the ground. They spun their heads around to see old man Uthren standing in the doorway behind them.

"You shouldn't be here!" He continued, "this is a dark and dangerous place. Do any of your parents know about this? This cave is *strictly* prohibited! You shouldn't even know about it! Why, when I tell them where you've been, I…" He stopped, his eyes fixed on the amulet in Torren's hand.

He stood, motionless, wordless for nearly a minute, his eyes never leaving the gaze of the amulet. Finally, a shaky finger pointed towards Torren's hand, and a voice even shakier than his hand escaped the old man's mouth.

"Boy… what do you have?"

"I- I don't know," Torren replied weakly. Clearing his voice he continued, "Sylas found it."

Old man Uthren walked slowly towards him, as if the amulet would suddenly jump out of Torren's hand and bite him.

"Let me see it," Uthren whispered.

Torren quickly handed the amulet over to Uthren, eager to be rid of it. Uthren lifted the amulet to his face, his eyes wide with fear. He studied the amulet and the stone for several minutes, his breathing growing slightly shallower as his mind worked out a hidden mystery within himself.

"How did you find this?" He finally asked.

Sylas swallowed, confused and scared at all of the events that had just transpired. He did his best to recount the experience to Uthren, Samara and Torren filling in their side of the story where appropriate.

"Hmm," Uthren said, uneasily, stroking his white beard. Sylas watched the old man, taking in his physical presence. Uthren was very intimidating, especially for being an older man. His arms were toned and thick. His face was stern and strong, the face of a warrior. How had he ever believed Torren that Uthren was nothing more than a storyteller? Looking at him in this new light, it was obvious that Uthren was much more powerful and wise than he ever would have guessed.

Finally, his deep blue eyes met Sylas. "Do you remember any of the images that you saw? Can you explain them to me with any level of detail?"

Sylas shook his head. "Maybe, but there was just so much information that I don't know if I could remember it all right now, I'm still pretty… shook up."

Uthren pondered his thoughts again, his gaze fixed upon the amulet in his hand.

"Wait a second." Torren piped up, his courage returning to him. "Why are *you* down here if this place is so dark and dangerous?"

"Because," Uthren said, his eyes not leaving the amulet. "I was minding my own business when one of the Magick wards that I had placed near the entrance of the cave went off. I came to see who had set it off."

"Magick ward? What the heck is that? And how do you even know about this place?" Torren asked, his mouth obviously moving faster than his mind.

Samara looked at him with a glare, trying to send the message to shut his mouth.

"I should be asking *you* that question, young man." Uthren replied, finally moving his eyes towards Torren. "I was on the Council of Light when we came here and destroyed Aracorn and his evil works. You, on the other hand, should have *no* knowledge of this place."

"You were part of the Council of Light when they killed Aracorn?" Sylas asked in astonishment.

"Yes. I'm one of the only ones left from that council. The rest have all passed away or have been killed by Maelos, may the Light be with them always." His eyes lingered back down to the amulet, then a look of determination passed the old man's face.

"Enough about that. I fear that you have come away with *much* more than you three bargained for in finding this stone and amulet. In looking for treasure, you have somehow stumbled upon something that I and the council of Light catastrophically missed… it's almost as if it were fate…" His deep blue eyes pierced into Sylas, causing a chill to run up his back.

"We have much to discuss with your families. So, if you don't mind, I'll hold onto the amulet for now, and you three will follow me back to Shilvrst."

Uthren placed the amulet into the pocket of his robe. He was wearing what seemed to be an old battle mage robe, probably from back when he was in the Council of Light. It was yellow with white and gold trim around the hems. The symbol of Light Magick sat in the center of his chest, which was a star that had two short arms on the left and right, a medium-sized arm on the top with a more extended arm at the bottom.

Uthren paused for a moment, then pulled the Amulet back out of his pocket and looked at Sylas.

"On second thought, why don't you hold on to it for now, Sylas. If you were able to find it when the entire Council of Light and I were not able to, there must be a reason." Sylas hesitated, but eventually took the amulet from Uthren.

"Come now, let's get back to Shilvrst, and we can discuss the consequences of your actions."

Uthren pulled his hands in front of his chest, his fingers making a symbol in front of his body. The tips of his thumbs together with his palms facing out. He then curved his pointer fingers and joined them together in a heart formation. Next, he pointed the rest of his fingers in a diagonal until they joined from each hand, creating a diamond symbol above the heart. His hands and eyes then began to glow a bright yellow color, spreading additional light throughout the crypt.

"Oh, wow!" Samara said, finding her voice. "Are you really going to do some Light, Magick?"

"Yes. I believe that would be the best way to get out of here, and most definitely the fastest. Now come and join hands in a circle with me."

"Woah," Sylas and Torren said in unison. Uthren looked even more powerful with the yellow glow of Magick flowing around his body. Sylas had heard of the ancient art of Elemental Magick growing up, but he'd only ever seen it used once, on the most terrifying day of his life, when Maelos had attacked.

"Are we using Light to teleport?" Samara asked in excitement, "I read about that in one of the books that you gave me."

"Yes. Now come and join hands."

Torren and Sylas both looked at each other, stunned. After the moment of confusion, they eventually joined hands with Samara in a circle. Uthren then closed his eyes again, and the yellow light that was surrounding his hands started to spread until it covered his entire body. He joined hands with the others, completing the circle, then the light began to spread around the circle from Uthren's arms down into Sylas, then to Torren, and finally to Samara. When the light reached Sylas, he was surprised to feel a warm, soft, comforting feeling from the light. It felt almost as if it was alive.

The light continued around the circle until everyone was submersed entirely, then *whoosh!* A bright light, almost as bright as the sun, yet somehow not damaging to the eye, came down as a pillar in the middle of the circle. About three seconds later, the light dissipated, and they were all standing on the road outside of the crypt.

"Wow! Oh wow, that was amazing!" Samara exclaimed.

Sylas looked at Torren, whose expression told the exact same story as his thoughts did. *What in the world just happened? And how did something so incredible just come from old man Uthren?*

"Now then," Uthren started. "How in the name of the Light did you all get past the guards?"

Sylas looked between Torren and Samara, "It's a long story… but it involves a cart that we stashed in a grove of trees."

Uthren nodded, "Very well, let's retrieve that and head back towards Shilvrst. There is much that we need to discuss about your discovery."

Then looking directly at Sylas, he continued, "Your role in this war may be more important and pivotal than you could ever imagine… especially for you, my boy."

CHAPTER 3
THE COUNCIL

Torren led the group back to their wagon and belongings. A slight fall breeze in the light of the lowering sun sent a cold gust through the air, blowing several orange and yellow leaves off their branches and onto the ground.

"We were in there longer than I thought," Sylas said out loud. "I told my mother I would be home before dark, we'd better hurry and get back."

"What were you doing in the crypt anyway?" Uthren asked. "It's not a place for children, and how did you know it was even there?"

Sylas told Uthren about his plan for finding some old trinkets to sell to try and help their families financially. He also told him about the time that he, Torren, and Samara had snuck out of town and accidentally stumbled upon the cave. Purely dumb luck. Rumors of a cave housing the dark dealings of Aracorn had whispered through the town on occasion after the Council of Light had cleansed the crypt, but they never thought they'd actually find the place.

"Hmm, I see…" Uthren responded.

"I have a question for you old- err Uthren," Torren corrected himself. "Samara said that you were in the Council of Light back in the day. I didn't believe her at first, but now that I saw what you did to get us out of the cave so fast, well, it was awesome! Do you think you could teach me how to do something like that?"

"It's a lot harder than you think, Torren." Samara butted in, "I've been trying to get that healing spell down all summer and still haven't quite got it right."

Uthren didn't answer. His mind looked fixated on something, as if he were pondering many difficult questions.

"I suspect," he finally said, "that I'll have the chance to teach all three of you how to use Magick in the near future."

Torren hooted into the air with a fist pump, but both Sylas and Samara picked up on an air of uneasiness from the words of the old man.

"Why would you need to teach us in the near future, exactly?"

Uthren placed a hand upon his wise, bearded chin, "Finding that amulet is no small ordeal, Sylas. Seeing visions is even greater, even more concerning to me. Maelos must be stopped. His dark reign has gone on for far too long. There are mysteries in this world, things that you'd never even dream possible out there. He's destroying them, destroying the lives of countless souls, countless families as he enforces his rule. By finding that amulet, you may have unlocked the very *key* that is needed to stop him. I have a sinking suspicion that you will play an important part in ridding the world of his darkness. All of you will."

"Us?" Sylas gulped. He exchanged glances with Samara and Torren and found their expressions of confusion just as visible as his own.

"Yes," Uthren continued. "The amulet that you hold is not some measly trinket, nor is the stone that sits in its center. No, the truth is far more spectacular. It's actually an ancient key."

"A key? You mean like, a key to a door?" Samara asked.

"Yes, but not just any door. It's a key to *the* door. The door that hides behind it the power and knowledge that has been lost for over a millennium. It is a key to the Vault of Kings."

Sylas thought that the name sounded familiar, but he couldn't remember why.

"Wait, *the* Vault of Kings? Like the same one from the stories of the original six Kings?" Samara asked in amazement.

"Nah, no way." Torren piped in. "That's just a myth, it's not actually a real place."

"It is indeed real, Torren." Uthren continued, "The original 'Kings' as we call them, were the first to unlock the knowledge of using Magick. Six of them, each one dedicated to a different basic element: Light, Nature, Air, Fire, Darkness, and Water. They each focused on their own respective elements, mastering them to perfection. They taught what they learned to worthy followers, spreading the knowledge of Magick and other secrets as well."

"Later, they uncovered the power behind the mystic arts we call *combination Magick*. They learned how to create a wide array of truly spectacular and powerful effects. They showed many of their successors how to use Magick, and even taught the more skilled how to do combinations, which has all been passed down from generation to generation."

"However, some things were not taught, and those secrets have been sealed away in the Vault of Kings. Secrets hidden from the world, which are said to give the one who knows them almost God-like knowledge and power. No one truly knows what mysteries lie in the vault, not even the royal bloodlines from the original Kings."

He paused for a moment, pondering something, then shook his head and continued, "If Maelos were able to get the six stones and unite them with the amulet to forge the key to the Vault of Kings… If he were the one to gain knowledge of whatever it is that's hidden inside… It would truly be the end of Evendreil, and the entire world as we know it."

"And this is our problem now because…" Torren started.

"Because you snooped into places where you shouldn't have been!"

Uthren sighed and his voice softened, "It's no fault of your own. The Council of Light and I should have found it years ago… With the visions you saw, Sylas… it makes my mind ponder. There are many unanswered questions that need to be answered. It's as if by destiny you have been called."

“But we’re just kids,” Sylas complained. “What could we even do?”

“That’s what we need to discuss with your families and my trusted friend, Geode,” Uthren continued. “There is a reason for all things. Our questions may not be answered now, but in time, the light will be shed upon all things. Now that the amulet has been found, something must be done about it. We can’t just simply wait for Maelos to find out and come take it by force, that would be sentencing the world to an imminent doom.”

Sylas’s skin began to crawl with nervousness. It didn’t help with the strange and formal way that Uthren spoke either, it made everything seem so *official*.

A slightly awkward silence overcame the group as they continued their way to the cart. It didn’t take long to get back to the place where they’d dropped it off with their hurried pace; but all the while, their minds were spinning, regretting having come out to the crypt at all.

Sylas was especially worried. Thoughts of him having to do something, *anything* that involved Maelos put a knot in his stomach.

Uthren thinks because I saw that vision, I’m *going to be important in solving all of this? But I can hardly even remember what I saw! I can’t do this, I’m just... I’m not...*

His thoughts were stopped short at the arrival of their cart. Uthren gave them instructions to pack everything up and follow him. Worried thoughts continued to dance through their minds as they pulled the cart back towards Shilvrst, no one brave enough to break the silence.

Torren was the first to find enough air in his lungs to ask a question. "So… you did have a plan for getting back into town, right, Sylas?"

Sylas stopped walking. His face grew sheepish as he responded, "Umm, I guess I forgot about that part…"

"Are you serious?" Samara said, shooting him a glare. "Don't you think that's a *little* important?"

"I'm sorry! I guess I was so excited about going back into the crypt and having the possibility of helping out my family… I just forgot about coming up with an idea to get back in."

"Not to worry, I can get us back in the same way that I got out." Uthren chimed in. "You three had better think about your actions a little more carefully in the future, though. You must think things through, lest you find yourselves in inescapable situations."

His words continued to worry Sylas. Was this guy *actually* for real? Did Uthren *really* expect him to go on some grand adventure? To save the day? He wasn't up to the task; he was just Sylas! Nothing extraordinary, not skilled, not… not anything!

Uthren instructed them to leave the cart. Sylas's dad wouldn't be happy when he couldn't find it later, but it seemed the least of his current problems.

Uthren then instructed that they once again join hands. Excited at seeing another display of Magick, the three of them joined hands with Uthren. He made the strange symbol with his hands again, and a bright, warm, yellow light began to engulf each of their hands and spread across the group.

Once entirely engulfed in the light, another bright pillar descended from above, splashing onto them like a direct beam from the sun. Sylas blinked his eyes after the light dissipated, mind blown to see that they were once again inside the town.

"Find your parents," he instructed. "Tell them it's quite urgent, and that I sent you to do so. I'll get Geode. We'll meet at the old town center building and figure out the best course of action. Pray that the Light be with us, to help us be guided."

Sylas arrived at his home just as the sun was setting. A deep orange glow of sunlight filled the sky, several thin clouds glowed bright pink as they floated just above the horizon. Sunbeams radiated out from behind the clouds covering the setting sun and reflected off the window of the front door to his home. Pausing for a moment to collect his thoughts, he took in a deep breath and walked through the door.

"Cutting it a bit close there, eh, Sylas?" He heard the stern voice of his father say.

"Sorry, Dad." Sylas said, looking towards his father. He was sitting in a slightly broken, wooden chair near the kitchen and had *that* look on his face. The look he always had when Sylas got into trouble. But this time, he looked a bit troubled himself.

"Your mom and I have something to discuss with you," He continued.

"Actually Dad," Sylas said hesitantly, "I have something that I need to tell you and Mom. It's… about where I've been all day. We need to go to the town center building. Old man Uthren will be waiting for us there."

A look of confusion crossed Thren's face. "Did you get yourself into trouble again, son?" He said, raising his eyebrows.

"No… Well, maybe? Not really?" He sighed, "It's complicated, dad."

His stomach rumbled, a mixture of both nervousness and hunger. "Can I eat something really quick, and then we can all go?"

Thren eyed Sylas with fatherly concern. "Sure thing, buddy. Dinner's on the table. You eat and I'll get your mother."

Sylas went into the kitchen and tried to calm his nerves with a bit of food. Potatoes again, this time with only butter as a topping. After eating, he walked into the main room of the house and saw his mother and father sitting together. His mother looked at him with worried eyes, "What's this all about, Sylas? Did you get yourself into trouble? Where were you all day?"

Reluctantly, Sylas told his parents what he, Torren, and Samara had been up to. He spared them of some of the details of what happened inside the crypt, especially his little tour through the darkness or whatever that was. Then he told them about how Uthren had come and helped them to get back into the city. Sylas then pulled the amulet out his pocket where he had it concealed.

"This is the amulet," he said, looking at the trinket coldly. The deep purple light within the stone at its center swam eerily in a slow, unscripted circle.

"Uthren thinks that because I found it, *I* should be the one to help figure out what we should do with it.

That's why he wants us to go to the town center building and meet him."

Thren stood up and took the amulet from Sylas. He turned it over several times in his hands and looked into the black stone in its center. The purple glow reflected off the strong eyes of his father, almost seeming to whisper ancient secrets that couldn't be heard.

"I've heard stories about these stones… but I never thought they were *actually* true. We used to talk about them while I worked in the king's guard. I've never heard of this amulet, though… A key to the Vault of Kings… could it all really be true?"

Sensing the worry and anxiety that swelled within his son, he handed the amulet back to Sylas and looked at Iriana. "Let's go see what this is all about then."

Turning back to Sylas and with a stern but loving fatherly voice, he continued, "Everything is going to be okay, Sylas. Let's go figure this out."

A fatherly embrace came next, one that spoke without the need of words that all would be well.

****

Sylas approached the town center building with his parents. The sun had set entirely now, so they relied on the fire burning light of nearby homes to direct them. The town center building was a large stone building that sat in roughly the center of the town, hence its great name. It was used often in the past for meetings led by the King of Shilvrst. In it, officials would discuss what needed to get done to help the town grow, as well as decide punishment for criminals. It no longer served much of a purpose, the government was run entirely by Maelos and his minions now, so the need to discuss what was best for the town was no longer needed because Maelos obviously had all of that under his control.

Sylas entered the building through its large wooden doors, his shoes echoing across the smooth polished stone as he stepped through its corridors.

Several intricately designed stone pillars with carvings that depicted the story of Shilvrst, its history and founders, as well as the history of Evendreil, rose from the stone floor up to the ceiling to help support the roof. The top of the ceiling was painted with murals showing the original six Kings, all glowing in the color of their respective elements. Spiral staircases sat at the edges of the room, each leading to an indoor balcony.

Sylas's eyes caught movement. He looked up to see Uthren standing at the end of a hallway.

"Come, Sylas. The others are waiting."

Uthren led Sylas and his parents towards one of the rooms on the main floor of the building, just to the side of one of the staircases.

Entering the room, he saw Samara and Torren sitting with their parents, as well as one other person that he did not recognize. The man was an absolute mountain. Arms that looked like they could rip trees out of the ground were folded across his chest. He wore a robe that looked very similar to the one that Uthren wore, the robes of the battle mages.

Sylas remembered the scene that haunted his dreams at night. He'd seen men and women wearing this type of clothing as they came to the aid of Shilvrst when Maelos attacked. Though, he'd only ever seen them in the colors that Uthren wore. Instead, this man's robes were a deep forest green. Instead of the golden trim, it was a woody brown color. The symbol in the middle of his chest was different, too. Instead of the four-pointed star, there was a symbol of a tree inside of a circle. The tree trunk was slightly curved to one side. Four branches that filled the upper part of the circle were covered in bright, green leaves, looking almost like a leafy silhouette of a cloud.

Uthren shut the door behind them and asked politely that they have a seat. The room was lit with bright yellow orbs of Light Magick, brightening the room as if there were large windows open to a sunny day.

Sylas sat down next to Samara in nervous anticipation, wishing that he could be anywhere rather than here. He'd even rather be back in the plane of darkness that he found himself in while at the crypt than here. Regretting his choices of the past day, his train of thought was broken by the voice of Uthren, who sat down at the desk in the middle of the room.

"I'm sure there are many questions as to why I have gathered you all here this evening. I don't want you to worry, your children are not in trouble. For any of you that don't know who I am, my name is Uthren, Lightbringer. I served on the High Council of Light under King Grindal of Sindmyr for many years. This is my dearest friend, and one who I can trust above all others, Geode. He is as wise as he is powerful." Geode nodded but said nothing.

"He served for many years in the Council of Nature in our neighboring city of Gelendor."

A Nature mage? Sylas thought, *I wonder what kind of crazy things he can do with Magick...*

Standing up, Uthren walked over to Sylas and held a gentle hand out towards him, "May I see the amulet that you found, please?"

Sylas reached into his pocket and pulled out the amulet. As he did, his fingers brushed against the dark purple stone in the middle. An immense cold ran up his fingers and into his arm, as though it had been sitting under a pile of ice for the past several hours instead of his warm pocket.

"Does anyone know what this is?" Uthren said as he returned to his seat and held the amulet in the air.

Thren spoke up first, "I'm not sure what the amulet is… but I believe that the purple stone in the middle is called the Stone of Darkness."

Uthren nodded his head and looked towards the others. "Does anyone know anything else?"

Torren's dad spoke this time; he had long brown hair like Torren did and the same muscular build.

"If Thren is correct, then that means that the Elemental Stones of Power are not a myth or legend. And that would mean that somewhere in the world there exists the stones of Nature, Water, Fire, Air, and Light as well."

"That's correct," Uthren responded.

He then looked at Samara and her parents, "Do you know anything of these stones?"

Samara's parents looked at each other and shook their heads. "Unfortunately," her father started, "I've never been very knowledgeable about Magick. I've always just focused on my own trade and raising my family. So, they're quite unfamiliar to me."

"I know a little bit," Samara added in. "I know that the original six Kings, the same that were painting on the ceiling of the main room in this building, were the ones that discovered the secret behind Magick. Eventually, the stones were supposed to be hidden… but I don't know why."

Uthren smiled. "Very nice Samara. I see that the books I've given you have not gone to waste. Samara is correct, and to make this a lot easier for everyone, I think I'll go ahead and just start from the beginning."

Uthren cleared his throat, "Over a thousand years ago, a very religious man named Zephyr climbed to the tallest peak of the Kandarin mountains and prayed to the Gods. He asked them to bestow upon him knowledge that would allow him to be more than a man, but still less than a God. The Gods found favor in Zephyr and blessed him with knowledge on what we refer to as 'Elemental Magick' today. Zephyr became the first of the original six Kings and the first to learn Air Magick. He returned to his people and taught them what information he was given and some of his more devout followers asked him if there was more knowledge to be gained. Curious, he climbed back to the top of the Kandarin mountains and petitioned the Gods for more knowledge. They told him to bring back five other worthy followers, and that they would grant him further light and knowledge."

Uthren paused for a moment to make sure everyone was still following, then continued.

"Zephyr returned to his home and gathered five of his most devout followers: Magnar, Nymphara, Amphilia, Freyr, and Chemosh. Together they ascended the mountain and petitioned the Gods for further knowledge. It's said that the Gods themselves came down and bestowed upon each one of them individually the knowledge of the separate Elemental Magick techniques. Fire to Magnar, Nature to Nymphara, Water to Amphilia, Light to Freyr, and Darkness to Chemosh. They then returned to their village and taught others on the use of the Elemental Magick techniques they had been taught, including teaching each other how to use the other elements."

Uthren tapped a finger on the desk, "Eventually, Zephyr, the first of the six, was able to learn how to combine different elements together for surprising and wild results. This opened up a plethora of new possibilities. They again taught the very most elite the techniques of Magick Combinations. For mysterious reasons unknown, the original six 'Kings' as we call them, got together and using their combined powers constructed the Vault of Kings and in it, hid a secret."

Uthren stood from the table, his voice rising slightly, "A secret that's said to give the possessor an immeasurable amount of power, and knowledge that in this day is only known to the Gods themselves. The story is vague on how exactly they obtained each of the Elemental Stones of Power, but the Kings in their wisdom used the stones and their combined powers to make the amulet that you see here, as well as the Vault that hides in it their ultimate secret."

Uthren sat back down, lifting the amulet from the desk and peering into the purple stone in its center.

"Each of the stones holds in itself a great mystery. By studying the stone, you can learn the deeper and more powerful techniques of that element and have additional power in that respective branch of Magick. As I said before, some secrets the Kings felt were too important, too powerful to share with the world at that time. Believing that the secret needed to be hidden away from the world, they sealed the secret away in the vault and constructed a key that could only be activated when one had collected all six of the Elemental Stones of Power and placed them into the key. The stones were then divided, separated, and kept well-guarded."

Uthren paused and looked around the group noting their expressions. "This amulet you found Sylas," Uthren held up the amulet again, "is indeed the *unpowered* key to the Vault of Kings. And the stone that sits in the middle of it is the Stone of Darkness. If this were to fall into the wrong hands and with it, the other Elemental Stones… Our world, as we know it, would be destroyed. If Maelos discovers that this amulet has been found, he will do *anything* in his power to obtain it."

Sylas gulped and scrunched deeper into his chair. Sweat was dripping down his back now, leaving a cold trail of regret.

"So, what do our children have to do with all of this?" Samara's mother asked. "Shouldn't we give that to someone in one of the High Councils and have them figure out what to do with it? Or better yet try and destroy it?"

"It cannot be destroyed," Uthren responded. "The way I see it, and I believe my friend here agrees with me…" Geode gave another nod. "The only correct course of action now that the amulet has been found is to try and locate the other five Elemental Stones, place them into the key, and unlock the Vault of Kings before Maelos can. Then we'll be able to use whatever is inside the vault *against* him, ridding us of his dark power and oppression once and for all."

Uthren grew solemn as he looked at Samara, Torren, and finally, Sylas. A small smile curled up his lips as he added, "And despite what all logic would have me to believe, I think these young people are the ones to take on that quest."

Sylas felt like he had just turned into a pile of mud. He couldn't feel any of his limbs and sunk so far into his chair that he almost fell out. He saw the mouths of Uthren, Geode, and the other adults moving, obviously arguing about the subject but couldn't hear anything they said. Shock had entered into his body and was swimming around his innards along with fear, regret, and a million other depressing emotions. They clouded his senses and sent his reality spinning. Eventually, he was awakened from the trance by his father's voice.

"Everyone hold it!"

The room went quiet, all eyes glued to Thren. Sylas watched his ultimate hero, the greatest man who had ever lived in his eyes, as he waited to see what his father had to say. The trust and respect that he had for his father overflowed to the point that it calmed his fears and bridled his anxiety.

"I would like to say something," He continued. "I agree that these kids all seem a little young to be taking on such a big and dangerous mission. I agree that they're not very experienced and that there are probably more qualified individuals that would be up to the task."

His eyes fell upon Torren's father, Fenrin. "But… deep down in my gut, I also have a feeling that this is the right thing to do. I, for one, believe in destiny, and I believe that it's not by chance that they were the ones to find both the amulet and the Stone of Darkness when the entire Council of Light together searched the crypt for anything dangerous or evil and were not able to find it."

Uthren bowed his head in agreement and Thren continued, "Maelos has destroyed so much of what we love and hold dear, and he must be stopped. If our children are the ones to do it, then all the better I say. I'm willing to help in any way that I can and hope that I'll be able to once again pick up my sword and join the front lines to bring back freedom to my family."

His eyes fell upon Sylas, wisdom and experience from a true hero. "And I believe that *they* have been chosen by destiny to fulfill this cause."

Thren folded his arms and sat back in his chair, his expression a mix of courage, worry, and concern for his son.

"Thank you, Thren," Uthren continued. "I've decided that with the permission of all of you, myself and Geode will accompany the three of them and help them along their journey. We both have extensive experience in Elemental Magick, myself mostly with Light, and Geode mostly with Nature. We've seen our fair share of battles and will be committed to keeping your children safe, even at the cost of our own lives. If you all agree to let them go, then we will be their guides and protectors."

The group sat in silence for some time until finally, Sylas felt a surge of courage from some unknown source and spoke up.

"I think that Uthren's right. As scared as I am to say it… when we were in the crypt, I felt something pulling me in the direction of the amulet. I also heard a voice calling my name. I saw… things that I don't understand yet, but I feel like I'll have an important role to play in finding the rest of the stones. As much as I don't want it to be me, I feel like it *has* to be. And I wouldn't want to do it without my two very best friends."

His mother, Iriana, tearfully grabbed his hand. Sylas looked into her beautiful blue eyes, his fear and determination both peaking at the same time. She smiled, tears welling in her eyes. She looked at Thren, then met Uthren's gaze.

"You have our permission to train Sylas and take him with you on your journey, Uthren."

"Thank you, Iriana," Uthren responded with a kind smile. After several minutes of pondering and quiet conversations, Samara and Torren's parents agreed and gave Uthren permission to take them on the journey as well.

"It's against *every* bit of logic and sane thinking… but I feel it too…"

A slight chill ran up Sylas's back. Perhaps it was all in his mind, but it almost felt like the entire room had just gotten slightly colder. The eyes of every person in the room told the same story. They could *all* feel it. As if the Gods themselves had just descended into the very room and confirmed that fate and destiny were being realized.

"But!" Samara's father added, "You have to give us your word that you will *die* before letting them perish."

"I give you my word." Uthren said with sincerity. "I swear to you that I'll do everything in my power to protect your children and to teach them the skills necessary for them to be able to take care of themselves."

He placed a fist on his chest and bowed slightly, looking more and more like a warrior by the second.

"And give to you my oath that I will die before I let anything happen to them."

Uthren walked to the center of the room with authority and power that Sylas would never before been able to assign to the old man.

"Now, it's time to make our preparations. We will leave first thing tomorrow morning, early. We need to be on our way before any of this information gets spread into the wrong ears. It seems as though no matter how well kept a secret is, the word always gets out. You will all need to put together some packs for the journey. Tomorrow, we head for Gelendor."

CHAPTER 4
THE SECOND MIND

Sylas watched his breath rise above his view in the cool, crisp morning air. He breathed softly, nervously, in anticipation for the grand journey in front of him. He, Samara, and Torren sat at the doorstep of Uthren's house, waiting in silence for him and Geode to finish discussing their plans. Sylas yawned, his eyes still feeling heavy from rising at such an early hour. Little bits of orange and yellow from the oncoming sunrise were just starting to creep above the horizon.

Torren yawned and stretched his arms, "Nervous?" he said as he finished his stretch.

Sylas nodded, "Aren't you?"

Torren shrugged, "Yeah, I guess I am. I'm really more excited though. If we're heading to Gelendor, it's going to be awesome! My dad was telling me a bit about it last night. It sounded incredible!"

Sylas smiled, his spirits slightly lifted.

"I guess I'm just nervous about all the other things… Learning to fight, use Magick, all that. At least you and Samara have a bit of a head start. She's already started trying to use Magick and you've known how to fight ever since you were little. I don't have anything…"

Samara scooted herself closer to Sylas, grabbing his hand with her own, "Don't worry, we'll help each other out. Plus, we have Uthren and Geode to help us. I think we're going to find out what we're *really* made of, and it's going to surprise us all."

Sylas looked into Samara's beautiful, emerald-green eyes. She smiled at him, nearly melting his heart. Her smile and face radiated perfection. Sylas truly believed that he had never seen anyone more beautiful in his life. Her perfect complexion and proportions begged his inner feelings to be released. He could have kissed her at that very moment. He desired it more than anything, to feel her lips against his…

"Are you kids ready?" Uthren's quiet, deep voice said behind him.

Sylas jumped and let go of Samara's hand, spinning around to meet Uthren's gaze.

"Don't sneak up on us like that!"

He felt his cheeks blushing and didn't know whether it came from the embarrassment of being startled, or that he was just *one ounce* of courage away from kissing Samara smack on the lips. *It's a good thing I didn't get too brave,* he thought to himself. *Or I probably* would've *gotten a smack, and not on the lips either.*

"Well?" Uthren continued, unphased by Sylas's words. "Do you have everything you will need for our travels? Remember, it will take us several weeks to make the journey to Gelendor. You will need to be prepared to survive in the wilderness. We will have to hunt and gather our own food, find our own water, and live with only what we can carry on our backs."

Sylas thought again about the items that he had packed and the advice that his father had given him.

"Remember, Sylas, trust your instincts. When you are faced with tough decisions, be sure to trust your mind and your heart. There are many dangerous things in this world and plenty of evil. But if you keep your heart and mind focused on what's right, darkness won't be able to overpower you."

Nodding Sylas responded back to Uthren, "Yeah, I think I'm all set."

"We are too," Samara added.

"Good," Uthren said, giving a quick nod. "Then we should be off. If Geode is correct, we will have but a very short window to make our escape without being noticed. We've decided it's too risky to teleport using Light Magick. Somehow, against all reason, the both of us have an uneasy feeling that whispers of our plans have already spread… We have to leave now, as quickly and *stealthily* as possible. Onward, to the east gate. And by the Light, try to remain unseen."

Sylas followed Uthren, Geode, and the others as they walked towards the east side of town. The warnings of Uthren in his strange, almost *holy* way of talking repeating in his mind as they walked in between buildings, ducked behind carts and stacks of hay, and tiptoed through the shadows of the early morning to avoid the view of any patrolling guards.

"Does it feel like there are more guards than usual this morning?" Torren whispered to Sylas as they were crouched behind an old horse barn. "I've never seen it like this before, even when I've had to get up this early for chores. Do you think that somehow Maelos could know what we're up to?"

"We'll have to hope that's not the case, Torren," Uthren whispered, intercepting his conversation. "I agree though, something is not right. Maelos was in possession of the Stone of Darkness for several years, it could be that he has some connection with the stone that is telling him it is no longer in its hiding place."

"It's almost certain that he knows," another deep voice added. Sylas turned his head to look at the extremely muscular, intimidating man. His dark, black hair and a long scar across his right cheek added to his intimidation level.

"From what I know about Darkness Magick, there are several ways that Maelos could be directly connected to the stone. It wouldn't surprise me at all if he were the one that directly ordered Aracorn to hide it in the crypt for who knows what purpose. Now that it's no longer there, he can probably *feel* its absence."

Sylas watched one of the guards patrolling directly in their path of escape wave his hand, beckoning a second guard to approach and start a conversation. "Is the Stone of Darkness, evil then?"

"It's… *complicated,*" Uthren sighed. "While not inherently evil, it has the tendency to bring out the worst in people. As you will learn, some elements are more naturally attuned towards evil, good, or other emotions than others. Light naturally wants to do things that are good and holy, commanding justice in all things. Darkness on the other hand, especially in the hands of someone with already not so good intentions, tends to bring out evil and corrupt desires. It doesn't mean that all practitioners of Darkness Magick are inherently evil, but it's much easier to sway in that direction when using Darkness than any other element."

The group sat in silence for a moment, then watched as a pair of guards left their post and began walking towards one of the market buildings. It wasn't an uncommon sight; they were most likely wanting to force the poor owner into selling them something for far less than it was worth. With the morning drawing near, people would start opening their shops soon.

"Now! We must go now, or I fear our window of opportunity will be too short at the gate," Geode whispered to the group, cautiously walking towards where the guards had been standing.

They made their way quietly and carefully through the streets. Each step through the once small, yet great trading kingdom brought additional questions to Sylas's mind.

Geode gave a signal, then quickly ran behind a building near the east gate where two guards stood at the ready.

"What's this window of opportunity that Geode keeps bringing up?" Sylas whispered as he stepped behind Uthren.

"You have much to learn still, Sylas," Uthren responded. "We'll teach you more as soon as we're out of Shilvrst and into the wilderness. Suffice it for now, I'll tell you that Geode is an exceptionally talented Nature Mage and possesses advanced knowledge of divination because of it."

"Divination?" Samara said, an edge of confusion in her voice.

"Yes," Uthren continued. "The ability to both transmogrify simple objects, as well as see tiny glimpses into the near future."

"The future?" Samara asked, her jaw dropping. "So, what did he-"

"Uthren, we must go now!" Geode's deep voice cut in.

"Hurry!" Uthren quickly replied. "Stay close behind me."

Uthren dashed out from behind the horse barn with a speed that defied his age. Sylas ran with the others towards an old rundown building near the east gate. Sliding behind the slightly crumbling walls of the building, Sylas risked a peek around the corner. One lone guard stood at the ready near the gate.

Most of the town gates were large and had several guards near them, as well as a small building where the guards could relieve themselves, sleep, or do other mundane tasks. Several of the gates were smaller, however, and were installed in places where the town walls had been broken down during the time when Maelos made his attack. These gates still had the small building next to them, but usually only had one guard on post.

Large lanterns hung on either side of the gate, swaying gently in the wind. Sylas pondered what the window of opportunity that Geode was talking about might be when a sudden movement from the guard caught his attention. The guard bent over slightly, putting one hand on his stomach and used the other to wipe sweat from his brow. He bent over, putting both of his hands on his knees and began breathing deeply. After a minute or so, the guard began looking around to see if anyone was watching. Seeing no one, he grabbed one of the lanterns from the gate and ran into the small building, slamming the door behind him.

"Now!" Geode said to the group and began to sprint towards the gate. Slightly startled, Sylas saw Samara, Torren, and Uthren run past him. Collecting himself, Sylas joined the race for the gate, still bewildered on how Geode could have possibly known that the guard was going to retreat to his little building at that exact moment.

Geode reached the gate first. Upon arriving, he slowed himself to a stop and began fiddling with the chain that was wrapped around the two doors of the gate. Trying to avoid the loud clanking of metal on metal as he unwrapped the chain, he carefully pulled the gate open. It made a loud creak as he swung the gate open and motioned with his hands for everyone to run through.

As Sylas approached the gate, he turned to look at the guardhouse and saw through one of the windows the dim glow of the lantern the guard had taken. He turned back towards the gate and slipped through past Geode. Geode then walked through and closed the gate behind him, wrapping the chain around the gate as it had been before, then motioned for the group to continue without him.

"Keep going, I'll catch up."

Sylas followed Uthren, Samara, and Torren as they ran towards a small group of trees. Sylas felt the crunch of dry fallen leaves under his feet as he entered the grove. They waited in silence, breathing their worry into the air while they waited for Geode to join them.

Sylas looked towards the gate. It was too dark to tell, but he didn't think he saw the shadow of the guard yet, just the bouncing lights of the one lantern that remained. A rustle of leaves caused his heart to jump, but relief quickly washed over him as he saw Geode enter the grove.

"Well done everyone. I think we were able to get through without him noticing us," Uthren said in a relieved tone.

"Why did he all of a sudden run into that guardhouse?" Samara asked, breathing heavy from the run and the adrenaline of escape.

"It looked like he was about to puke," Torren added in, not nearly as winded as the rest of them seemed.

"That's precisely what he was doing," Geode responded. "Last night I sent one of the merchants that was headed home with some sweets that were, let's just say, not too delightful. I gave him the instruction to make sure that the guard at this gate got one of them as a gift…" Geode winked, a charming, devious smile upon his warrior face.

Sylas instantly grew a liking for Geode, a smile spreading across his own face at the prank that had allowed them to escape.

"So, you were able to use divination to know *exactly* when it would get to his stomach and when he would be sick enough to have to leave his post?" Samara asked.

"More or less, yes. There's a bit more to it than that, but it's a different story for a different day. For now, we need to get moving. I don't *think* we were seen, but it's better to be safe than sorry. If someone did see us leaving, we need to put some distance between us."

"Keep each other safe," Uthren added. "If we run into any danger be sure to stick together. Don't hesitate to leave Geode or me behind. You mustn't engage in *anything* until we've been able to train you. I know that you are already quite good at fighting, Torren, and I expect you to use that knowledge to protect your friends if they fall into any danger. Is that understood? Keep them safe, that's your number one priority."

Torren nodded, "I understand. I'll keep them safe." His tone was much more mature than Sylas was used to hearing.

"Good," Uthren continued. "Let's be off then, we will head east until we reach the mouth of the river. We can make camp there tonight."

****

The sun began to peek up over the mountains to the east, spreading a warm orange glow over Sylas.

The birds were out now, singing their songs and beginning their searches for food. Thoughts of learning Magick and of a mysterious city called Gelendor swirled amongst his thoughts, along with a growling stomach.

"Uthren," Sylas finally started, "why exactly are we headed for Gelendor? Is there another Elemental Stone of Power there?"

Uthren slowed his pace just slightly, "My apologies, I haven't explained myself very well to you all yet. My mind has been deep in thought about the reasoning behind all the guards back in Shilvrst, and I tend to allow myself to jump to conclusions. In answer to your question, we're headed to Gelendor because there are currently many Nature mages that live there who we believe will be able to help us find some clues as to the whereabouts of the Stone of Nature. Geode used to live there and believes that they will be willing to help."

Samara increased her pace to put herself next to Sylas, "Uthren, I guess I still don't quite understand something. If the Stone of Darkness is so powerful and the amulet is literally the *key* to The Vault of Kings, why would Maelos have hidden it back in the ancient crypt?"

Uthren frowned, "That's something I have been puzzling over for a while now… it's a very troubling question. If he knew where the amulet to the Vault of Kings was hidden, there is no way he would ever let it out of his sight. I am wondering if perhaps Aracorn was the one that had discovered the amulet and for some reason never told Maelos. Perhaps he had thoughts of betrayal and was not able to act on them before the Council of Light ended him? It's a mystery that I have not yet solved."

"What do the stones do exactly?" Sylas asked.

"The stones are an additional means of power for the person who wields them," Uthren said, resuming his previous pace. "When opening the second mind and connecting your will with the elements, the stones provide the user with additional strength and focus, as well as more persuasion to bend the will of the elements towards what you desire. They are also essential for the amulet to work as the key to the Vault of Kings, as I had mentioned before."

"Second mind?" Sylas said in a confused tone.

Uthren sighed, "There's so much to explain… I believe we've been making good time thus far. Let's stop and rest for a moment. We can eat, and I can clarify a few things."

The group came to a stop in a group of trees not far from the road. Finding a fallen tree, Sylas, Torren, and Samara sat down on the slightly rotting trunk. Geode sat on a nearby rock and pulled out some bread from his pack. Sylas eagerly tore into his rations as Uthren stood in front of the fallen tree and talked.

"There are four basic steps when it comes to channeling the ancient art of Magick. The first step is to make the correct hand symbol to initiate the *type* of element that you are using. There are six different symbols, one for each element. The element of Light, which is the one that I'm most familiar with, has a symbol that's made like so."

Uthren put his hands out in front of him and made the symbol of Light. He held his hands out so the others could see as he explained.

"With the palms facing outward, the thumbs and pointer fingers are connected, making a heart symbol. Next, the middle fingers are brought upward and touch, creating a diamond above the heart. The ring and pinky fingers align with the middle finger."

"Once that symbol has been made, the next step is to tap into what is called the inner life. Everything has an inner life. All the objects around us are filled with it. The birds you hear, the worms under your feet. The log that you sit upon, even the air that you breathe. Inner life is what connects us all, it is the foundation of all things. For us, our inner life is found within the stomach."

Uthren broke the symbol he was making with his hands and put his right hand over his stomach.

"This is the basin to your inner life. It needs to be brought forth out of the stomach and into the hands to be used."

He resumed the symbol that he had made with his hands before and continued, "After you make the symbol, focus your mind upon this basin. Once you have found its spark, the third step is to bring that inner life from your stomach, up through your torso, into your chest, down your arms, and into your hands."

Just as Uthren finished speaking, his hands began to glow. A bright yellow light filled the symbols of the heart and the diamond shapes that his fingers made, then spread to cover the entirety of his hands until just above the wrist. Sylas looked in awe and wonder at the light display. It was beautiful, giving off a warm glow and emanating an energy that made Sylas feel that the light was almost alive. The soft glow continued radiating from Uthren's hands as he continued to explain.

"The final step is the most difficult of the four. After moving your inner life to your hands and creating the elemental glow, you need to open what is called the second mind."

Uthren again released the energy from his hands and elaborated.

"The second mind is an extension of yourself. It allows you to be connected to the energies of everything around you. Think of your conscious self as your *first* mind. The thoughts that you are having right now, the desires that occupy your heart, your inner thoughts and workings, they are all a part of your first mind. Once you connect your first mind to the inner life of the energy that surrounds you, your very soul is lifted from your body and connected to these elemental powers. A completely *new* body is created from your soul. This new body is called the second mind. It is half you, and half the element to which you are connected, coexisting in balance and harmony."

Torren rubbed the sides of his head with his fingers, "Okay, I am *super* confused right now… So, you're saying that you can have two *separate* bodies or minds or whatever at the same time? Does that mean that I would be able to think about two different things at once?"

"I wish I had a better way to explain it, but you don't truly come to understand the feeling until you have experienced it. It's as though your body and soul become separate, but you are still in control of the actions of both. And your soul, or second mind, is heavily influenced by the element you are connected with."

Torren folded his arms. "That seems complicated..."

"Indeed. That's why it's the hardest step for beginners to learn. After you open your second mind for the first time you will know what it feels like and be able to do it again with more and more ease until it's second nature."

Uthren again made the symbol of Light with his hands, and they began to glow. Taking in a breath, Uthren's eyes started to glow the same color as his hands. Sylas could no longer see the blue coloring that was once centered in his eyes, only a radiating yellow light. It was somewhat frightening seeing someone's eyes glowing so unnaturally. It reminded him of his memory of Maelos and his glowing eyes and made the hairs on his arms stand up.

"I am now connected to my second mind," Uthren continued. "At this stage, the only thing left to do is to bring into unison the desires of your first mind and your second mind so that they align. Once that happens, the Magick will take effect."

Uthren broke the symbol that he was making with his hands and held his hand out towards Sylas. An orb of Light Magick appeared in his hand and floated just above his outstretched palm. It radiated with power, a slight hum buzzing around its edges. The powerful ball of Light pulsated as Uthren continued.

"As I said before, your second mind is only *half* you and half the element you are channeling. Sometimes, it is difficult to get your desires to align because of that. Each element has unique, natural desires of things that it would like to accomplish. For example, the Light wants to heal, protect, and bring justice upon what it deems as 'wicked'. If I were to try to command it to burn down a tree in front of me, I would have a really hard time persuading my second mind to come to that desire. There is a little bit of persuading that can happen, but ultimately the Light will only deviate so far. Part of knowing how to use Magick is knowing the natural desires of each element, and how to use them appropriately. A true master knows where the limits of the element lie, for you cannot control the elements and force them to do things that they do not naturally desire to do."

"How do you know what the elements naturally desire to do?" Samara asked.

"When you have opened your second mind, you will *feel* those desires. They will literally become a part of you."

Uthren allowed the ball of Light to fade into the air, then held up one finger, "One part you, knowing what you desire." He held up another finger on his opposite hand, "The other part the element, telling you what it's willing to let you do." He put his fingers together, wrapping them as one. "Coming together, in unison, allowing your combined wills to be done. The more time you spend with your second mind opened, the more you will discover both about the elements *and* about yourself. The more time you spend with the elements, the more that they will truly become a part of who you are."

Uthren looked at Samara then over to Torren and finally Sylas. "After you have learned to open your second mind and cast your first Light spell, maybe we can ask Geode to teach you some Nature Magick. But for now, we had better be on the move again. I would like to get to the river before nightfall."

The light from Uthren's hands and eyes faded as he closed his connection to the Light. Sylas, Torren, and Samara finished eating what they could then put the rest away in their bags. Tossing his bag on his shoulder, Sylas made a silent vow to himself.

I'm going to learn how to open my second mind and become a great mage. No matter what it takes.

The group returned to the road and continued their way eastward towards the river. Sylas was grateful for the cooler weather of the season. He imagined that it would have been quite hot and miserable to do all this walking, with all the gear that he had in his pack, in the middle of the summer. He shifted the weight of his pack on his shoulders as he walked, his mind reflecting on the items that his father had helped him pack: A small hunting bow with several arrows, a knife, some extra clothes, rope, flint, a small hatchet, gear to pitch a small tent, blankets to sleep with, and a short sword he had used while in the King's Guard, as well as a couple days' worth of rations.

Uthren announced after several miles that their path would deviate from the main road to help avoid the chances of running into trouble.

They walked through the grassy hills and trees for the rest of the afternoon, occasionally asking a question to Uthren or Geode or reminiscing childhood memories between Sylas, Torren, and Samara.

The sounds of rushing water over rocks finally reached their ears and a short distance later, the sight of the river came into view.

"We'll make camp here," Uthren announced. "When you're finished setting up for tonight, meet me by the riverbank. We'll begin your training tonight."

Excited to start his training, Sylas looked around for the best place to set up his sleeping arrangements. "Where do you think we should sleep?" He asked Samara.

Samara got a slightly disgusted look on her face. "What do you mean where *we* should sleep? I'm sleeping somewhere where I can get some privacy, *away* from you two. So don't even think about setting up anywhere near me."

Sylas's face turned bright red, "No, that's not what I… what I meant to say was-"

Torren laughed a loud, hardy laugh and patted him on the back.

"Come on, Sylas, let's go find a spot over by the river and leave the princess to find her own spot where we can't spy on her… at least, not without her noticing." He looked at Samara with a devious look and raised his eyebrows several times.

"Torren, I swear if I catch you spying on me or coming over and trying to scare me in the night, you won't live to see Gelendor!"

Torren laughed again, his face growing sly. He then turned toward Sylas and spoke in a whisper just loud enough for her to hear, "She said *if* we get caught."

Samara dropped her bag and stomped over to Torren.

"Ahh help!" He yelled and began to jog away from her. She chased him as he ran away laughing.

A smile crept up Sylas's mouth, his heart grateful for moments like these that took away from the ever-growing stress.

Samara finally gave up the chase and returned to her bag. She picked it up and pointed a finger at Sylas's chest, "I mean it. Far away. You got it?"

Without waiting for a response, Samara set off to find a private place to set up her tent.

He and Torren picked a perfect place, right on a sand bar near the river. They pitched their tents and got everything set, then looked for Uthren. They found him sitting on a small grassy area near the large body of water that connected the northern sea to the river which would narrow as they continued south.

As Sylas and Torren approached him, Uthren motioned for them to sit down. They sat next to each other on the grass and awaited further instructions. Their respect for the old man had grown substantially after seeing what he could do and hearing him talk about Magick. He was much more powerful and wise than either of them could have ever thought possible.

"First, we will have both of you try to tap into your inner life," he began. "As soon as we can get to that point, we'll move on to opening the second mind, but first, we need to understand the very basics. Both of you make the symbol of Light as I showed you before."

Torren and Sylas looked at each other, and then both tried to replicate the symbol of Light with their hands.

"Not quite," Uthren said, examining their hands. "Torren, you need to make sure the last three fingers on your hands are all aligned with each other. And Sylas, you need to bend your pointer fingers more so that you make a heart, not a circle."

Trying again, the boys adjusted their hands until Uthren was satisfied. "Excellent, now commit this symbol to memory. Before you are to begin using Light Magick, you must first initiate this symbol. Once you have opened your second mind, you can break the symbol and won't have to use it again until you either change elements or close your second mind and need to re-open it again. You must also learn to make these symbols quickly, if you are ever in trouble and need to quickly cast a spell, you don't want to be stumbling with your hands while someone is trying to kill you. Next, I want you both to focus your minds upon your stomachs and search for the sensation of your inner life. It will be small, and somewhat difficult to find at first. When you are first learning, I find it easier to actually start by listening to your heart. Close your eyes and focus on your heartbeat."

Sylas and Torren closed their eyes. Sylas focused on his heartbeat. At first, he couldn't feel anything at all, but as he sat and listened, he could start to feel the steady rhythm of his heart.

"Once you have focused on your heart, which is what gives life to your body, change that focus, and move it down, deep within your stomach. You won't be able to feel a physical beat like you do with your heart, but you will be able to feel a slight tingle. Your pools of inner life will be small right now but will grow over time as you become more and more powerful."

Sylas mentally moved his focus from his beating heart downwards until it rested upon his stomach. He focused on his breathing, the slow inward and outward movement of his diaphragm, and then moved in deeper. He didn't feel anything for what seemed like a long time but was determined to see results. He blocked out all the surrounding noise, from the river water running gently past them, to the birds softly chirping in the trees, to the breeze gently brushing against his ears. He felt as if he had removed himself from the world and entered his own domain of peace. *It feels good to block out the world*, he thought to himself.

Just then, he felt an extremely faint but nevertheless present tingle deep within his stomach. He redoubled his focus, letting the sensation grow within himself. The tingle seemed alive, almost shy, hiding itself deep within its secure domain. He found himself almost coxing the little feeling to come out, assuring it that it was safe. The tingle gained in strength and began to spread until it no longer felt shy, but curious. It grew and grew until Sylas felt his entire torso tingling.

"I think I've got it," he said softly, opening his eyes. The feeling of peace and inner security continued to flow through him, granting him confidence and happiness. He had never felt so good in his entire life.

"This is incredible!"

"Very good, Sylas. Now move your inner life from your stomach through your arms and into your hands."

Sylas closed his eyes again and focused on the sensation. It felt so good, so welcoming. It felt as if a part of his very being had just been awakened from a dormant state. He moved the sensation from his torso to fill his arms and then down into his hands. Keeping his eyes closed, he felt his hands start to tingle with the same sensation, but this time with an added warmth. It felt as if he were holding a small rabbit in his hands, or something else that was alive and giving more heat than his normal body would produce on its own.

"Well done!" Uthren said, "Very well done."

Sylas opened his eyes to see his hands glowing with the bright yellow color of Light Magick. The Light warmed his hands and strengthened his confidence. Turning his head towards Torren to view his progress, he saw Torren still sitting with his eyes closed tightly. He seemed to be struggling with no outward sign of success. He could see sweat forming on Torren's forehead, the veins on his neck bulging under the strain. He was just about to offer some words of encouragement when he was interrupted by Uthren.

"Maintain your focus Sylas, you're not done yet. The next part is the most difficult in the process. You must now focus the energy from your hands, back up your arms and into your head. As it enters your head, you will feel a very *specific* sensation. The feeling is different for everyone, but you should know it when you feel it. Allow that feeling take over you, then allow your consciousness to be released. That part will almost feel like you are allowing your soul to leave your body as if you were dying. Don't be alarmed, you won't die. You will just allow part of your life energy to exit and form the connection to your second mind."

Sylas looked at his hands again. His confidence bolstered at his early success. *I can do this…* He then closed his eyes and focused on the energy in his hands.

He felt the energy, still alive, still as welcoming as ever. He willed the energy to move from its current position back up his arms. The warmth crawled ever so slowly into his arms and up into his shoulders, the tingling sensation ever-present. It continued to rise until it entered his neck and then up into his head. Once it entered his head, his entire body started to pulsate with energy. He could feel every inch of his body all in unison. He felt the blood pumping through his veins, the air entering and exiting his lungs. He was aware of every muscle, every ligament, every cell in his body. He felt in complete control of his very being as if he could simply tell his heart to stop beating, and it would obey. A warm, almost burning sensation came from his pocket where the amulet was concealed as well, as if it knew that he was attempting to use the ancient power of Magick.

This must be the feeling, he thought, then felt a tingle run up his spine as if his body was affirming the thought. Focusing on the energy that now coursed through his body, he let out a breath of air and imagined his soul leaving his body. A part of his soul seemed to raise up above his mortal capsule, and then stopped.

Darkness flooded into his body, invading his mind. Despair and fear entered and overtook every other feeling. What once was light and warmth and peace, suddenly became darkness, cold, and destruction. He willed the feeling to go away, but it denied his pleas. Terror overcame him. He tried to release the energy and break the symbol that he was making with his hands, but the Darkness seemed to grab hold of his muscles, weaving their way into his bones and ligaments, forcing its dark will upon him.

He felt himself fall onto his back. He opened his eyes but saw nothing, only darkness. He tried to scream, calling out for help from Uthren and Torren, but only a cold wheeze came out. He felt as if his body was going to be decimated, reduced to a cold, dark ruin. Just when he felt as if all hope was lost, that he was banished to a dark realm, several images flashed in front of him, which he immediately recognized from when he was in the Ancient Crypt.

He saw an illuminated tree, standing on the top of a hill. A stream appeared next to the tree, slowly trickling water towards it before fading off into the nothingness in the distance. Birds were chirping and landing on the lower branches of the tree, picking at bright white fruit that was scattered about its branches. Something flashed to his left, then darkness consumed the tree. The scene in front of him changed to a great fire burning in the darkness. The flames were dark purple, almost black, consuming everything in their wake. Buildings and people that Sylas didn't recognize were being destroyed by the dark heat that it emitted.

He ran away from the flames in search of his home and his family, but the dark fire immediately surrounded him, sending an indescribable pain coursing through his body. He fell to his knees in agony and confusion, seemingly sentenced to an immediate doom. An echoing, evil laugh caused him to again jump to his feet and spin around.

Standing in front of him was the Dark Mage, Maelos. He wore black robes and a hood that covered his head and face. All that Sylas could see were his dark, glowing purple eyes through the shadows of his hood. Maelos laughed again, sending terror flooding through his body. He collapsed in fear and wrapped his arms around his head.

The flames of the dark fire and the cruel, mocking laughter of evil incarnate tormented his soul. Just as he felt he would be consumed by all the things surrounding him, everything fell silent.

He opened his eyes to see that the flames had disappeared, along with Maelos and the destruction of the city. A giant, breathtaking door stood in front of him. It was made of wood, so pure and white that it looked as though it had been made from trees that only grew in the heavens. The top of the door was rounded, and six, brightly colored symbols that glowed softly stretched across its arch. Where Sylas expected a door handle to be, there was instead an indented hole about the size of the amulet.

Sylas approached the door, cautiously reaching his hand out and touching the wood. Just as he felt the wood, the vision ended, and he found himself back on the riverbank lying on the ground. Pain coursed through his body as he lay there, struggling to get a breath of air to enter his lungs.

"Sylas! Are you alright?" Uthren said, kneeling beside him. He had one hand upon Sylas's chest and a look of concern on his face. "What happened? You were doing so well, then you suddenly looked to be having a seizure or something, are you okay?"

Pain continued to pulse through his body, though it was starting to subside. He sat up, terrifying images continuing to pass through his mind like the remembrance of a nightmare.

"I- I have no idea… I was just trying to open my second mind, but- but right when I thought I had it, I started seeing things again."

Uthren raised an eyebrow. "Seeing things again? Like another vision? Were they the same things you saw the first time?"

"I- think so…" Sylas responded, holding his head. "No, this time I only saw small pieces. Just more vividly a couple of pieces of what I saw the first time."

"What was it?" Torren asked, an obvious concern for his friend in his voice.

Sylas explained the vision to Uthren and Torren, describing the tree, birds, and stream as best as he could. He then moved on to the fire and destruction of what he assumed to be Shilvrst, as well as his encounter with Maelos. Finally, he recounted his view of the giant door.

"What could all of this mean, Uthren?" Sylas asked after he had finished. "Do you think any of it is going to come true? Is Shilvrst going to be destroyed?"

Uthren sat and pondered for a moment before speaking. "I'm not sure to be honest. In your vision, Maelos was looking *at* you? You feel like he saw you?"

"Maybe," Sylas said, rubbing the side of his head. "I don't know."

"What if it is true?" Torren exclaimed, "What if Sylas just used divination like Geode and saw the future? What if Shilvrst really is going to be destroyed? We have to stop it! Or at least warn them that something could happen!"

Uthren put a hand on his chin, "I don't think we have to worry about Shilvrst… at least, not yet. I do think it would be a good idea to at least warn them though. Perhaps send a message to Thren and have him tell others to keep an eye out. We can have Geode return to Shilvrst and deliver the message. We'll wait for him here. I truly believe that the sooner we can make it to Gelendor, the better. We can't risk Maelos or his henchmen finding us alone in the woods."

"Uthren," Sylas said, his mind unable to focus on Uthren's words. "Was the door that I saw… was that the Vault of Kings?"

"It's a good guess," Uthren responded. "I don't know what else it could be. As far as I know, only the original Kings themselves have ever seen the door to the Vault of Kings. These visions you're having, they trouble me… I'll have to ponder them."

"Why did they come back when I was trying to open my second mind?"

"It's hard to know. It could be that when you touched the stone in the crypt that you set off some kind of Darkness spell that the Council of Light and I failed to detect. Perhaps some of that Darkness remained within you all this time? I know that Darkness can be used to cause people to see things… to have nightmares… but this- I just can't be sure. I do wonder if there are any hidden messages within these visions that could help us in our quest… We'll have to keep a close eye on these visions whenever you have them. Perhaps we will be able to see more into what Aracorn and Maelos were up to through them."

Sylas opened his mouth but was cut off by the sight of Samara and Geode.

"What's everyone up to?" Samara asked, "Did you start training without me?"

Uthren motioned for both Geode and Samara to sit in the grass and then proceeded to tell them of the events that had just transpired. Sylas added in details where necessary and assured them both that he was alright.

"It can't be true… Shilvrst won't really be destroyed right, Uthren?" Samara said fearfully, "We have to do something. We can't just sit here if we know that something bad is going to happen."

"I was going to ask Geode if he would return to the town and warn Thren. He could then warn others and they could keep watch."

Uthren looked towards his comrade of many years, "What do you say, my friend? In the morning, would you return to the town and warn them of what Sylas has seen and meet us back here?"

Geode nodded, "I don't like it either. There isn't a reason I can think of that Maelos would attack Shilvrst again… But you never know with that mad man. I'll move swiftly and give a report to Thren. I'll be back before you know it."

"Thank you, my friend. As for the rest of you, I swore to protect you, and I vowed to myself that I would teach you how to protect yourselves if something ever happened to me. Get some rest. Tomorrow Geode will head back for Shilvrst, and we can continue our training."

CHAPTER 5
LESSONS OF LIGHT

Sylas laid in his tent, listening to the gentle flow of the river pass by him. Crickets and other insects chirped in the distance. A soft pitter-patter of a light rain fell upon the canvas of his tent. Typically, a night this peaceful would have lulled him into a deep sleep, but there was too much on his mind for sleep.

He pondered all that had happened to him over the past couple of days. The trip to the Ancient Crypt, the discussion about finding the rest of the elemental stones, the crazy vision he had seen… Not to mention he had almost conjured Light Magick already. True, he hadn't cast any spells yet, but he was surprised at how fast he was able to tap into his inner life and *almost* open his second mind.

Still pondering why fate had chosen him to find the amulet and embark on this crazy journey, Sylas thought that he heard something crack off in the distance. He sat up slowly and strained his ears, trying to filter out the gentle rain on the canvas and the flowing water behind him. He heard another sound, this time a rustling of leaves that sounded like they had been stepped on by a wet boot.

Sylas held his breath and slowly positioned himself on his knees and crawled over to the door flap of his tent, then with one finger pulled the fold of the door open just enough that he could peer out into the darkness. It was a Light Moon year, so even though the moon was only about three-quarters full tonight and there was a slight cloud cover, he was still able to see with only some slight limitations to visibility.

Four figures were slowly walking in the shadows, their silhouettes just barely noticeable. He wasn't able to see much detail, but it looked like they were looking for something.

Maybe they're bandits? Or friends of Uthren? Sylas doubted the last thought, Uthren would have told them if he had friends coming to meet them. Not knowing what to do, Sylas reached for his short sword that was lying just inside of his tent door flap. He steadied his breath as he quietly unsheathed the blade. The prospect of actually using it against another person terrified him, but he needed to be ready for anything.

Looking around to try and determine if it was just the four of them, Sylas noticed another figure crouching right next to Torren's tent. Sylas squinted his eyes upon the character and then realized that it *was* Torren. He must have been awake and heard them walking around too.

Torren turned his head and looked right at Sylas. He slowly put a finger up to his mouth and began to stand up. Sylas could see that Torren was also holding his sword and had already put his boots on. Sylas swallowed, unsure if he was ready for what was surely soon to come. He quickly reentered his tent, pulling his boots upon his feet with shaky fingers. Just as he was finishing lacing them up, he heard a brave yet scared yell enter the night air.

Scrambling out of the tent, Sylas looked up to see Torren exchanging blows with his sword against one of the dark figures, the other three charging towards him. Sylas jumped to his feet and ran towards his friend, screams of confusion and a plea for help escaping his lips.

One of the figures stopped running at Torren and turned towards Sylas. Sylas readied his sword and gritted his teeth.

The man stepped towards Sylas, raising his sword and swinging it down at his head. Sylas was barely able to bring his sword up to block the blow in time. Their swords clashed and bounced off each other, sending a loud ring throughout their camp. The man brought his sword to his side and swung out in an arch, this time aiming for the chest.

Sylas jumped backward, barely dodging the blade in time. Lifting his sword for the counterattack, he swung his blade at the man's upper arm. The man parried the sword away as if it were a stick and slashed again at Sylas. He tried to dodge it, but it came down with too much speed and caught Sylas on his left forearm. The blade sunk deep into his arm, burning like he'd just dipped his arm into liquid fire.

Pain coursed through his arm, forcing him to drop his sword. Blood poured out of his arm and into the ground, mixing with the rain and mud. The man lifted his sword to deliver the killing blow. Sylas helplessly lifted his right hand into the air as if to block the sword with his hand.

"Say goodbye, boy." The dark robed figure said, rain dripping down an evil smile.

The man swung his sword down at Sylas with a yell, but the sword stopped just before making contact. A glowing yellow sphere surrounded Sylas, its warm energy radiating over his body. The sword, unable to penetrate the shield of Light, bounced off unexpectedly and put the man who wielded it slightly off balance. Sylas looked to his left and saw Uthren standing with his arms stretched out towards him, his eyes and hands glowing the same color as the sphere.

"Uthren!" Sylas yelled. Raindrops glowed yellow as they fell around the powerful mage. He looked back down at his arm, the pain almost seeming to subside ever so slightly at the presence of his protector.

The man's stunned look turned into a scowl as he pulled his sword back into a fighting position and turned to face Uthren. Uthren looked at Sylas and instructed him to find Samara and hide.

"Don't come out until I call for you, do you understand?"

Sylas nodded, forcing himself to stand and push through the pain in his arm. Adrenaline surged through his body as he splashed through the rain and mud in search of his friend. A curious eye turned several times to focus upon Uthren.

The man tilted his sword, looking at Uthren with disgust, then spat at his feet.

"You have something that we need. Give us the stone, and we'll be on our way."

Completely ignoring the man, Uthren pulled his hands in towards his body and cupped them at his side. The shield that was protecting Sylas dissipated as he saw a ball of Light appearing in Uthren's hands.

With a yell, Uthren extended his hands out in front of his body, shooting a bright beam of Light towards the man. It rippled through the air with incredible speed, and before he even had time to blink, the Light beam pierced him in the chest and exited his back.

A gaping, cauterized hole sat where his chest cavity once was, allowing the light of the moon to shine right through his body. He fell to his knees, splashing muddy water into the air. A deathly wheeze joined the pattering of rain as he slowly tipped forward, falling face first into a dark puddle.

Turning from the sight of the corpse, Sylas put his hand over the gash in his arm, trying to stop the blood from exiting as much as he could. His mind was swirling with the loss of energy, but something deep down within forced him to continue. His eyes found Torren, still locked in combat with one of the other intruders.

Their blades danced in the night, clanking against one another in a deadly display. Torren surprisingly looked to have the upper hand. He swung at the man's leg with his sword, then threw his left fist at his enemy's face. The man was able to block the sword but didn't see the fist coming. Torren struck him right in the jaw, causing him to stumble backward.

Torren took this opportunity to bring his sword back around and jab at the man's side. He parried the blade, just in time, then took another swing at Torren.

Torren blocked the sword, but the man continued with added fervor, swinging with increased speed left and right. Torren was barely able to keep up, parrying the blade, but each time losing more and more ground. Rain splashed off dark robes as a black blade quickly changed positions, striking at Torren's head. Torren was quick to react, but not quick enough to avoid a swift shoulder as it slammed into his chest. The blow sent Torren sprawling backward onto the ground, a splash of muddy water rising into the air to meet the rain.

Torren reached for his blade that had fallen from his hands into a puddle, but the man introduced his muddy boots to Torren's chin with a swift kick, sending him back to the ground.

"Torren, no!" Sylas screamed, running towards his friend.

The man placed his muddy boot upon Torren's chest then lifted his sword high above his head, thrusting it down with a yell towards his heart. Just before the blade penetrated Torren's chest, a slightly glowing vine from a nearby tree sprang forward and wrapped itself around the sword. The man grunted and struggled against the vine as he looked around in confusion.

A deep green glow penetrated the darkness to his side. Sylas spun his head to the source, his eyes landing upon Geode.

Geode expertly spun a wooden staff, cracking it against his enemies head, then spinning it to block the attack of his second opponent. He held one arm extended towards Torren, controlling the vines with twitching fingers. His eyes and hands glowed with a deep forest green, causing the rain around him to appear as tiny falling emeralds.

He commanded the vines to throw the sword to the side then wrap themselves around the man like a woody serpent, starting at the ankles and working their way up his body. As if he were able to see in two directions at once, Geode expertly swung his staff with one hand, twirling it with astounding speed. He blocked incoming blades, parrying their attacks and smacking his opponents with spinning movements. His staff whirled in the wind before cracking against one of the man's arms, then swiftly returned to block a blow sent at his back. Geode pivoted and spun his staff above his head several times before slamming it down once again.

Glowing, emerald-like rain continued to fall around him, his dark black hair glistened in the light of the moon above. His attackers stood absolutely no chance.

A flash of light to his left pulled Sylas's attention. Uthren was engaged with several other dark figures, yellow Light Magick filling the air as he quickly incapacitated them. The growing number of enemies confirmed to Sylas that he had obviously not seen all of them when first peering out of his tent.

Torren rubbed his chin and pushed himself to his feet. His long hair dripped over the front of his face as his mouth dropped open, "Sylas your arm!"

"I'm fine," Sylas replied, the amazement of his two mentors in battle almost causing him to forget his wound. "Come on! We have to find Samara!"

Torren sent a quick glance towards Uthren and Geode. Yellow and green light glowed around them like strange auroras in the night. Enemies fell around them like flies, no hope for the forces of evil tonight. Torren nodded, springing to his feet, and joining Sylas as he ran towards Samara's tent. Wind whipped past their ears in the night as they sprinted through the rain, their eyes scanning the darkness for other intruders hiding in the shadows.

Please let her be okay. Sylas kept repeating to himself, *please let her be okay.* Approaching the tent, Sylas watched as a dark shadow slipped inside the door flap.

"Samara, watch out!" Sylas and Torren both yelled in unison.

They heard a scream coming from the tent and redoubled their speed. Moments later they came crashing through the canvas entrance where they saw a man holding Samara with a knife at her throat.

"Don't come any closer, 'r the girl gets it!"

Samara whimpered at his gruff voice, tears running down her face as her body shook with fear.

"Help me!" She whispered in a choked voice.

"Let her go!" Sylas yelled, his voice cracking slightly.

"I said stay back! Now, 'nless you want sweet cheeks 'ere to get it, you're gunna do exactly as I say. Back outta the tent, now!"

Sylas and Torren hesitated for a moment, not wanting to comply.

"Did I stutter? I said back *out*!" The man pressed the knife firmly against Samara's neck, drawing a bead of blood.

"Okay! We're going!" Torren said, raising his hands.

Keeping their eyes fixed upon Samara, they both backed out of the tent slowly.

"Hang the door op'n, so I can see ya leave," the man instructed, keeping the knife firm against Samara's neck.

Torren drew the door flap open and secured it to one of the main frame poles so that it would stay open.

"Now, keep movin'!"

Torren and Sylas continued backing up until they were out of the tent. The man exited the tent, keeping a tight hold on Samara. "Now, one of you's got the stone, yeah? Bring it t'me, or I'll slice 'er neck!"

"What stone?" Torren said, trying to delay for as long as possible, "There are rocks all over the place. Just pick one out yourself."

"Don't play games with me, boy. I know ya have it… The Stone of Darkness, it's all I need. Give it 'ere, or she dies!"

The man's eyes widened, he jumped backwards, tightening his grip around Samara, "Stay back! I'm warnin' you!"

Taken aback by the sudden movement, Sylas turned around and saw both Uthren and Geode approaching them. They had finished off the other men and still had the power of Magick glowing in their eyes and around their hands.

Samara's body was shaking involuntarily, her eyes pleading for help as she gazed upon her two protectors.

"Help me," A dry squeak slipped from her throat.

"Stop! Nott'a step closer!" The man said, pressing the knife against Samara's neck even harder, drawing more blood. "I'll hill 'er. Don't think I won't do it! I'll kill 'er dead!"

Uthren and Geode stopped walking, hands slowly rising in a defensive position.

"It's going to be okay, Samara," Uthren said, slowly pointing a finger towards her. A bright glow of Light Magick radiated at the tip of his finger, sending yellow reflections into the falling drops of rain.

A bright yellow Light appeared around Samara, covering her body with the protective Light energy that Sylas had seen Uthren use on him just moments before.

The man gritted his teeth, "I warned ya!" He twisted his body, slicing his knife across Samara's neck.

"No!" Sylas and Torren both shouted.

Samara's scream filled the air as the knife slid across her neck. Instead of falling to the ground in a destroyed heap, Samara remained standing, a bright flash of yellow Light around her neck acting as a protective barrier.

Uthren then raised both hands high above his head and pulled them down, causing a brilliant beam of Light to descend from the sky. A boom that sounded like it had descended directly from the heavens smote the man with holy power. His grip on Samara released, and the knife fell from his hand. He took a step backward, then fell to the ground, incinerated by the deadly beam of Light Magick.

Samara ran to Uthren, tears flowing down her cheeks as she wrapped her arms around him. Uthren returned the hug, and the Light from his eyes and hands faded into the night.

"Are you alright, Samara?" He asked softly.

She nodded and wiped the tears from her eyes, "I- I think so."

Relieved, Sylas released a breath of air he had been holding, then feeling light-headed looked back at his arm. The giant gash continued to pour blood onto the ground, his arm now completely numb. Stars glittered in his vision as he fell to his knees, trying to resist the urge to faint.

"Sylas!" Uthren exclaimed.

Kneeling down beside him, he again made the symbol of Light, and his hands and eyes began to glow. He placed his hands on Sylas's arm, causing him to scream in pain. Resisting the urge to pull his arm away from Uthren's hands, Light began to circle around his arm and enter into the giant gash. He felt the same warmth that he had felt when attempting to conjure Light Magick earlier that day. The heat entered his arm, and he instantly felt the pain start to subside. The blood stopped flowing from his arm onto the ground as his arm muscles began to weave themselves back together, working their way up towards the outer layer of skin. Finally, his skin pulled itself together, leaving a long white line where the blade had penetrated.

He looked with astonishment at his healed arm. The pain had completely left, the only sign that he had even been injured at all was just the thin scar that he now wore. Uthren tended to Samara, healing the small cut that she had on her neck, then proceeded to ask Torren if he needed any healing.

Torren simply shook his head, his senses still completely overwhelmed at the terrifying action that had just taken place.

Uthren nodded, and the yellow glow left his eyes and hands. He then turned and looked at the man in the distance who was still wrapped up in vines.

"Let's find out exactly who these people were. We need to know who sent them and how they know we have the stone."

They all walked over to where the man was lying on the ground. He struggled against the vines that held him captive but to no avail. Geode made the symbol of Nature with his hands and resumed the dark green glow of Magick. He stretched out his hand, and the vines around the man tightened, lifting him into the air so he was floating upright, just slightly off the ground.

Uthren walked up to the man and with an open palm, slapped him across the face. "Who are you? Who sent you to find us?"

The man spat at Uthren. "Do what you want, I ain't talkin'."

A strange look flashed over Uthren's eyes. It was as though he were casting holy judgement upon the evil that the man had just tried to perform. He made the symbol of Nature, and just like Geode, his hands and eyes began to glow a dark green. He raised his hand in the air and then clenched it into a fist. A small thorn sprouted from one of the vines wrapped around the man's chest, poking outwards away from his body.

"It would be a shame if more of these thorns were to continue growing from these vines, but *inward* instead of outward…" Uthren said, his voice cold.

The man swallowed, but his resolve held firm, "Do your worst!"

Uthren's face tightened as he held the gaze of the man. Rain continucd to fall, a low rumble of thunder in the distance. He raised his fist, then slowly started to squeeze. Several small thorns sprouted out from the vines that wrapped around the man's chest and arms. They pierced into his skin and continued to grow. The man shrieked in pain, a bead of sweat forming at the top of his forehead as his breathing rapidly increased.

"The thorns will continue to slowly grow in size until you are skewered like a kebab. Now tell me, who are you and who sent you here? Was it Maelos himself? Or do you work for one of his puppets?"

The man tried to hold firm, biting down hard against his lip as he endured the agonizing pain. A slow screech left his lips as he arched his back slightly, the pain too much to bare, "Alright, alright, I'll talk! Make it stop!"

Uthren waved his hand and the thorns that pierced the man's body retreated. Red spots of blood began to mark the man's clothing where the thorns had exited.

"Gah!" The man spat, his breathing heavy. "My name- My name's Raymond. I'm part of a band a thieves called the Black Hand. We've worked under Maelos goin' on ten years now. We were stationed atta encampment just outside'a Shilvrst when we got word from the Dark Mage that the Stone of Darkness 'ad been moved. He told us that he'd 'ad a vision that the stone'd been taken from its hidin' place. Told us it was crucial he get it back. He commanded us t' retrieve it and bring it t' him at any cost. We went t' Shilvrst searching for clues when we got word that he'd seen another vision. He said and the stone was near the river to the east."

The man grimaced again from the pain that the thorns had left in his body. "That's when found yer camp. Figured it was you who'd have the stone. No one else fer miles 'n miles. Has 'ta be you."

The man stared deeply into Uthren's eyes. "We're just his minions, the ones th't happened t' be closest to where the stone was when he felt it. He'll send more… He can *feel* where't is. He'll send powerful mages, ruthless warriors more skilled than us!"

His face darkened with hate and malice as he spat the next sentence, "You won't survive the onslaught that he'll send! He *will* get th' stone, and then he'll bathe the world in darkness!"

"He's already done that, genius." Torren mocked back at him.

The man chuckled, "Nah, bein' the s'preme ruler of Evendreil isn't his end goal, boy. He *needs* it back. He's still yet t' unlock his full potential. He's not done 'till he's become the ultimate and *immortal* ruler of the world."

Torren's eyes widened, but he played it off as cool as he could, "Pff, *immortal.* Looks like you chose the wrong side buddy. It's not gunna happen."

The man tipped his head back a hideous laugh exiting his throat. "You don't know the *half'a* what's goin' on. His power is *limitless!* He'll find a new hiding spot for the stone until the time is right. He'll continue buildin' up his armies until no one can stand in his way! The world you know'll be-"

The vines started squeezing Raymond tighter and tighter. He wheezed out in pain, unable to finish his monolog. Sylas heard the sickening cracking of bones as his wheezing scream turned into nothing but a gurgling whisper.

A loud *crack* followed, and Raymond's body fell limp. The vines dropped the lifeless body to the ground and retreated back to the tree from which they sprang.

"Geode," Uthren spat, almost angrily. "I wasn't done!"

"We heard enough, Uthren," Geode said as he lowered his hand. "There wasn't anything else useful he could tell us. Besides, if Maelos really knows the general whereabouts of where we are, then that means I need to leave for Shilvrst to warn them *now* and return to you as swiftly as possible. If he's going to continue to send people to hunt us down, you'll need me here."

Uthren still looked frustrated but agreed. "You're right, as usual. Leave for Shilvrst right away, we'll await your return here. I'll keep the others safe."

Geode nodded, turning towards the town of Shilvrst. "I'll be as fast as I can, but if I'm not back by tomorrow night, you must go without me. There will be others that can help keep you safe in Gelendor, and it would be much safer there than in the middle of the wilderness."

"We will wait for you, but we'll leave if it becomes too dangerous to wait." Uthren responded. "Meet us just a bit further down the river when you return. I'd like to move away from this battle scene in the morning."

Geode looked up at the moon. The rain was slowly starting to let up as patches of clouds began to part themselves to allow the moon to shine down upon them. Turning, he hurriedly jogged off towards Shilvrst.

Sylas looked back down at the now almost unnoticeable scar on his arm. *It's only been one day and half of a night since we left home, and I've already almost died.*

Uthren saw the concern on his face and walked up to Sylas, putting his hand on his arm.

"It should be as good as new by morning. Light can't get rid of all scars, but some, if healed quickly, will fade until it's like they were never there. You did well, Sylas."

He then looked at Samara and Torren, "You *all* did well. I'm sorry that we've already run into trouble. Try to get some sleep if you can. I'll keep watch for the rest of the night. We shouldn't be too far off sunrise."

Looking off into the distance where Geode had left, Sylas asked, "Will Geode be alright on his own?"

"Geode is one of the most skilled warriors I have ever met Sylas, not to mention a powerful and deeply knowledgeable mage. He can take care of himself. Now, you three go get some rest. I'll teach you how to heal with Light Magick in the morning while we wait for his return. I can already see that this will be quite necessary for you all to learn."

Looking back at his scar and then to Torren and Samara, who both nodded, Sylas agreed and started off towards his tent. Samara, still shaken from the night's events, opted to stay awake with Uthren. Sylas didn't see his sword on the way back to the tent, which made him nervous, but the knowledge that Uthren was keeping watch calmed his nerves.

He crawled into his tent and laid down on his back. Closing his eyes, he thought of his family back in Shilvrst, pleading to the Gods above that they were all safe.

****

Sylas awoke to the sound of birds singing in the trees around him. He sat up in his tent, his back cracking as he rose. To his surprise, he slept reasonably well and felt rejuvenated upon waking up. He found his boots and laced them up and then exited the tent. It was a beautiful fall morning. A crisp, cool air filled his lungs as he smelled the sweet scent of rain and dew upon the forest plants.

He stretched his arms, then remembered that his sword was still lost somewhere on the ground. It didn't take him long to find it, pulling it out of a slightly muddy puddle.

He wiped the dew and mud off the blade on his pant leg, then sheathed the sword and started off in the direction of Torren's tent. His eyes found Torren, stretching his arms into the morning air with a yawn.

"Hey, how's the arm?"

"Fine. It feels like nothing happened. I can hardly even see the scar."

"Pretty cool that healing Magick, right?" Torren replied. "I can definitely see how it would come in handy."

Sylas nodded, "I bet Uthren teaches us the same thing Samara was trying to do when we met her to talk about going to the crypt. She'll probably pick it up really fast."

Torren shrugged, "Yeah, maybe. But we can't let her think she's better than we are. We have to keep her humble, ya know?"

He gave Sylas a wink and then stretched his arms, and in the middle of the stretch, flexed his biceps, then raised an eyebrow and looked at Sylas. "Man, I'm looking *big* this morning!"

Sylas tried but couldn't keep back a smile and laughed. "Okay, Mr. Humble, let's go find her then and meet Uthren. I thought I might have heard her go back into her tent early this morning."

Torren chuckled and followed Sylas towards Samara's tent. Approaching the dew-covered canvas, Torren gave a couple knocks on one of its outer poles.

"Samara? Are you still sleeping?"

No answer.

Torren looked at Sylas and shrugged, "Do you want to take a peek inside?"

"Are you kidding me? No way! She'd kill me if I looked in there without her first giving permission."

Torren smiled, "Okay! Sylas is coming in, so I hope you're dressed!"

"Torren! No, I'm not coming in, go ahead and take your time Samara."

Torren laughed and then looked up and saw Samara and Uthren near the bank of the slow-moving river.

Torren slapped Sylas on the arm, "She never went back to the tent. Look, there she is with Uthren already. Oh well, guess you won't get to take a peek after all."

Before Sylas could say anything, Torren walked off towards Uthren and Samara. Sylas shook his head and took off after him.

Uthren greeted them as they arrived at the riverbank. The sound of gently trickling water filled Sylas's ears as Uthren directed both of the boys to sit down next to Samara.

"As you can tell from last night, we will run into our fair share of trouble during our quest. I believe that because of this, the most crucial spell for you to learn as of now will be a healing spell, closely followed by some basic combat spells."

"Torren and Sylas, I've caught Samara up to about the same point that you two got to yesterday, so now all three of you should be at about the same page. I realize that Torren still has yet to tap into his inner life, but we can work on that some more today. So far, Sylas is the only one to open his second mind, and he didn't really do it successfully. I hope that we don't cause another episode for you in trying again Sylas, are you willing to give it another shot?"

Sylas nodded.

"Good. Now, all of you again make the symbol of Light and tap into your inner life. Bring it forth into your hands and hold it there until I give further instruction."

All three of them made the symbols without any errors and closed their eyes. Sylas reached down and found the pool of his inner life. It was much easier to find this time, and he assumed it would continue to get simpler as he learned to recognize the feeling.

He brought the tingling sensation up from his stomach, into his torso, down his arms and into his hands. His hands felt warm and alive again. He opened his eyes and looked over at Samara and Torren. They were both still sitting, concentrating on finding their inner life.

"Remember to clear your mind and focus all your energy into finding that small spark within you. Once you find it, let it take control and work its way into your hands. Imagine it inside of your blood, pumping its way from your stomach into your hands."

They sat for just a bit longer until Samara's hands began to glow. She let out a sigh of relief at her success.

"Very good, Samara."

They all turned and looked towards Torren, whose eyes were now open. He broke the symbol with his hands and placed them in his lap.

"Go ahead without me, I'll watch for now."

Uthren nodded and returned his attention to Samara and Sylas.

"Now, bring your inner life from your hands up into your head and open your second mind. Once you feel the Magick take its place, let it embrace you and imagine yourself removing your soul from your body, allowing it to rise into the air. As it leaves, you will gain the ability to think and observe with both your first and second mind, and we can move on."

Sylas closed his eyes again and moved the energy from his hands up his arms and into his head. Upon entering his head, he felt the energy pulsing through his entire body, the same feeling that he had last time. He was yet again aware of every fiber of his being, every bone, hair, and drop of blood, all performing their functions while awaiting his next command. Sylas was about to imagine his soul leaving his body but then hesitated. Fear swept over him at the thought of having the dark visions again.

He stopped, and the very blood inside his body seemed to stand still. He was about to back out when he heard the voice of his father echo in his mind, "If you keep your heart and mind focused on what's right, darkness won't be able to overpower you."

The words of his father helped calm his nerves and reinvigorate his focus. He pushed away all thoughts of darkness and only focused on what was good and right. Then imagining his soul leaving his body, he felt again as if a part of his soul seemed to rise up above his body. After it exited, the strangest feeling overcame him. He felt his natural body, with his regular thoughts focusing on the task at hand, but he also felt as if he had gained a new *ethereal* body that could not be seen, floating above him in the air.

Slightly startled, Sylas opened his eyes and looked around. He felt as if he was controlling two persons at the same time. His physical body turned around and he saw the trees and land around him. Like exercising a muscle he'd never used before, he felt the newly gained ability to also turn the ghostly body of his second mind. Through its perspective, he was able to see the exact same scenery, just from a different point of view.

"Well done, Sylas! Very well done. Your second mind has been opened!"

With eyes glowing, Sylas turned back to Uthren with both his physical and ghostly head, still trying to make sense of what exactly he was feeling.

"Concentrate upon the second mind that you have just opened, Sylas. Try and think with just the *new* mind. Feel its influence, its tug. What differences can you gather between the thoughts you normally have and the thoughts of your second mind?"

Sylas concentrated upon his newfound ghostly body and homed in on its desires and thoughts, trying as best as he could to ignore the thoughts and feelings of his mortal body.

"I feel like- like it's me, but not entirely me… almost as if it's half of me and half something else…"

"That's *exactly* what it is. Your second mind is an extension of yourself, with the addition of the living element that you have conjured. It's not visible, but it exists nonetheless and can be independently controlled. Half of it belongs to you, and the other half belongs to the Light. They are combined to make one person, and that person is an extension of your physical self. You are now two instead of one, and your second self is shared half-and-half with the Light."

As confusing as his words sounded, it actually made perfect sense now that he was feeling it. He felt as if he could control his body just as regularly as ever, but at the same time had the ability to control this new ethereal body to do something completely different at the exact same time. This new body, however, seemed much different than his original. It was both attached to his normal body but also able to act and do whatever he wanted on its own. It also had different desires than he usually had. He felt as if he were righteous, holy, and justified in all things and refuted everything that was evil, unholy, and dark.

"I feel… good. And by good, I mean, holy. Like I'm righteous, and it's my duty to banish evil from existence. I also feel like I want to help people and smite those who would cause evil and destruction."

"Yes. That's because your second mind has been bound to the element of Light. Those are the feelings of Light mixed with yourself. Light would normally have an even greater self-righteous desire and demand for justice, but since it's only half Light and half you, those feelings have been toned down. The same thing goes the other way as well. Because you are bound with the Light, your normal desires have been amplified towards the good and banishment of anything dark or evil."

Sylas looked over at Samara to see that she had also broken the symbol and was watching him.

"The hardest part is complete. Now, you can cast your first spell."

Uthren took a knife out of his pocket and unsheathed it. He placed the blade on the palm of his hand and slowly slid it across his skin. He winced slightly, a thin line of blood slowly rising from his hand.

"Now, come over here and place your hand upon mine."

Sylas watched with his invisible body as his physical body moved towards Uthren. When it had moved a short distance, he found his new, second body drifting towards his physical body as if it were attached by some sort of invisible rope. He kneeled down in front of Uthren and placed his hand upon Uthren's.

"Now, I'm asking your physical self, the Sylas that's kneeling in front of me. Do you want my hand to be healed?"

Sylas nodded, "Yeah, of course."

"Now I'm asking your *second* mind, the new body that you have just received. Do *you* want my hand to be healed?"

Sylas felt his second mind grow ecstatic as the answer clearly flooded over his thoughts, *I need to heal you! And I will punish the blade that caused you injury.*

Sylas raised his eyebrows, surprised at the firmness of his own thoughts. "Not only do I want to heal you, it's like I also want to destroy your knife for cutting you!"

Uthren chuckled. "As you learn to control your second mind more, you will be able to temper the desires of the elements. They can be overbearing at times. The more you can persuade the elemental half of your second mind, the more powerful of a mage you will become. The more you get used to the way the elements *change* you, the more you can temper them and control your desires and passions towards your end goal. Try that now by using both your first mind and the half of your second mind that is you to persuade your feelings. Persuade them that, although the knife did something unjust, it's not your intent to destroy the knife, only to heal my hand."

Sylas focused upon the feelings of his second mind. The desire for righteous vengeance was still strong, but he reasoned with himself that Uthren was the one who cut himself, it wasn't the knife's fault.

After some time debating, the desires of his second mind calmed down and resolved that they wanted to only heal Uthren's hand… for now.

"Alright, we're one in our desires." He shook his head slightly, it sounded *weird* the way he'd said it.

"Then *will* it to be done."

Sylas focused on his desires, willing the effect to take place. A warm radiance began to fill his hands as the Magick began to flow.

The Magick seeped from his palms into Uthren's hands, glowing with a brilliant yellow Light as Uthren's wound began to mend itself. After only a few moments, the Light slowly dissipated. Uthren wiped the remaining drops of blood from his hand on the grass, then raised his hand and showed it to Sylas.

"Well done."

His hand was completely healed, a small white line spread across his palm the only sign that damage had been there just moments ago.

"That was *excellent* Sylas. Now, end the connection with your second mind. To do that, just allow your ethereal body to enter into your physical body, then allow the connection to the Light to be released."

Sylas concentrated his efforts into moving his ghostly body into his physical body. It slowly floated into place, then entered. A strange resistance followed, and Sylas allowed the connection to fade. The Light bid him a noble farewell as it left. His vision and other senses went from two back down to one, and the tingling feeling of his inner life slowly flowed down his body, back to its resting place in his stomach.

Sylas leaned back, his heart pounding quickly at the exhilaration. A smile curled up his lips, an immensely strong sense of accomplishment bubbling to the surface.

"You have a gift, Sylas," Uthren said softly. "There aren't many who are able to progress with the speed and success that you have just demonstrated."

Uthren looked at both Samara and Torren. "Don't feel bad that you weren't successful this morning. It's not a simple task to learn how to tap into your inner life and ultimately open your second mind."

Torren cleared his throat, "Uthren, I think I've decided that Samara and Sylas can go ahead and learn how to use Magick, but I think I'd rather do what I'm already good at. I've always been pretty gifted with a sword. Do you think you could teach me more?"

Uthren smiled, "Of course, Torren. There are many advantages of knowing how to defend yourself with a sword. I’ve been in many situations where I had to rely not on the elements, but on my physical abilities to save my life. I will teach you what I know, but Geode would be better suited to be your master, as he has much more experience than I do. When he returns, I’ll let him know your desires and he can teach you. He won’t be as good as your father, but his skills are excellent, and a greater master would be difficult to find.”

Torren smiled and jumped to his feet. “Alright!”

Samara stood and extended her hand to Sylas. Sylas received the gesture as she helped him to his feet.

“Good job, Sylas! That was amazing! Maybe you could give me some pointers sometime? I feel like I was *really* close… It’s just that last part that always gets me. I’d take any help you’re willing to give.”

Sylas grinned, “Yeah, of course! I’d love to help any way that I can.”

“I would expect nothing less,” Uthren said, rising to his feet. “Help each other to learn. We are all in this together, and there’s no room for jealousy or hoarding of secrets. The only way we’re going to be able to find all of the stones, enter the Vault of Kings, and ultimately stop Maelos, is by using our strengths to help where others are weak. Now, get your things together, let’s pack up camp and move downriver.”

CHAPTER 6
A WARNING TO SHILVRST

"Gah! Piece of garbage!"

Thren put the tip of his left thumb into his mouth to try and soothe the throbbing pain. He looked back at the nail and though it was now stuck in the wall, it bent to the left defiantly. Tossing his hammer on the ground, he picked up the last slice of bread he had been eating for lunch and ate it with a scowl. He looked back at the nail and asked, "Why? Why won't you just do as I ask?"

The nail stood just as still as ever, ignoring the plea directed towards it. Thren sighed and sat down on the ground. He'd been working on patching a hole in the wall of his chicken coop all morning. Due to his shortage of good nails, he was forced to use some old rusty ones that had been laying in a pile outside his house for who knows how long. Taking his last bite, Thren scooped a nail off the ground and rose to his feet.

"Now, you listen here..."

"Are you talking to that nail?"

Thren spun around, his heart jumping at the sudden voice behind him. His wife, Iriana stood behind him, her hand over her mouth trying to suppress a smile.

"I- No, of course I wasn't talking to the nail! I was just- It was-"

Iriana laughed. "Oh alright, I must be hearing things is all."

She smiled and walked up to Thren, giving him a kiss on the cheek.

"How is it coming along?"

Thren looked back at the bent nail and almost thought he saw a malicious grin rusted into its side.

"It *was* going alright, but I've run out of good nails and am having to use some of these old ones I found by the house, and they aren't cooperating with me."

"Well, shame on them. Don't they know who you are?"

Thren smiled, "Exactly! You'd think they'd show me more respect!"

Iriana laughed again, "Come on back to the house, Geode is here and says he has some questions for you."

Thren's eyes widened, but Iriana quickly shut his thoughts down, "Don't worry, he assured me that Sylas is doing fine. He says they just forgot to mention a few details is all."

Thren's hands began to sweat. *Why would Geode be here and need to talk to me if nothing has happened? Surely that can't be the case...* Masking his worry, Thren agreed and took Iriana's hand.

"Let's see what's going on then."

As he and Iriana approached the house, he saw Geode sitting with his eyes closed on the front steps.

"I found him Geode," Iriana called to him. "He was working with some *rebel* nails!" Iriana released his hand, letting out an anxious breath. A look of worry crossed her face, but her trust beat out her worry as she turned towards the house. "I need to finish hanging out the clothes, I'll be just around back if you need me."

Geode thanked her and gestured that they should go inside. Leading the way into the house, Thren's mind spun with possibilities of horrible things that could have happened to his son and the others. Anger and sadness wrestled inside of him, combated by a small sliver of hope that Geode did indeed tell the truth to Iriana and that they were all still okay.

Subconsciously, he led Geode into Sylas's room and shut the door. Pulling up a chair and bracing himself for the worst, he cleared his voice.

"What's this all about Geode? You wouldn't be here if you'd just forgotten to tell me something. What happened? Is Sylas alright?"

"Yes, Thren. Sylas is fine, I promise. We ran into a bit of trouble near the river, some bandits working for Maelos. No one was hurt, your boy did a mighty fine job of keeping himself safe. I hate to report so early that we've run into trouble, but you would know how dangerous it is out there, being part of Shilvrst's guard in past years."

"Yes, but this soon? You've only just left! How could Maelos possibly know what we're doing already?"

"That's what I'm here to talk to you about. Has anything strange happened in Shilvrst since we've been gone?"

Thren pondered for a moment then shook his head, "Now that you mention it… there were some strange people that came the morning you left. I didn't think much of it at the time, Maelos is always sending guards in and out. But these guys, they did have something *different* about them. They didn't stay long though, they left that evening."

Geode sat down on Sylas's bed, his mind putting the pieces together. "The timing all lines up. It must have been the same group that attacked us."

"But how would they know?"

Geode sat motionless for a moment, his mind spinning. "It's just a theory, but I'm starting to think that there might be a connection between Maelos and your son."

Thren's heart stopped in his chest, his throat growing dry, "What do you mean?"

"The Stone of Darkness, I think it might be the center piece. When Sylas found it, he said he had a strange vision. It showed him things that he couldn't possibly know about by any other means. I'm guessing that the very moment that he had that vision, Maelos was aware that the stone had been taken from its hiding place, so he sent some men to go and get it. They came here, the general location of where it was last hidden. While we were on the road, Sylas tried to use Magick, and must have accidentally tapped into that connection again. He saw another vision, which must have set off something so that Maelos knew where we were. That's why his men left, they knew where we were."

"Then they found you by the river," Thren finished.

"Exactly. There has to be a connection of some kind, Darkness that has seeped from the stone into your son."

Thren ran his fingers through his hair in frustration, his breathing growing heavier. "He's in danger then! All of you are! Maelos knows exactly where you are and will keep sending his goons! Or worse… he'll come down himself and kill you all and take the stone!"

Geode stood from the bed, pacing back and forth across Sylas's cold room.

"I think we still have a chance. I'm almost positive that he's *only* able to know where we are when Sylas has those visions. I don't think he can tell where we are otherwise. So, if we take slightly obscure paths and figure out a way to stop Sylas from having the visions, I don't think he'll be able to find us so easily. Also, I don't think we have to worry about himself coming to find us. At least, not yet. He's the kind of man that let's others do the dirty work for him, until he has no other option. By the time that happens, we'll be in Gelendor. We'll have the forces of Nature on our side, and it will be too late for him."

Geode stopped pacing, turning towards Thren, "You haven't gotten any impression of an incoming invasion, have you?"

Thren looked up, "What? Here in Shilvrst? No, I don't think so… Why?"

"Sylas was convinced he saw Shilvrst burning in the most recent vision he had," Geode said, starting his pacing back up again. "I think it would be wise to start keeping watch. Perhaps round up others that used to be in the Kings Guard to watch for signs of an invasion."

"I'd almost *want* them to come," Thren said, his voice low. "Torren's father, Fenrin, feels the same way. We talk about it often… the guards here would hardly stand a chance if we rose up against them. The only problem is what would happen if Maelos came down to put us back in our place…"

Thren shook himself, ideas of liberating the town fading from his mind. "I'll keep an eye out, tell a few people that were in the Kings Guard about it too. There's still a few of us left. We won't let them catch us by surprise."

"Good," Geode replied, "For now, that's probably the best we can do. Maybe someday though, Thren. I feel that someday soon, you might get your wish."

The thrill of battle started to rise once again in his mind, but he shut it down quickly, "Was there anything else that you needed to tell me?"

"No. Just that we appreciate you letting your son come with us. It's crazy to put so much upon the shoulders of one so young… but I *feel* something special about him, Thren. I don't know what it is yet, but I really do feel it."

Thren nodded, a tear of pride starting to form in his eye, "He's a special guy. No doubt about it."

Geode started for the door, turning back just before leaving Sylas's room, "Once we have our edge, we'll fight back, Thren. I promise you."

Thren smiled, "I'll hold you to it. No way I'd miss out on that fight."

****

Samara's inner life flowed up her arms like a warm river. The tingling sensation filled her chest, then slowly entered her head.

Nothing, she still felt *nothing!* Words of encouragement from both Uthren and Sylas filled her ears, but it was only distracting.

She let out a frustrated breath, pushing the inner life back into her chest, then inhaled as she focused on bringing it back to her mind once more. Uthren had said that the *feeling* was different for everyone. He described his own trigger like a slight chill that slowly ran up his spine. Sylas's had been much easier to recognize, like he felt his entire body being energized.

Her *feeling* was proving to be much more subtle than both of theirs… which was annoying her beyond belief. Up and down once again, she let the power of her inner life flow. She searched for the change, searched for the slightest of triggers that would tell her that she was ready to 'release her soul and open her second mind'. Even that part didn't seem to make much sense.

Release my soul? She thought. *Just let it fly up, up and away!*

She shook her head. She knew the inner sarcasm was *not* going to help her. She also knew that dwelling on the fact that it came so easily to Sylas was destructive.

Her spirits lowered slightly at the thought. She wanted to be *good* at this. She *needed* to be good at it. The previous night had been the most terrifying night of her life. Even sitting next to Uthren for the remainder of the night, she constantly thought she saw shadows in the trees, lurking towards her to come and snatch her up… place a knife on her throat and slice her neck. She feared she might never get a good night's rest again.

"Come on," She whispered a prayer, so softly that no one else could hear. "I *need* to do this. I have to be able to protect myself."

As the prayer left her lips, a calmness greater than any she'd ever felt seemed to fill her chest. It wasn't anything physical, no warmth or cold or strange tingling sensation. It was simply a feeling, like a knowledge that had been gently placed within her, telling her that all would be well.

It was as if there was an ancestral spirit whispering into her ear, letting her know that she was being watched over. The cares of the world seemed to fade away, their meaning and significance blurred away by a peaceful calm.

Without questioning the feelings, Samara imagined her soul leaving her body. The strangest sensation came over her, as if a small piece of herself that she rarely felt was slowly leaving, rising above her physical body, and hovering above her.

She gasped, opening her eyes as the feeling cemented itself. Upon opening her eyes, she noticed that instead of just one plane of vision, she was met with an additional view she had never seen before, one from the perspective of a ghostly apparition floating directly above herself.

"By the Light!" Uthren exclaimed, his eyes widening. "Samara, you've done it! You've opened your second mind and connected to the Light!"

Samara's heart raced with excitement. She looked to her left and with her physical eyes was able to see the surroundings that sat to her left. From her spectral body, she saw her physical body beneath her slowly turn. She then willed her second mind to look to the right, and her ghostly eyes saw the river gently flowing beside her. She could see and perceive the sight of two *different* directions all at the same time!

No way... Excited to see what the body of her second mind looked like, she turned her physical head to look behind her and at the same time tried to look down at her body with her second mind. To her surprise, she didn't see anything floating behind her. The vision of her second mind saw her physical body, look of confusion and all, staring right through her.

"Don't confuse yourself too much," Uthren said with a chuckle. "The body of your second mind isn't visible to anyone, not even yourself."

"This is- Wow! I just, I don't know how I can take *all* of this in at the same time! How can I look both left and right… It's-"

"It's confusing at first. But with time and practice, it becomes much more natural."

A noticeable shift came across her thoughts as she observed the world. She felt more noble and proud. She almost felt… *holy*. Her thoughts and desires were still her own, but there was a definite influence tugging at her now that seemed to want *justice* in all things.

"Light is very… confident," she said, trying to come up with the word that fit her feelings correctly.

"The Light is very influential. All the elements have their own pull and a lot of times if you are not careful, you will find that they can even influence you to do things that *you* wouldn't want to do. Never let the element have full reign upon your desires. The perfect balance is to bring the desires of the element to a happy medium with your own. The Light is *constantly* wanting to banish darkness and destroy evil, but sometimes it can't recognize the good in some things. If Light were able to use Magick on its own, it would be completely overzealous and probably end up doing more harm than good. It's the *balance* that you create that makes it truly good."

The power of the Light surged through her body, exhilarating her senses.

"I want to try to cast a healing spell like Sylas did," she said excitedly.

Uthren pulled his knife out of his pocket. He slowly unsheathed it and gently slid the blade across his hand, drawing several small beads of blood across his palm.

"Just as I instructed Sylas, you must bring into alignment the desires of both your first and second minds. When they are both in unison with your end goal, place your hand over mine and will it to be done."

Sylas watched as Samara concentrated on most likely the same process he'd used to convince the Light within herself that she did not need to enact holy vengeance upon the knife, but just to heal what was wounded. Samara concentrated for a moment, then slowly placed her hand upon Uthren's. Almost immediately, the glow from her hands spread into Uthren's hand. A flash of yellow surrounded their hands, then faded. She pulled her hand away eager to see her success.

Uthren smiled, revealing his unwounded hand. "Very good, Samara. Now you have *both* successfully cast your first Light spell."

"I want to learn more!" She exclaimed. "Teach me something else! I don't want to close my second mind yet."

"I appreciate your enthusiasm, but before we get into any more basic spells, I want to help both you and Sylas to become efficient at opening your second mind swiftly. It won't do you any good to know how to cast spells in battle if you will be overtaken while trying to focus on opening your second mind. It needs to become something that you can do in an *instant*, without even having to think about it."

Uthren made the symbol of Light. The very instant that his fingers completed the symbol, the brilliant yellow glow of Light surged within his hands and in his eyes.

"The mark of a true master is when they can enter and exit stages of Magick in a moment's notice. I don't expect either of you to be this fast for quite some time, but I do expect you to become much quicker than you are now before I teach you any more spells."

Uthren released the Magick, and the Light faded out of existence. With a smile, he added, "This way, you will have motivation."

Disappointed that they were not going to learn anything new, but excited at the challenge of getting faster at opening their second minds, Samara and Sylas looked at each other. Sylas knew that Samara was quite competitive, as was he. The race to mastering the Light was on.

****

Torren wiped the blood from his knife on the tall grass beside him. "Three rabbits ain't too bad if I do say so myself."

He wrapped the meat he had just skinned inside of a cloth and put it in his bag along with the fur skins. "At least it'll satisfy until Geode gets back."

He remembered catching a glimpse of Geode fighting off the two men with his staff. Grandeur thoughts of becoming the greatest swordsman alive spun through his head wildly. He could almost see himself challenging his own father to a sparring match, beating him with techniques that not even the greatest of the greats could dream of. *While Samara and Sylas are off learning their silly Magick, I'll be learning the cool stuff.*

He jabbed at the air several times with his knife, stabbing his invisible opponents with grace and ease. Disappointment swirled in the edges of his mind at not even getting the first step of Magick down, but he didn't let it get to him. His father was the best swordsman in Shilvrst, possibly the world if his mother's stories were true, and he had a legacy to uphold.

I'll be the greatest swordsman ever! No one will be able to cross blades with me and live to tell the tale! The strange technique that his father always kept a secret flashed in his mind. He'd learned it from Torren's grandfather, someone he *really* wished he knew more about. So many secrets were kept in his family… Maybe once he *proved* to his father that he could stand toe to toe with him, he'd spill all the secrets. He took another swing, slicing the head off his last imaginary opponent and then shoved the knife into its holster. *Master Torren, they'll call me. The greatest of all time!*

Making sure that he wasn't leaving anything behind, Torren turned back towards the river. With daydreams of epic battles and legendary victories, he made his way back to camp. Upon arriving, he noticed both Sylas and Samara sitting with Uthren near the riverbank. Approaching them, Torren asked if they were still planning on packing up and heading out this evening.

"I imagine that Geode will be back before dark," Uthren responded. "Either way, we'll probably stay one more night. He's been traveling nonstop and will need to rest."

"I got some rabbits while I was hunting," Torren said holding up his prize. "So, I was just wondering if I should prepare them for travel or if we were going to stay one more night."

"Looks good," Uthren said with a sincere smile. "We'll have them tonight while we wait for Geode."

Happy with Uthren's answer, Torren jogged towards his tent to get the meat ready for cooking.

"Excellent progress today," Uthren said, placing a fist on his chest. "Your speed has increased significantly. Rest now, and we'll await the return of Geode."

****

It was several hours after dark before Geode finally returned. Sylas was beginning to worry that he might not come back at all. *What if more of the Black Hand found him before he made it back to Shilvrst? Or what if the town was being destroyed as he arrived, and he tried to help but was killed in battle?* Ominous thoughts continued to peruse through his mind until Geode finally arrived.

He and Uthren talked privately for a while, after which Geode returned exhaustedly to his tent.

"Shilvrst is still in one piece," Uthren said sitting next to them around the fire. "Preparations have been made to ensure that any attempt to attack the town will not be a surprise. You need not worry about your family's safety for the time being."

All three of them let out sighs of relief. The tension had been building during Uthren and Geode's private conversation. It was hard to tell whether the fact that they had decided to discuss things privately was a good or bad sign.

"However," Uthren added. "Geode and I both agree that not all is well. We believe there may be a curse upon you, Sylas. Something that not I, nor the Council of Light could have foreseen. When you have your visions, we believe that it is a trigger that allows Maelos to see where you are. There's a connection between him and you, and we think the connecting point may be the Stone of Darkness."

Sylas felt the cold of the amulet in his pant pocket radiate, as though it knew that they were talking about it.

"Aracorn's power was admittedly much more accomplished than we gave him credit for, which has proved to be a grave mistake. His knowledge of dark, ancient arts and the utility of Darkness far surpasses anything I would have guessed him to possess."

"Utility?" Samara asked, tightening the blanket she had wrapped around her.

"A word I use to describe how *useful* some Magick can be. Healing is not something that can be used offensively in battle, but is still very useful in practice. For example, an offensive spell that you have seen would be what Geode did, where the vines came forth from that tree and incapacitated the man who was fighting Torren. One that you have not seen him use that's much more utility-based would be something like when he talks to animals or uses divination."

"He can talk to animals?" Torren shouted, about falling off the tree stump he had been sitting on.

"Indeed, he can," Uthren responded with a smile. "And it's more useful than you think. An innocent squirrel or bluebird can be much greater of a spy than any human. The point is, however, that some spells are used almost exclusively for utility purposes rather than for offensive or defensive combat.

Darkness seems to give thoroughly when it comes to useful spells… It gives a *lot* of knowledge to those who are willing to bind themselves to it…"

Uthren shook himself, "Needless to say, I think that Aracorn and Maelos must have found the Stone of Darkness a long time ago, learned many ancient secrets from it, then, for some evil purpose still unknown to me, hid the stone for safekeeping so that no one else would be able to find it."

He wasn't sure why, but a strange curiosity seemed to fill Sylas, and he couldn't help but ask, "Why is Darkness so useful?"

Uthren sighed, "Ultimately, the elements are only as useful or powerful as the mage that wields them," Most mages will tell you that the elements are equally balanced, some with greater power and less utility, and others with more utility than power. Others, however, truly believe that a master of Darkness is the most powerful that a mage can aspire to become, without the use of combinations that is. The amount and quality of Darkness spells that have been discovered throughout the ages is mind boggling compared to other elements. Darkness seems to almost *guide* the user to new discoveries. Some of them are quite terrifying as well…"

Uthren's gaze flicked towards Sylas, a mystery hidden behind his old, wise eyes.

Crickets and other insects, along with the flowing river in the distance and the crackling of the campfire, provided the only competition to the silence that surrounded them until Uthren spoke again.

"I'll tell you one thing. If there *is* a connection between you and Maelos, then there is a chance that a truly ancient evil has been awakened. Knowledge of such things is not supposed to exist… not anymore. I hope to the Light that I am wrong, that I am overreacting. Perhaps this old fool is dreaming up nightmares, but one can never be too sure when talking about Maelos."

Uthren put his hands on his knees and rose to his feet. "We've gone into more detail than I wanted to. Now, get some rest everyone, we'll leave for Gelendor first thing in the morning."

CHAPTER 7
DARK VISIONS

Sylas walked with heavy feet along the grassy trail in front of him. Birds chirped in the surrounding trees, almost as though they were laughing at his pain. *How many days has it been now? Four? Five?* He was beginning to lose track. The muscles in his legs felt stiff as they carried his body closer and closer to the city called Gelendor. He couldn't wait to get there. Geode was doing his best to keep many stories about the city a secret in order to 'surprise' them when they arrived. But Torren, Samara, and himself had been able to squeeze a few details out of the warrior. The Capital of Nature… if anything that Geode had said was true, it might just be the most amazing place that Sylas would ever visit.

A curious sensation- like a whisper- told him that Gelendor would only be the beginning. It tickled the back of his mind, but the feeling quickly faded as the bottoms of his feet ached and complained.

Looking up from the ground in front of him, Sylas directed his voice towards Uthren. "How much further is it to Gelendor? *Please* tell me we're getting close."

"We still have about another week's journey until we get there," Uthren replied. "I would estimate we are about halfway there."

Audible moans came from not only Sylas but also Samara and Torren. Uthren turned his head towards them, a sly smile curling up his lips. "You are all going to have to get used to traveling long distances. We aren't going to be in Gelendor for too long I'd imagine. There will be much more strenuous, long, journeys ahead of us yet."

"Can't we rest for just a minute?" Samara complained, slowing her pace slightly. "I'm starving and need a break."

Uthren looked into the sky, noting the midday position of the sun. He sighed, shaking his head, "We really *should* keep a good pace. But I suppose a small rest wouldn't kill us. I'll agree, as long as we can put in a small training session while we rest."

"Deal!" Torren, Samara, and Sylas exclaimed in unison.

Taking a few more steps towards an inviting grassy area, Uthren dropped his pack and sat down on a slightly rotting, fallen tree.

"Geode, if you and Torren are not too fatigued, this would probably be a good time to continue with your combat training as well."

Geode looked over at Torren. Torren grinned widely, "I'm always ready for more training!"

Torren reached into his bag and pulled out some dried fruit, shoved it in his mouth, then drew his sword and held it high in the air as if he were trying to channel a lightning bolt to come down and energize his blade. He let out a battle cry then slashed his sword down and did a spin move.

Cocking his sword arm to a jabbing position and holding his left hand out in front of him, thumb and two fingers extended, he raised his left knee to his chest, closed his eyes, and let out a controlled breath of air.

He opened his eyes and saw the rest of his companions frozen in their actions, staring at him wide-eyed. He turned his head and saw Geode with his face in his palm.

Torren's face turned red, a bead of sweat forming at the back of his neck as he lowered his leg and sheathed his sword. Clearing his throat, he sheepishly notified everyone that he would be 'over there' and quickly scurried away.

Laughter quickly filled the trees as the group teased Torren. Although he was still embarrassed, Torren couldn't help but smile. He was glad that he had a gift of lightening the mood and making people smile, even if it was spawned from an embarrassing moment.

Geode pushed himself to his feet, still stifling a bit of laughter, then headed off to begin his session with Torren.

Uthren cleared his throat, "I promised that we would learn more techniques after your speed at opening your second mind had improved, and neither of you has left me disappointed. You will continue to get faster and faster as we train, but for now, your speed is sufficient. However, before moving on to offensive techniques, I have one very important defensive spell that I would like you to learn."

Uthren made the symbol of Light, and his hands and eyes began to glow. He then broke the symbol and held one of his hands outstretched.

"As you both have already witnessed, shielding can be very useful during the heat of combat. It can be used to protect yourself or an ally from danger. While the shield is very powerful and will block almost any amount of damage directed towards you, it's not fail-proof. If too much damage is directed towards your shield, the damage will be blocked, but the shield will then dissipate, and you will need to conjure another to take its place. For now, however, we shouldn't be running into many enemies that will challenge the strength of your shields."

A yellow sphere appeared around Uthren's hand as he finished talking. The Light swirled in a slow even pattern, almost like a liquid caught in a slow whirlpool. It was deceptively thin and looked as if a blade would easily penetrate its shell, although Sylas knew better. Uthren reached into his pocket with his other hand and pulled out his knife, handing it to Sylas.

Sylas hesitated for a moment, then called to remembrance the shield that had been placed around him when the Black Hand had attacked, as well as the shield that Uthren had placed upon Samara, protecting her from getting her throat slit. He took in a small breath, then stabbed at Uthren's hand with the knife. The tip of the blade struck the glowing yellow power of the Light Magick, feeling like it had just been slammed into a wall. The tip of the blade shot to the side, as if the Light had not only blocked the blow, but also commandingly rebuked it. His wrist twisted at the impact, almost making him lose his grip on the knife.

"Light *naturally* wants to protect, so conjuring powerful shields is a simple task, even for beginners. One is also able to control the size of the shield, like so…"

The Light swirling around his hand quickly expanded, the energy pulsating like a living, alien form of liquid. In moments it was large enough to surround Uthren's entire body, encasing him within the protective barrier.

"I can also shape it to my body, dawning the armor of the Light."

The Light again glowed more luminous as the size changed, shrinking down to just around Uthren's one hand until it looked almost as if it had turned into a thin glove of Light.

"The size of the shield is the easy part to control, but the strength of it, how much damage it can block without being broken, is where the practice and mastery kicks in. The stronger you are as a mage, the more powerful your shields will become."

The Light faded from Uthren's hand, and his eyes stopped glowing as he gestured to Sylas to return his knife. Sylas handed the knife back to Uthren as he continued to speak.

"As I was saying, Light naturally wants to protect those whom it deems worthy, so providing protection is not difficult. The more that you can persuade the

Light that the object or person that requires protection is holy and just, the stronger the protection will be. If you are trying to convince the Light to protect yourself, it makes it even easier. Now, it's your turn. Both of you open your second minds, and we'll continue from there."

Sylas and Samara both made the symbol of Light with their hands. Within a couple of seconds, their eyes and hands began to glow with the yellow color of Light Magick.

Uthren nodded in satisfaction, "We'll start with shielding *yourselves* before moving on to protecting others. Concentrate on your second mind and align your wills together with the desire to create a shield around your right hand."

Almost in unison, Sylas and Samara broke the symbols they were making and stretched their right hands out in front of them. Sylas concentrated on his second mind and its desires. He tried to think in words that Uthren might use, telling his second mind that he needed to prove himself worthy of further instruction in the sacred art of Light Magick, by creating a divine shield around his hand. His second mind seemed to *really* like the flowery language, immediately agreeing that this cause was just and that the task should be done.

Sylas noted how much the influence of Light tugged at the conscience of his second mind. It *wanted* to be used and show forth its power. It just needed a vessel, a vessel that was provided by himself.

With his desires aligned, Sylas willed the task to be done, and a yellow sphere of Light encircled his hand. Samara had similar success, a brilliant yellow glow radiating around her hand as well.

Uthren held his knife out in front of Sylas and asked him if his desires were pure and just. Sylas nervously nodded, then felt the rebuke of his second mind. It told him to be confident, to not shy away from his divine potential. Feeling the boost of confidence, Sylas nodded once more.

Uthren's hand shot forward, stabbing the knife towards Sylas's shield. The Light around his hand glowed brightly as the tip of the knife bounced off its edge. The Light grew as his confidence at seeing his success increased. His sense of holy power and desire to provide protection from evil flaring the power of his shield spell.

"Light is a very *confident* element," Uthren explained as if he'd read Sylas's feelings. "As your confidence in yourself and the element increases, your power with the Light will also increase. Well done. Samara, are your intentions pure, and your actions holy?"

"Yes! You will not harm me!"

Uthren smiled at the apparent influence of Light in her voice. He flipped the knife in his hand, displaying an expertise with the blade that Sylas wouldn't have guessed the old man to have, then slashed the knife at Samara's hand. The blade bounced off just as it had done with Sylas but added to it, a slight booming noise and a flash of Light that sent Uthren's arm sprawling backwards.

Uthren shook his arm, rubbing out the pain, "Outstanding Samara! You seem to have an aptitude for Light Magick. Time will tell… Now, I want each of you to concentrate on moving the shield from your hands, and this time placing them upon each other. Change your desires from being self-centered to being protective of your friend. Increase the size of the shield as well, so that it's covering the entire body."

The two apprentices concentrated, slowly moving their orbs of Light towards each other. Sylas focused on how much he cared for Samara as he pushed the shield towards her. A burning sensation filled his soul, a deep desire within his second mind to protect her at any cost.

The Light from his shield radiated even brighter as his desires aligned, and he found it easy to extend the sphere around her entire body. Samara also had success in moving her sphere around Sylas and extending it to cover his whole body.

Uthren readied his knife, his eyes becoming fierce, "Samara! Protect your friend!" The old man lunged out with the knife, stabbing it ferociously at Sylas.

Sylas winced slightly but was relieved when once again the blade bounced off the shield that was surrounding him and was sent backward defiantly. Uthren shook his arm from the rejection and with a pleased look, congratulated Samara for her excellent protection.

Readying himself, he once again took an aggressive position, this time towards Samara. "Sylas! Protect your friend!"

As Uthren swung his knife towards Samara, time slowed nearly to a stop. His second mind flared with rage, the Light dominating his thoughts.

He tried to control his anger, knowing that Uthren did not intend to *actually* harm Samara. It wasn't enough, his second mind was being dominated by the Light. Its desires to prevent Uthren from attacking Samara were overwhelming. The Light forced it's will upon his own, taking complete control of his actions. Time sped back up as he yelled, "Don't hurt her!"

The energy from his shield grew brighter and brighter, the shield expanding outward and actually *attacking* Uthren. Its circular, shield form changed shape to form a deadly point of Light, like a spear cast down directly from the heavens. The spear lunged forward, eager to sink its tip into his opponent, striking down his enemy in holy vengeance.

With the speed and mastery of a true legend, Uthren moved his hands into the symbol of Light and quickly radiated with the same holy energy. He swirled his hands in front of his body, catching the spear of Light within his palms. Sylas felt the Magick slowly fade from his body, its will and power obeying a new master now. Uthren's long, white hair flowed wildly, as if a powerful wind hand suddenly been blown towards him. The Light swirled in between his palms, as he slowly pressed his hands together, then all at once disappeared into nothing, the power having been completely absorbed by the powerful man.

Sylas fell to his knees and felt his second mind close as the Light left him completely. Breathing heavily from the loss of control, he looked over at Uthren.

"Uthren! I- I'm sorry. I don't know what happened! The Light, it took control..."

Uthren closed his eyes, releasing a breath of air as the Magick around his body faded.

"You can't let the elements take over you, Sylas. It's *imperative* that you always stay in control. If you lash out with the untamed and unbridled power of the elements when they are out of your control, it could prove fatal not only to those around you but also to yourself."

His voice was stern, but in it there was a kind understanding. "I know it's hard. The elements can be difficult to control at times. As you continue to practice it will get easier. I'll help you to control those outbursts as best as I can with tips that I have found helpful during future training sessions."

His sternness faded as a smile curled up his lips, "Good job on protecting Samara, though. If I weren't quick, I would have been in trouble."

Sylas allowed himself to release a small chuckle, but the painful thought of almost *attacking* Uthren still ate at him. "I'm really sorry, I don't know what came over me…"

"I felt something similar when Uthren was attacking you, Sylas," Samara said, touching his arm.

"I didn't want to see you get hurt. I knew that Uthren was just trying to teach us, but still a part of me wanted to lash out and stop him. But I was able to focus my thoughts and tell myself that my desires were only to *protect* and not to harm. I sort of whispered it to myself, and it seemed to help me."

"There have been many mages that have been consumed by the elements they were attempting to wield," Uthren explained. "The power that the elements contain cannot be treated lightly, and one must always proceed with caution when attempting to use them. Remember, you are not just using them, you are *uniting* yourself with them, then directing them in a manner that *you* desire. Control is the true key to mastering Magick."

Sylas nodded, feeling slightly better.

"All in all, I think you both did quite well. There's still a lot of room for improvement, of course, but you are both progressing much faster than I could have hoped. Perhaps tomorrow we'll talk about control and do some *planned* offensive Magick."

Uthren gave him a wink. "Until then, we'd better keep moving. Sylas, can you please let Geode and Torren know that we're ready to leave?"

Sylas headed off towards where Geode and Torren were sparring. He was still upset that he let the Light overpower his will and take control…how could he not be? In his heart, he vowed to himself that he would *never* let that happen again.

The images of two sparring figures grew closer as he approached, the sound of wood-on-wood clanking together with audible thuds.

****

Torren took a step back and ducked under the swing of Geode's staff, then lunged his wooden training sword towards the chest of the Nature mage. Geode easily parried the blow as he spun his staff in front of him in a quick circle.

Geode's eyes met Sylas, and Torren took the moment of distraction as an opportunity of attack. He attempted to use the momentum from being parried aside to spin around and make a mighty swing at Geode. As soon as his back was turned, Geode brought his staff down on Torren's back with a loud slap, dropping him to the ground. Torren gasped for air his face hit the dirt.

"What have I told you about turning your back to your opponent?" He said in a gruff voice. "Those types of moves are never practical and will only get you killed. By the time you actually spun your body to face me again, I could have struck you several times."

Torren choked on air that refused to enter his lungs. He slowly pushed himself off the ground and onto his knees. He tried to respond, but the wind had been forced out of his body with the blow, and all he managed was a wheeze.

"You need to learn to focus on what strikes are most *efficient*, not the ones that everyone will tell stories about around the campfire. I know that you want to live up to the reputation of your father, but you aren't going to be able to do that while making these silly moves of yours."

Geode walked to the front of Torren and held out his hand. Taking it, Torren stood and after a few more moments of breathlessness, was finally able to take in a gasp of air.

"Yes, master." He finally said. "I guess I was just, I was trying to be like him… I won't do it again; you have my word."

Geode placed a kind hand on his shoulder. "I've heard stories about your father, Torren. Believe it or not, I've even heard about your grandfather. One day you'll be just as skilled as they are. I know you will. For now, though, let's keep our focus on the basics." He smiled and patted Torren's shoulder. "Are we ready, then, Sylas?"

"Yeah. I was just coming to get you. We're headed out soon."

"Very well, let us be off." Geode faced Torren and put his fists together, giving him a respectful bow.

Torren repeated the gesture and bowed back, then bent down and picked his wooden sword up off the ground and slid it into its leather holster.

Torren and Sylas walked together, following the mighty Geode a few paces behind his own.

"How did your training go, Sylas?" Torren asked.

With a slight hesitation, Sylas responded a bit less enthusiastically than Torren expected.

"It was good… we went over shields today."

"Oh man, that sounds awesome! So, were you able to do it then? Did you make a shield?"

"Yeah, I made one, it even blocked Uthren's knife when he tried to stab through it."

"That's great! So, why do you seem so down? I thought you'd be happy with that."

Sylas let out a breath of frustration and recounted his little mishap to Torren.

"It was like… Like the Light's influence was more powerful than my own. It just took over and made me lash out. I feel terrible about it."

"Don't let it get you down, Sylas," Geode said, turning his head towards them. "Taming the elements and learning to control the desires of your second mind isn't easy. Especially with the elements that have strong wills. Light is kind of a tough one, to be honest. Not that it's particularly hard to use, just that it's hard to… tame it. It just seems to have an unyielding will to do what it sees as *righteous* all the time. It can sometimes be hard to sway it in the direction that you desire."

"Is Nature that same way?"

"Nope," he said with a smile. "Nature is *much* different. Well, I guess I wouldn't say it like that. Nature wants to do good, just like the Light does, and it has a strong desire to *protect*, just like Light. Why, it can even heal just like the Light does! But, Nature is much more *calm* and easily persuaded. As long as the user has a calm and peaceful mind, it simply wants to be used to further growth and life and to protect against anything that would destroy life. It's content to let you steer it in whatever direction falls into those simple categories."

Sylas kicked a pebble and watched it roll across the dirt. *It would be nice to use a more relaxed element…*

"Maybe one of these days you could teach me about Nature Magick?" Sylas asked. "I'm also really interested in learning combinations, too. Uthren keeps telling me about them and how useful and powerful they can be."

"Ahh, now *that's* where the Magick gets fun." Geode said with a smile. "It's not easy, and I'd recommend you at least get down the basics, plus some more advanced stuff before trying to combine the elements. But I'm telling you, *real* Magick, is when you can mix them all together to *exactly* fit your needs."

He slowed himself so that Sylas was walking directly by his side. "I'd be happy to teach you some Nature Magick sometime though. That way you can see the difference between it and the Light. Maybe after you get both of 'em down, we can work on mixing the two. You'd like that… it's a real… *colorful* combination, useful too."

A mysterious, almost mischievous look passed over Geode's lips as he continued walking.

"Aren't you going to tell us what it is?" Torren asked.

"Nope. Basics first, my young apprentices. Basics first." He ended his sentence with a slight laugh, obviously proud of his little secret.

"Is there any advantage to choosing one element over another?" Sylas asked, eager to dig deeper into Geode's knowledge. "Or even advantages with using combinations or sticking to one element?"

Geode shrugged, "It's kind of just preference. Well, there's a bit more to it than that, but I'll bet Uthren teaches more about that later. Some like to focus solely on one or two elements, like Uthren for example. You haven't seen it yet, but I've never seen someone able to bring so much *spark* to the battlefield. And that suits him just fine. For me, I like to explore. I like to have a good understanding about *all* the elements. Sure, Nature comes the most easily to me, but that doesn't mean that I can't branch out and discover new things too. In the end, it's all up to you. Pick one, or pick 'em all. Your only as powerful as you work hard to be."

Arriving at the others, the group once again set off towards Gelendor. Geode mentioned to Uthren that Sylas had the desire to learn Nature Magick, and Uthren agreed that it would be a good idea.

"It's important that you find out which element naturally attunes to *you* and that you learn it well. If you want to be equally rounded, that's always an option, but you should figure out which one you are naturally gifted in first. I think that it's beneficial, especially when you are first learning, that you find which element really speaks to you and get your basics cemented with that element first. Of course, I expect you to learn all of the elements and be at least somewhat proficient with each of them eventually, but I'd advise you to find and focus on the one that feels right to you first."

"Do you know how to use all of the elements then Uthren?" Samara asked.

"I, along with Geode, do know the basics of all of the elements, yes. But I would not say that I'm skilled with all of them. As you know, the elements all have their opposites. Water and Fire, Nature and Air, Light, and Darkness. As I have found that my strengths belong to the Light, you can naturally assume that my weakness would be that of Darkness. I know several basic spells and have learned about what others can do with it, but I can't do anything very impressive. If you fancy learning Darkness, Geode would probably be a better teacher than I as he is very well rounded with most elements."

Uthren hesitated, his step slowing just slightly before resuming, "But, I would caution against starting with Darkness so soon… It has a tendency to… bring out some of the bad in you. But perhaps I'm just somewhat biased, as I'm naturally pulled towards the Light."

Sylas shook his head. "I don't think I want to learn any Darkness right now anyway. I do think Nature seems really cool though!"

He hoped that maybe Nature would be what he was 'naturally attuned to' whatever that meant. The abilities that Geode displayed when they were attacked by the Black Hand were incredible. And although he could see how useful it would be to be a master of Light, Nature seemed very appealing to him, especially the *easy-going* part.

"I can teach you the symbol of Nature tonight when we make camp and we can go over some of the basics," Geode offered. "If that's alright with Uthren, anyway."

Sylas turned towards Uthren and was pleased to see him nodding in approval. "I think that would be appropriate. I'll continue to teach Samara about shielding in the meantime, and you can decide where you want to go from there, Sylas."

Sylas agreed and the group continued their journey towards Gelendor. A smile spread across his face as he eagerly awaited the long day to end.

Thoughts of controlling the trees, speaking to animals, and generally being like Geode danced in his mind as he walked. A strange feeling brushed against him between one of his thoughts. It was cold, like a shadow had been cast over him for just a moment. He stopped walking for a split second, looking around to see if anyone else had felt it.

He quickly resumed his walk, the strange coldness now gone from him. He waited for the feeling to come back, but even after walking for some time, it never returned. Doing his best to shrug it off, he focused his eyes on the horizon. *One day closer to Gelendor.*

****

Frogs and other boggy animals croaked in the night as Sylas finished putting up his tent. The ground sank slightly beneath his boots, squishing water up between the blades of grass at his feet. It was a *terrible* place to camp. But the ground in this area seemed to be like this *everywhere,* so they'd just have to deal with it for tonight.

Samara finished with her shelter as well, staking it out mere feet from Uthren's. Sylas didn't blame her. Even he had fearful thoughts crossing his mind in the night ever since the attack, and no one had held him at knife point.

After setting up their tents and getting something to eat, Sylas approached Geode, anxiously hoping that he would agree to start the Nature training.

Geode extended his muscular arm in front of him and motioned for Sylas to sit down. A smile passed over his face, as it seemed to do the more that Sylas interacted with the strong warrior. "Have a seat Sylas, we'll start with a brief history."

Sylas excitedly sat down and focused all his attention towards Geode. The Light Moon was full tonight, shining brilliantly and lighting up the area around him. A silvery beam of moonlight almost seemed to illuminate the silhouette of Geode, as if the Light Moon was *attracted* to him. He shrugged the idea off and paid close attention to the mighty mage's words.

"As Uthren has already taught you, the original King of Nature, who just so happened to be a woman in this case, don't ask me about their naming conventions, was Nymphara. She was bestowed with the knowledge of Nature Magick and its source of power. Look around you, Sylas, and tell me what you think the *source* of power is for Nature Magick."

Slightly confused, Sylas looked around and saw many things that could have been a source of power for Nature. The trees, dirt, rocks, grass… none of them really stood out more than the others though.

Sylas scratched his head and then looked up again at the moon. It didn't really seem connected to Nature, but yet tonight, it shone so brightly and seemed so alive…

"Is it the moon?"

"Very good. Yes, the *Light Moon*, specifically is the source from which Nature gains its power. During a Light Moon year, mages who use Nature Magick are able to feel greater power and clarity as they control that element. When it is a year of Dark Moon, you will not be able to feel that additional power, as the Dark Moon is the source of power for Darkness. The trees and the earth and all living things have Nature Magick flowing within them, but it's the Light Moon that *truly* gives us strength and life. A night like this is *perfect* for learning to use Nature Magick. So, as the source of power for Nature is the moon, the symbol for Nature Magick is appropriately shaped like a moon."

Geode held his hands out in front of him and made the symbol of Nature by curving the fingers in his left hand to form a crescent shape. Then with his right hand made an open circle and touched the middle of his bent pointer finger to the bottom of his outstretched thumb.

"You'll find that tapping into your inner life and opening your second mind is the same with any element that you decide to use, so you should be able to tap into Nature Magick with little to no problem. Once it has been opened, however, your second mind will vastly differ from what you are used to feeling when using Light. Nature is calm and collected, observant, and peaceful. It's highly protective of all living things and destructive towards that which would harm the earth and its inhabitants. Go on, try it yourself. Make the symbol of Nature like this and open your second mind."

Sylas did as he was instructed and made the symbol of Nature with his hands. Cupping his left hand to form a crescent, and then making an open circle with his right and placing it below his left hand, middle knuckle on his pointer finger touching the fingernail of his thumb. He then reached into his pool of inner life and moved it from his stomach into his hands and saw a green glow start to emanate from them. He then closed his eyes and moved the energy to his head and, like he had done so many times before, began to imagine his soul leaving his body.

****

Sylas opened his eyes, but to his dismay did not feel his second mind open, nor did he see Geode sitting right in front of him. Instead, he found himself in a vast graveyard.

It was dark where he was. That and somehow… there was a large dark void in the stary night sky where the moon should have been. It almost appeared as if time had impossibly transitioned to a Dark Moon year.

Confused, he continued to survey the landscape around him and tried to orient himself. The graveyard was massive. Gravestones littered the ground around him, and large dead trees cast eerie shadows across the grass at his feet from large torches that surrounded the graveyard. The torches were unnatural, glowing with an eerie purple flame.

Most of the gravestones were small slabs of stone with names engraved upon their faces. Others were massive pillars that stood several feet in the air with varying designs, cracking, and faded with age.

A flash of black and a loud *Caw!* made him jump. A black crow took flight from a sizeable tomblike building that stood off in the distance.

As he peered into the darkness towards the building, he suddenly felt himself being whisked through the air until he was standing right in front of it.

The tomb was made from a dark stone material and stood at about the same height as a one-level house. Two stone pillars sat on either side of the door, holding up a stone slab which acted as a porchway. The pillars were cracking and faded, showing that they had been here a long, long time.

The door to the tomb was made of a dark, thick, heavy wood with large iron braces holding its frame. Above the door was the same symbol that he had encountered in the Ancient Crypt, a large black skull that seemed to scream evil. The very image seemed to whisper dark thoughts into his mind.

Sylas quickly stepped back away from the tomb and heard what he could only describe as the sound of bones clanking against each other behind him.

He spun around and met the purple gaze of a reanimated skeleton. One by one, additional skeletons seemed to fade into view, an entire host of once living warriors standing where he had been only moments before.

The air inside his lungs choked in his throat. He tried to scream, but no sound came, neither did his lungs allow him to breathe. His heart raced. His blood turned ice cold. A chill ran throughout his body, sending goosebumps down his neck and arms.

The skeleton stared right at him, dark purple eyes peering directly into his soul. No, it wasn't looking at him… it was staring directly *passed* him. The air he had been choking on softened, and he let it out slowly.

He moved out of the skeleton's line of sight. Gratefully the terrifying creature didn't react in any way. Each of the thousands of skeletons were glowing with the slightest of auras, a dark black color with a hint of purple radiating from their dry bones. The aura reminded him of flames, but flickering in a much slower, much softer fashion, like burning shadows.

Their eye sockets were filled with a floating orb of dark purple light, centered where eyeballs would have been who knows how long ago. Each of the skeletons made a terrible clanking noise as bones rubbed on bones with every slight movement. Their dark eyes continued to stare at something unseen, something terrible. With terror gripping his soul, Sylas slowly turned to see what the animated skeletons were looking at.

The scenery immediately changed, and he found himself standing in a dimly lit room. The smell of dust and stale air unwillingly entering into his nose.

Coughing, he found himself staring into a large mirror. The mirror was leaning up against a wall and showed his reflection at just a slightly skewed angle.

Sylas approached the mirror. The closer he got, the clearer his image became. Coming to a stop in front of the mirror, he observed the bit of stubble that had formed on his chin and upper lip. He touched his face, his reflection exactly mirroring his movements. Like a nightmare, his reflection suddenly seemed to gain a mind of its own. He watched in horror as his reflection in the mirror started to smile. The smile stretched across his face, unnaturally long and thin. Evil dripped from the edges of his mouth deviously. His reflection then put its hands out in front of it and made a symbol that he had never seen before.

His reflection made a small circle in each hand using its pointer finger and thumb. It brought the two circles together then extended each of its other three fingers in a diagonal, meeting them together at a point above the circles. It then proceeded to tip its hands forward until the symbol was upside down.

The symbol greatly resembled the symbol of Light. It was just different enough though… different enough to almost *mock* the Light. That, and it was turned upside down as to add even more mockery to its cheap imitation.

His reflection's eyes and hands began to glow with dark purple Magick energy. Slowly, it stretched its arms out to either side of its body. A dark purple ball of energy then formed in each of his outstretched hands, and with a laugh that was not his own, it threw the Magick towards him.

Acting purely out of instinct, Sylas quickly made the symbol of Light with his hands and attempted to open his second mind to create a shield of Light around himself. As he tried to open his second mind, a deep purple light, accompanied with the terrifying whispers of countless souls swept over him, knocking him to the floor.

Sitting up, he found that he had again been transported to a different place. This time he was somewhere near the mountains. He wasn't sure which mountains they were, but they did look somewhat familiar. Moments later, he was in the darkness of a small room.

In front of him stood a giant statue of a man in armor that had the same symbol that Uthren's battle mage robes had, sitting right in the center of the breastplate. The statue held a large maul, the length of the maul looked to be almost as tall as the man was if stood upright. The head of the maul was a large bulky rectangular cube with intricate designs carved into it. As he looked at the maul, it began to fade slightly, and he found himself looking straight through the statue.

Inside the head of the maul sat a bright yellow glowing stone, the only reason he was not able to see it before was most likely due to the thick metal that covered it. The statue then gained its thickness again, and he was no longer able to see through it.

The statue started to crack and shake, and a gust of wind blew past it, crumbling it into dust. As the plume of dust faded away, a shadowy figure entered into his view.

Maelos sat on a large black throne, dark battle mage robes covering his body. His hood rested on his back as he sat, his eyes closed as he hunched forward and stared at the ground.

Sylas took a step backward in fear, the very aura of the Dark Mage's evil presence causing him to shake. As his foot touched the ground behind him, Maelos opened his eyes and looked directly at him. His eyes met Sylas's and terror flooded into his entire body.

Maelos stretched his hand out towards him, and Sylas felt his soul being torn from his body. The pain was unreal! He felt as if his second mind was being *forcefully* opened, like his soul was about to be rent from his body unwillingly. Just as it seemed as though it was about to exit, a bright light swept over him, and Sylas lost his strength and fell onto his back, his vision fading into darkness.

****

His ears were ringing as he heard the muffled voices of people around him. He slowly opened his eyes and saw Geode, Uthren, Samara, and Torren all gathered around him. The ringing in his ears slowly began to dissipate as his senses faded back into existence.

"Sylas! Are you alright? What happened?" Uthren said, reaching his hand towards him and placing it on his forehead. "Are you hurt?"

"I- I think I'm alright," Sylas said as he sat up slowly. "I think I just had another vision… I- I saw Maelos."

Geode and Uthren looked at each other, fear spreading across their faces.

"We must pack up and leave immediately," Uthren whispered. "Torren, Samara, get your things and hurry!" He exclaimed, raising his voice. "Maelos will know where we are, we'll have to travel through the night."

They nodded and immediately did as they were asked and ran towards their tents.

"Sylas, can you get up?"

"Yeah- I think so."

He forced himself to yawn to try and get rid of the rest of the ringing that invaded his ears, then pushed himself to his feet.

"I'm alright. I'll get my stuff."

Uthren held his shoulder with his strong hand, his old eyes worried as he peered into Sylas's. He nodded, then left with Geode towards their tents to quickly pack for their untimely departure.

Sylas started running towards his tent, thoughts of having to face more warriors sent by Maelos to kill them giving additional speed to his legs.

The group finished packing then traveled swiftly and silently through the tall grass and trees. The swishing of the grass joining the choir of insects and other animals in the night. After their first confrontation, Geode and Uthren decided that instead of taking the most direct route towards Gelendor, it would be safer if they took a more roundabout way to the city to try and throw off any inclination of what direction they might be going. If any of their suspicions were correct, Maelos was most likely able to pinpoint their latest location because of the vision, so it was essential to put as much distance between themselves and where they were as possible.

Who knows how close his soldiers could have already been? After his first batch had failed, he probably sent more to pursue and track us down. Now that Maelos saw right where we were, it's probably a matter of when *not* if *they find us...* Sylas thought in anger. *Stupid! Why did that happen again?*

He continued to ponder why he'd been successful in opening his second mind so many times while training with Uthren with no incident whatsoever, just to let it happen to him again when trying to open it with Nature Magick for the first time.

Several hours passed, and thankfully no incidents. They continued to travel as silently as possible, only allowing their steps and labored breathing to make any noise. Sylas watched the Light Moon as it slowly changed positions in the sky, along with the millions of stars that surrounded it. It was a beautiful clear night, despite the temperatures continuing to grow colder and colder. He wished that he could enjoy looking at the stars in peace rather than running away from potentially a band of murderous henchmen.

His train of thought was cut off when Geode immediately stopped moving and raised a hand into the air. He crouched down slightly and motioned for everyone else to do the same and drop their packs onto the ground. Sylas's heart rate increased dramatically as his anticipation for horrible things he was sure were about to happen grew.

In a low whisper, Geode told them that he thought he heard something. Like a silent bolt of lightning, a whooshing sound came flying through the air. A muffled grunt escaped Geode as a sickening *thwack* rang in the air. Sylas's heart stopped as his eyes caught the terrifying sight of an arrow embedded into Geode's shoulder.

CHAPTER 8
CONFRONTATIONS

A painful yell echoed through the trees as Geode clutched his arm. The sounds of voices yelling and leaves rustling took over the silence that had once prevailed.

"Use the Light!" Uthren commanded, opening his second mind in a fraction of a second. "Protect yourselves and get out of here!"

Sylas stumbled back slightly at the sight of the arrow protruding from Geode's arm, his stomach turning over as a sickening feeling started to fill his throat. A golden glow, like a newly formed sun, lit the area around them as Uthren radiated with the holy power of Light. His powerful voice filled the air as he charged towards the incoming attackers.

Geode let out a muffled grunt as he slowly moved his hands in front of his chest, creating a symbol that Sylas had never seen before. Less than a second later, Geode's hands and eyes started glowing with a deep, vibrant red. Sylas could almost *feel* the power that radiated off the warrior, his eyes ablaze as though his soul had just caught flame. His hands were like burning logs as he raised one powerful hand towards his injured shoulder. Geode's muscles bulged, nearly ripping the fabric of his robes. He reached his flame lit hand towards the arrow, grabbed its shaft, and without even wincing, tore the arrow straight from the flesh of his shoulder. His shoulder poured blood, the wound deep and gnarly.

Sylas himself nearly fainted at the scene, empathetically *feeling* the pain in his own shoulder. Geode rose to his full height, a flaming warrior that showed absolutely no sign of pain.

Bringing his hands back together, Geode twisted his fingers into the symbol of Light and his eyes and hands changed from red to bright yellow. Sylas could tell by the look on his face that as he switched to using Light Magick, the terrible damage that the arrow had caused was now sending its pain signals through Geode's body with a vengeance.

Placing a Light shrouded hand upon the wound, a warm, healing glow began to mend his shoulder. His tense face softened as the healing finished, and he quickly brought his hands back to his chest and created the symbol of Nature. Eyes and hands glowing a powerful green, he flashed his gaze towards Sylas and Samara, then set them upon Torren.

"Remember your training! Try to avoid conflict at *all* costs. Protect them, Torren. I'm counting on you."

The ground beneath his feet began to rumble, a pile of dirt and rock lifted him from the ground and threw him in the air towards the incoming enemies.

Their two protectors gone, Samara's breathing became frantic.

"Hey! Samara," Torren said, grabbing her wrists. "Listen to me, everything's going to be alright. Okay? Sylas and I got you. You hear me?"

Samara was on the verge of tears, her body visibly shaking. She returned Torren's gaze, then slowly looked over towards Sylas.

Sylas swallowed, but Torren's words brought the additional courage that he needed.

"That's right!" He said, his voice wavering slightly. "We won't let *anything* happen to you. Stay close! Let's get out of here!"

Bringing his hands together, he made the symbol of Light and opened his second mind. The strange feeling of having two points of view came as his second mind opened. The power of the Light, along with its fury of the evil around him filled his body as his eyes and hands glowed with its holy power.

He focused his desires until they were in unison with the Light and created a circular shield that covered the length of his left arm. He moved his arm left and right and was pleased that the shield floated alongside him as if it were physically attached. He then drew his sword and readied himself for a fight.

"Stay between us," he called to Samara." Torren, let's go!"

Torren spun his sword in the air, his back to Samara so he could cover her flank, "Way ahead of you, brother!"

Sylas looked once more at Samara's cowering face. The Light flared within him as the desire to protect her from harm grew tenfold. Embracing the call for justice from the Light, he let a battle cry fill the air, then charged.

Sylas found that the ethereal body of his second mind floated just above and behind him as if it were attached to him with a rope, never drifting too far away. He used this additional viewpoint to his advantage and took a survey of his surroundings. The Light in his eyes seemed to enhance his vision, allowing him to see in the dark with much greater ease.

His second mind caught a glimpse of the archer that had fired the arrow into Geode's shoulder. Feeding the Light's desire to enact holy vengeance on the evildoer, his shield flared with Light, and Sylas ran towards the man. He flashed his vision back towards Torren and Samara, but Torren's instincts were sharp. He quickly rotated around her, allowing Sylas to break off to try and take this enemy out.

The archer saw the oncoming assault and nocked another arrow. Sylas held his shield in front of his body as the archer shot the arrow towards him. Wincing as the arrow approached, he prayed that the missile wouldn't go right through the shield and into his chest. To his satisfaction, the arrow bounced off his shield of Light and flew spinning through the air. A slight ripple of Light waved through the energy of the shield after the arrow struck its surface.

Confidence surged within him at the successful block from his shield. With a slightly more worried look on his face, the archer pulled another arrow from his back and nocked it. Sylas was not far from the man now. Like a silent whisper, the Light suggested his next actions, and Sylas happily complied. Raising his shield arm up and flaring his Magick, he emanated a blinding flash of Light towards the archer.

Just as the archer was about to release his arrow, the Light coming from Sylas's shield hit his eyes. He reared back in pain and the arrow shot high into the air, missing its intended target. The archer dropped his bow and held his hands to his face in agony. Sylas took advantage of the opportunity that he had created and closed the gap between them. Slashing his sword at the man's torso, he cut right through the light leather armor that he had been wearing and sliced a huge gash into his stomach. Blood poured from the wound as the man took his hands from his face and pressed them against his now open stomach.

As the archer removed his hands from his face, Sylas was surprised to see that his blinding Light attack had done more damage than he'd thought. He intended to blind the man, giving himself an advantage for the rest of the fight but saw that along with the blinding, the Light had also burned the man's face to a crisp.

The man fell to his knees, then face down on the ground. With the Light coursing through him, Sylas could almost *feel* when the archer took his last breath. The Light within him suggested he offer a quick prayer, which Sylas did, wishing for his confused soul to receive safe passage to the heavenly gates of the afterlife.

Shock immediately entered into his mind after the prayer, the realization that, for the very first time in his life, he had just taken the life of someone else away. His heart felt sick, his stomach bubbling, but the Light within him immediately flared, calming his mind and easing his conscious. It reminded him that his intentions were noble, that his cause was just. It spoke into his heart that his quest was one of great integrity, and those who stood in his way and tried to stop his quest for peace needed to be vanquished.

"Darkness must perish, so that the Light can spread across the land once more."

He'd said it out loud, to no one but himself. Swallowing his regret, he knew that it was right, so he focused his eyes on his next target.

****

Torren parried the incoming blade to the side as his opponent swung it down towards his head. He resisted the urge to do a spin move and go for the decapitating blow, then instead kicked at the man's shin as hard as he could. Torren's foot made contact with the unarmored bone of the man's shin, causing him to hop backward and bend forward slightly. Torren dropped his left hand from the hilt of his sword and swung it upward, connecting it to the man's jaw with a *crunch*. Torren shook his hand as the man fell backward onto the ground.

Yeah, that's going to be swollen for a while, he thought. The man spat blood onto the ground and looked back up to Torren, who meeting his gaze gave a taunting smile. The man smiled back and wiped the blood from his mouth.

"You honestly think you have a chance, boy? I'm just getting warmed up."

Torren gave a disrespectful shrug and a fake yawn, "You know, I have a sister that I fight with at home, and to be honest… she's usually done more damage than you have by now."

The man chuckled. "Is that so? Well then, I don't think you will mind if I turn up the *heat* a little bit."

Torren pointed the blade towards the man, lowering his stance slightly as he had seen his father do during countless training sessions. "Bring it!"

The man chuckled again, spitting a drop of blood at the ground as he pushed himself to his feet.

"Alright… You asked for it."

The man sheathed his sword. He pulled his hands in front of his chest and made a strange symbol. His laughter grew deeper and more menacing as a red, fiery glow began to surround his hands and sparked deep within his eyes.

Torren swallowed, lowering his stance. "What? You don't wanna fight me like a *man*?"

"Heh- Oh, you'll get your *honorable* death. There's more to Fire than just shooting flames."

The warrior flexed his muscles, his chest and arms doubling their size in mere moments. The flames in his eyes grew wild, as if they were wildfires on the verge of becoming uncontrollable.

"Let's see you best me in this state, boy. I'll even give you an advantage..."

The crazed man tossed his sword to the ground, several feet away from where he stood. He bent his head backward, laughing into the air. He then pointed a finger at Torren, flames dancing in his eyes and around his fiery fists.

"Come at me, if you dare!"

Torren took in several deep breaths, desperately summoning his courage. He took a quick glance backwards. Samara was gone. She'd probably found a good place to hide until the action was over. Growling into the air for courage, he took several steps forward, increasing his speed with each step, then with all his strength, slashed his sword downward at the man.

Sparks fluttered from the man's eyes as he reached one hand forward, *catching* the blade in the palm of his hand.

Torren's breath caught in his throat, his eyes growing wide with fear. The blade had nearly severed the hand, sinking deeply into the slightly red glowing flesh. The man smiled, his eyes completely void of pain. The red in his eyes burned like a forest fire, rage and power consuming what used to be his pupils.

"What's the matter, *boy*? Is that all you've got?"

Torren yanked his sword from the man's grasp, cutting his hand more with the action. His mind raced, trying to come up with a solution to his deadly problem.

The man laughed, mocking Torren's surprise. "Come on, *boy*! Be a man! Attack me! Show me what you've got! Where's all that *talk* now?"

Torren took in several rapid breaths, his lips pressing together tightly. He ran at the maniac, thrusting his sword with everything he had, aiming for the top of his head.

Again, the man caught his blade as if it were nothing, this time with his other hand. The sword again penetrated his hand deeply, giving him a wound that should bring any sane person to their knees in pain. The man's biceps bulged, the veins in his arms visibly pumping his enraged blood throughout his body.

"I'm disappointed… you seemed so sure of yourself just a moment ago."

Gripping Torren's sword with his bloody hand, the enraged man yanked it from Torren's grasp. In a motion too swift to follow, he slammed his fist into Torren's stomach with so much power that it threw him high into the night air. Torren's lungs choked, air refusing to enter as he soared through the night sky. Stars glittered in the edges of his vision as he slammed onto the ground after several seconds of flight time. His body fought to stay conscious as he slowly slid to a stop, the entire front of his body agonizingly broken.

The surety of a slow, agonizing death flooded his mind. The sound of pounding footsteps approached. Cold, maniacal laughing squeezed its way into his ears, unrelenting.

The powerful man bent down over Torren, his flaming red eyes burning with torturous desires. He reached out and grabbed Torren by the neck, lifting him up off the ground, high above his head with one arm as he continued to laugh. His face then hardened, hatred and disgust forming on his expression.

"Too bad. Guess it takes only *one* little punch to take you out. I was hoping to show you more..." Torren tried to pull his hands to his neck, to do anything to defend himself, but his body refused.

The man pulled his fist back, yelling with delight as he threw his fist towards Torren's face. Torren closed his eyes, awaiting what would surely be this life taking blow to strike him. Just as his eyes closed, the blacks of his eyelids turned red, as if he had just turned his head towards the light of the sun.

Torren opened his eyes. An angel stood behind the man, pointing her beautiful, lifesaving hand towards Torren. No… no, it wasn't an angel…

Samara stood behind the man, her eyes and hands glowing with the color of Light Magick. A glowing yellow shield of Light surrounded Torren's entire body. Torren felt the sensation of flying through the air once more as he was angrily tossed to the side. He thudded against the ground once more, his vision fading to darkness.

****

Samara stood in front of the hulking man, her heart beating so fast she was afraid it would explode. She glanced to her right and saw Uthren and Geode again, both fighting against what seemed an entire army of enemies. It looked like Maelos had sent Fire mages after them this time. Bright pillars of flame exploded into the air, splashing against beams of yellow and green Magick. As the Fire and Light Magick connected, sparks of lightning crackled across the sky, leaving behind them booms of thunder. Samara decided she needed to ask Uthren about this interaction as soon as this nightmare of a night was over. She had no idea where Sylas was, last she saw him he was chasing after another one of the archers that were firing arrows at both Uthren and Geode.

"You'll pay dearly for that missy. I was going to enjoy smashing that ignorant pup's face in! You took that moment away from me. And for that, you will *pay*."

The man looked into the sky and buffed his body up again, the red aura surrounding his skin glowing slightly brighter now. Samara could have sworn she saw a slight jet of flame escape his mouth and nostrils as he enhanced the spell.

The man took several steps to the side, reaching towards the ground. He retrieved his sword, then held it high into the air. The blade of the sword ignited with a bright red flame, sending a heat wave towards her. Terror gripped at her heart as she lifted the shield from Torren's body and placed it around herself.

Somehow, I've got to get over there and heal Torren before it's too late…

"Your pathetic shields won't be able to withstand my onslaught. You will soon face the same fate as your friend. And once we've killed you all, we shall bring the stone back to the Dark Mage, and he will bathe the world in darkness!"

With a yell, the man began running towards her, flaming sword held high above his head. Samara felt her blood ice over. In her mind she immediately plead with the Light that flowed within her, "I trust your judgment and agree with whatever you decide! Just get me out of this mess!" Samara felt almost as if her second mind cracked its neck with a smile.

Giving in to each and every suggestion that was sent to her, as well as allowing her body to seemingly be *controlled* by the powers of her second mind, Samara raised her hands above her head. A yell escaped her lungs as the shield that surrounded her exploded outward in a dome shape. The Light struck the man, and although it didn't knock him completely over, sent him off his original course as he stumbled to maintain balance.

Samara held both hands outstretched to her side and filled them with balls of Light. Bringing her hands together, she cupped the balls together near her waist, continuing to pour Light energy into the palms of her hands. Gaining his footing, the man turned and bolted towards Samara, flames streaming from his glowing eyes as if they were dripping molten lava.

Without giving herself the chance of having second thoughts, she obeyed completely whatever the Light commanded her to do. She extended her arms in front of her, releasing a powerful beam of Light towards the man.

The Light ray rippled through the air, striking the man in the left shoulder, her aim just slightly off. It sent him spinning through the air, launching him backward to the ground. The man cursed under his breath then stood, revealing the grizzly sight of now only having one arm. He bent down and picked his sword up off the ground, then turned towards her, a furious rage swelling within.

The muscles on his remaining arm surged and swelled, the rage in his face exposing no outer signs of pain. His devastating wound had been cauterized by the intense heat of her blast, leaving dark black burn marks where blood would have been pouring.

The man yelled defiantly, cursing her for what she had done. Flames grew from his sword as though he had dipped it in lava. He took two furious steps towards her, then slashed the flaming sword in an arch, flinging molten drips and a fiery surge of energy towards her. The flames spat forward out of the tip of his sword like a geyser spews water from the earth.

Samara gave all her thoughts to the Light, allowing it to command *her* to create a shield around herself. The powerful yellow glow of the Light radiated brilliantly as the protective barrier formed. The flames from the fiery sword struck the shield, strange, hissing crackles sending miniature bolts of lightning spewing off either side of her shield.

Electric shocks arched between the inside of her shield and her body, zapping her with painful Magick jolts. She released the shield, not able to stand the pain of the electricity any longer and dove out of the way of the remaining fire blast. Rolling from her back to her feet, she shot her eyes towards her should-be-dead opponent. The man stomped towards her, flames burning beneath his footsteps, as he held his blazing blade high in the air.

The Light shot an idea into her mind. Accepting everything that it told her without question, she raised her hands high above her head. Channeling all of the energy that she could muster, she called forth a beam of Light from the heavens to come down and strike the tip of the sword.

His eyes radiated with pure, blind power, his pupils like an unquenchable storm. He tensed his arm, ready to slice Samara in half. Light descending from the heavens commanded its justice, striking the tip of his blade. The sword crackled with energy, lightning coursing down the metal into the man's powerful body. The hairs on Samara's head and neck stood upright as powerful energy sparked and zapped. Arcs of electricity connected with the ground all around the man in a powerful, deadly display. As the energy peaked, a loud *boom* followed, and a surge of electrical energy knocked Samara to the ground.

The Light surged within her as her eyes met the sight of the mans shattered sword next to his crumpled body. Justice, had been served. The Light commanded that she continue, that she seek for more evildoers to reprimand. Her mind felt like it might explode, that the energy that coursed through her body would consume her. With the ounce of control that she still held, she *forced* her second mind to enter her body, closing the connection before the Light could protest. Her entire body tingled with energy, her breathing was heavy and deep, as though she had just finished swimming up a swiftly flowing river.

It took several seconds for her to calm down enough to even think straight. Once she did, the immediate remembrance of Torren shot into her mind. She spied him, still lying motionless on the ground in the distance. With wobbly legs, she pushed herself towards him, praying that he was still alive.

Torren lay unmoving upon the ground. His chest completely motionless, his breathing nonexistent.

"Uthren!" Samara screamed, tears full of fear ripping themselves from her eyes. "Uthren! Help!"

She looked down at her childhood friend, her hands trembling as footsteps swiftly approached her.

"Samara! What happened?"

"It was- He, he was- He got him in the chest. I- I don't-"

Uthren gently pushed Samara to the side, assessing the damage for himself. He placed his hand on Torren's chest, rubbing it up and down his ribcage slowly.

Finally, he turned towards her, grabbing her by the shoulders. "Samara, listen to me! You *must* get control of yourself. Torren has *no pulse.* His ribs are also completely collapsed. I *need* your help to save him."

Samara could hardly breathe, the intensity of the situation threatening to cause her to black out.

"Look at me!" Uthren commanded. Then, softer he repeated, "Samara, look at me. Look into my eyes."

She did so. Uthren's bright blue eyes were glowing like sapphires. The wrinkles around the edges of his eyes were soft, yet overwhelmingly determined.

"You can *do* this," he said. "I know you can. I'm going to have to get his heart started. I need *you* to mend his ribs while I restart his heart. Do you understand me?"

Samara could barely interpret his words, but nodded, taking a deep breath to try and calm herself.

"Get ready."

Uthren pulled his hands to his chest, creating the symbol of Light. His fingers then expertly shifted, creating a new symbol that Samara didn't recognize. His hands and eyes then began to radiate an electric blue color, sparking with intense energy.

Samara shook her head, taking another deep breath before pulling her hands into the symbol of Light. Once again, she felt the power of the Light fill her body as her second mind opened.

Please, she thought, *all I want to do is to heal him... just heal my friend...*

"Ready?" Uthren asked, rubbing his hands together.

Samara nodded, watching the lightning that coursed in between his fingers as it sparked and began to hum gently.

"Now!" Uthren yelled, pressing his hands onto Torren's chest.

Samara slapped her hands down onto Torren's limp body, feeling as the Light began to pour from her palms and radiate into her friend. Torren's body jolted, a zapping sound echoing around him as the energy from Uthren's hands filled his body. Samara felt the energy spark against her hands as well, but she *refused* to take her hands off her friend.

Uthren rubbed his hands together again, the energy slightly more intense this time.

"Come on, boy!" He whispered.

Samara repeated a prayer in her mind over and over again, tears streaming down her face. Uthren hit Torren with a second blast, then a third, and a fourth. A choked cry exited her mouth as Torren's chest suddenly began to rise. She watched as the bones in his chest started placing themselves back in their place, his lungs once again filling with the life-giving air that he so needed.

"That's it, Samara! Keep it up!"

Uthren rubbed his hands together one last time, slapping them down on Torren's body. The blast of lightning hit his body once again, and Torren's eyes shot open, a massive gasp of air forcing its way into his lungs.

Samara began to cry as Torren gently laid his head back on the ground, coughing as he continued to suck in shallow gasps of breath.

Uthren sat back on his legs, his hands rising to his forehead in what looked to be a prayer of thanks. "You *really* gave us a scare there, Torren," he said, lowing a hand and placing it on Torren's forehead.

Torren coughed, his lips curling into a smile. "Yeah, I totally got you guys' hu?" He winced in pain as the words came out.

"Torren! Don't talk!" Samara exclaimed, tears still streaming from her eyes.

Torren chuckled softly and let his head rest on the ground. "Fine by me."

Uthren placed a strong hand on Samara's shoulder, then rose to his feet. "Samara, I need to go find Geode and Sylas. You stay here and tend to Torren. I'll be right back."

Samara nodded, the power of the Light finally finding a good balance within her as it flowed its healing power into her lifelong friend.

****

Uthren ran in the darkness towards two silhouettes in the night. Bodies of Fire mages that Maelos had sent were scattered everywhere. He took a quick glance, relieved that it appeared that the battle was finally over. Approaching the figures, he found Geode sitting with Sylas near several crippled bodies.

"Are you both alright?"

"Yes, we're fine," Geode responded. He put a gentle, loving arm around Sylas, "Sylas here gave us a bit of a scare, but we're both okay."

"What happened?"

Geode remained silent, his strong, kind eyes not wavering from their place. Sylas looked down, obviously ashamed of the events that had just transpired.

"I- I don't know…" Sylas started. "I was chasing after one of the archers who was shooting arrows at you two. He shot a couple arrows at me, but I blocked them with my Light shield."

He looked down at his calf, a tear in his pant legs exposing his skin. "A different archer from behind got me in the leg. It hurt so bad… I immediately lost control of my second mind, and it closed. The two archers saw that I was defenseless and ran up to me. They told me to give them the stone, then one of them drew a sword and stabbed me in the shoulder."

Sylas's voice started to quiver. Geode moved his hand to his back and slowly rubbed for comfort.

"I- I didn't know what to do! I thought they were going to kill me. Then, I- I just kind of *snapped*. It all happened so fast... I tried to use Nature Magick, like Geode did to use the vines from the trees nearby to grab them, but I must have done something wrong. My leg and shoulder hurt so bad; I just wanted the pain to go away. I wanted the man who had stabbed me to die..."

Sylas looked down at his leg and placed a hand over his shoulder, no wounds were there to be seen, only tears in his clothing.

"Then they did. Both of them. Several others ran towards me after that. I felt the power flowing through me again. I must have blacked out before they got to me. But the next thing I knew… *all* these bodies were around me, I had no pain, and Geode was shaking me."

Uthren looked at Geode for further explanation. Geode continued rubbing Sylas's back for comfort.

"Somehow Uthren," Geode started. "Sylas *combined* Nature and Darkness together. Not only that, but he also cast a very advanced, very… well, *dark* spell at all of them. He used Life Magick, Uthren. The combination of Darkness and Nature. I've heard of what these types of spells can do… how they seem to *drain* the very life from your enemies."

Geode pulled his hand from Sylas's back, his eyes full of concern. "He wasn't the Sylas that we know in the moment that I found him. He had killed all of these men, draining their life force and using it to heal himself. I saw what was happening from a distance, but by the time I arrived, he had already fallen unconscious."

Sylas stifled a choked cry, wiping at his eyes with the back of his hand, "Uthren, what's wrong with me? Why do things like this keep happening?"

Uthren placed a comforting hand on his shoulder, more questions than answers swimming through his mind. "I'm- not sure, Sylas. But, I promise you we are going to figure it out. We had better leave this place. I don't know if there are more people after us nearby or not, but I don't want to find out. Can you keep going?"

Wiping the tears from his eyes, Sylas nodded.

Uthren patted him on the shoulder. "I promise, I'll do everything in my power to figure out what's going on with you and *help* you. Samara and Torren should be ready to continue soon. I have to make sure they're alright. Meet us over there when you're ready."

Uthren stood, giving one last look of helpless concern, then ran off towards Torren and Samara.

"You're sure you are okay, Sylas?" Geode asked.

"I don't know," Sylas said, wiping the tears from his eyes. "I think so. Thanks for helping me, Geode. I'm sorry for all the trouble I've caused. This is *all* my fault, everything. If we would have never gone down into the Ancient Crypt, I would've never found the amulet or the stone, and we wouldn't be in this mess."

Geode grabbed Sylas and pulled him into a loving embrace. "No, Sylas. Don't you *dare* think that. It's because of you we have some troubles, yes, *but* it will also be because of you that we can *stop* Maelos. Without you, we never would have had that chance." Geode released Sylas from the embrace and stood up, extending a hand towards him.

Sylas gripped his mentor's hand and pulled himself to his feet.

"You keep your chin up. Before this war is over, we'll *all* question why we were called to endure our pains and trials. In the end, we'll never truly know until the next life. But, it is a surety that when we find out, we'll know that our trials and tribulations were for our own good and experience. Now come on, let's get out of here."

****

Every crack of a stick beneath someone's boot or the chirp of an animal in the night sent their hearts racing. Uthren helped to finish healing Torren, and they counted their blessings that everyone was able to walk away from the encounter alive. Luckily for them, the rest of the night came and went without incident and they found a secluded place to finish the night off with an hour or two of sleep.

The next morning they awoke and immediately continued their journey, taking another alternate path to try and throw Maelos off their trail towards Gelendor. During their morning travels, Uthren inquired as to what happened to each of them during the attack the night before.

Torren recounted his events with the man that 'all of the sudden got super buff,' and Samara filled in the minor details. She then recounted her battle with him and asked Uthren what technique he'd used to get so strong.

"One of the more useful spells in Fire Magick is to use it to enrage your body," Uthren explained. "Geode did the same thing when he pulled the arrow from his arm last night. When you use that spell, your body is much more resistant to pain and you increase your strength several times over. You also become extremely aggressive and cocky, so it needs to be used with caution. When in that state, it's easy to find yourself doing stupid things just to show dominance and power, like that man did when catching Torren's sword in his hand."

"Yeah, that was crazy!" Torren exclaimed. "I knew I was in trouble when he did that. Good thing Samara came to save the day!" He gave Samara a playful, yet grateful smile.

"The other thing I wanted to ask you about Uthren," Samara continued, "was what happened when the Light and the Fire collided. It looked like it was making *lightning.* Do you know why that would've happened?"

"Your observations are amazing, Samara," Uthren replied. "You are correct, Fire and Light combine to create Lightning. I used the same technique last night to jolt Torren's heart back into action. Although neither of you were intentionally combining both elements, because the two Magick energies struck each other, they were able to produce the same effect."

Uthren shook his head slowly, his old lips curling upward, "You children are continuing to surprise me every day. Samara, it's *extremely* rare that someone of your experience is able to discover new spells so rapidly. I would even call it prodigious. You might have already discovered your natural attunement. Either way, I believe that you will one day become a mighty Light mage."

His voice growing a bit more gruff, he continued, "I would caution you, however, in allowing your second mind that much control in the future. While it can be extremely powerful to always give in to its suggestions, if you are not careful, it can cause you to do things that you may regret before you can stop yourself. Think about the time where Sylas lashed out at me during our training by accident. When you allow your second mind to rule and control your actions, accidents are much more likely to happen. Nevertheless, I think you did amazing last night, and commend you for your actions."

Samara blushed, but the warning rang through loud and clear. "Thanks, Uthren. I promise, I'll try not to let it take control again."

Uthren nodded in approval and then continued, "As for you, Sylas, I've been thinking greatly about what happened last night. I believe I have come to several conclusions. How accurate they are is another matter in itself. Anyway, as I believe that Samara is naturally attuned to Light Magick, I think that you have also found your natural attunement. I think that you may be naturally gifted with Darkness."

Silence fell upon the group, all eyes darting towards Sylas.

"No- No, it can't be Darkness. I don't even know what the symbol of Darkness is! It just can't be. I don't know-"

He stopped, his eyes growing wide with realization.

"Sylas? What is it?" Uthren asked.

Sylas clenched his lips together, shaking his head as though he could nullify the truth. The more that he resisted, the deeper the realization sunk. He finally looked towards his mentor, then recounted the part of his vision where he saw himself in the mirror. He explained the awful scene of his reflection making a strange symbol, then using what looked like Darkness Magick.

Silence continued to surround the group, a chill wind blowing past them, causing eerily cold shivers to run up their spines.

Sylas continued, telling him about the graveyard that he found himself in and the large tomb with the skull symbol above the door. He also recounted how there were thousands of animated skeletons, their eyes glowing with a dark, purple light. He once again visited the scene of his reflection, and how his reflection made a symbol, which he now guessed was the symbol of Darkness. He told them about the massive mountains that he had been transported to, and the immaculate statue of what looked to be a powerful warrior. How inside of the great maul, he saw something glowing brightly. Finally, he talked about seeing Maelos, and the pain that he felt as he looked into his cold, dark eyes.

“Sylas, can you show me the symbol that your reflection made, do you remember it?” Geode asked, breaking the silence.

Sylas stopped walking, his mind calling to remembrance the images of his nightmarish vision. He could almost see his reflection in his mind, smiling back at him with that unnatural grin. He brought his hands together, making two circles with his pointer finger and thumb, and touched them together. He then extended the three other fingers on both of his hands and touched them together, arching over the circles. He then proceeded to twist his hands forward, making the symbol appear upside down.

Another gust of chill wind blew past them as he finished the symbol. Leaves scattered across the ground, as if they were trying to get away to a new resting place. Uthren looked at Geode, deep concern in his eyes.

"It's not all bad," Geode said, his voice lightening the mood slightly. "Perhaps Darkness is your natural attunement. Maybe it isn't. Maybe it's just the connection you've developed with Maelos and the stone that's bringing it out."

Geode placed a firm hand on his shoulder, waiting for Sylas to meet his eyes before continuing. "Either way, it doesn't change the fact that you are *Sylas*. That you have been called to carry a difficult burden, and that you have the potential to do a great *good* in this world. Not all Darkness mages are evil, Sylas. It may seem that way, but there was a time, even not that long ago, when there were many *good* users of Darkness that walked the earth. As Uthren explained before, Darkness is not inherently evil, it's just easier to *lean* that way with it a bit more than the other elements."

Geode ruffled Sylas's hair, smiling, "You know… Fire is actually closer to Darkness than you'd think. When I use Fire Magick, I have to be sure to keep my thoughts and desires under control, so I don't do anything I'll regret later. It has a lot to give, but it's up to you to make sure you use it the *right* way. It's become a lot easier to control over the years, but the urges still come. I've done a lot less with Darkness, but I know my fair share, and it's very similar. It really is an incredible element. It almost feels like it *guides* you throughout the learning process, like it's eager to allow you to become great. In truth, I've been meaning to train with Darkness a bit more myself… Perhaps I've put it off a bit too long. I think that you, Sylas, could become an excellent, powerful, and *upstanding* Darkness mage."

"You really think so?"

"I *know* so. Let's get some more of the basics of Light down, maybe throw in a little Nature here and there. But after that, I promise that I'll teach you what I know about Darkness. You should really master the element that is strongest to you, so if you're naturally gifted with it, there's no reason why you shouldn't learn it. We'll do it the *right* way. The good way."

Sylas wrapped Geode in a hug, his chest feeling like a massive weight had just been lifted from it.

"Thank you, Geode. Thank you! I- I don't want to be naturally attuned to the Darkness… but if I am, then I'd want to learn how to use it from you."

Geode smiled, returning the hug. "I'm actually kind of excited. There's a lot of *really* powerful stuff that I'm missing out on. We'll learn it all together. It's going to be great."

Uthren nodded his head, giving a silent thanks to Geode. "As for the other parts of your vision, it may have been a message from the Gods themselves. Based on what you saw, I believe I might know where the Stone of Light is. I think I know what statue you saw. If I am correct, it's in the Light capital of Sindmyr. If the stone really is inside of that statue, then our quest to find all the stones just got one step easier. Once we have visited Gelendor and done what we need to do, we can go search for it."

Uthren started walking again and motioned for everyone to follow, "If we pick up our pace, I believe we can make it to Gelendor within a couple more days. Once there, we'll be able to rest with ease. Make haste, and may the Light guide us."

CHAPTER 9
SKY

Several days had passed since their encounter with the Fire mages. The days of travel were long and hard as Uthren and Geode pushed the group to their limits to make it to Gelendor as fast as possible.

During their rest periods, Sylas had successfully opened his second mind using Nature as his element of choice with no vision attacks hindering his progress. Geode had also taught him several basic Nature spells such as healings- which were slightly less effective but not so different than the way Light could heal- basic rock-throwing, vine-whipping, and accelerated plant growth. Sylas really enjoyed using Nature Magick and wished that he was naturally attuned to it instead of Darkness.

Samara and Torren both increased in their skills as well. Torren learned several new fighting stances from Geode and would even wake up early each morning to practice these stances.

Samara was continuing to show a natural gift for Light Magick, and Uthren continued to praise her for her accomplishments. She even successfully learned her first advanced Light spell, which consisted of bending the natural light around objects in such a way as to make them appear invisible as long as they sat perfectly still. She found it quite hilarious after learning this spell to sit in front of Torren's tent in the morning, appearing out of thin air at the perfect moment to scare him. What she enjoyed even more though, was when she would *not* sit in front of his tent, and watch as Torren cautiously flailed his arms about looking for an invisible prankster to appear, only to have nothing happen.

"I'm just keeping him on his toes," she would always state in defense. "If he's going to be our *master swordsman* and *protector of evil*, then he needs to be conditioned to surprises."

Sylas was excited for tonight's training. They had all been discussing plans for what they were going to do to ensure that they could enter Gelendor safely, and part of these plans called for an advanced Magick technique. The Nature Magick consisted of talking to a squirrel, bird, or some other small animal to go into the city first in a stealthy, scouting mission.

Sylas begged Geode to let him be the one to try talking to the animal to which he agreed.

His excitement continued to grow when Samara broke his train of thought, "Uthren, If Maelos knows we came from Shilvrst and he knows the main direction we've been going, then how do we know we're even going to be able to make it into Gelendor?

Won't he just have the place surrounded by guards or something?"

Uthren shook his head, "although he would have you think otherwise, Maelos hasn't been successful just yet in taking over all the cities of Evendreil. His influence can be seen everywhere, yes, but he hasn't obtained supreme rule over *all* the land. His reign first started in the Capital of Darkness, Azrindal. From there, he moved to The Scorched Lands and Northrinde, taking over the powerful nations of Fire and Water. By that time, his forces had been weakened. Smaller cities, like Shilvrst, were still within his grasp, but the remaining elemental capitals of Light, Nature, and Air were able to hold strong against him. In the places where he has control, he *teaches* that he's the ruler over the entire earth, along with a multitude of other lies. He does his best to keep those beneath him in the dark, until he finds the power that he needs to take over the rest of Evendreil."

"So, we'll be totally safe once we get in!" Samara exclaimed. "He won't be able to do anything!"

"Not while I still stand," Geode said with pride. "Gelendor is a strong city. It is ancient and beautiful. The mages there are some of the most powerful in all of Evendreil. While the Great Tree still stands, Maelos will *never* have access to its roots."

"Great Tree?" Sylas asked.

"A more beautiful creation, you will *never* see," Geode replied. "Just you wait. The world is much bigger, much more incredible than you could ever imagine."

After several hours of walking over rolling hills of grass and trees, a sad sight of destruction met their view. Once tall, proud, trees and other foliage that had beautified the rolling hills of the valley had been reduced to black logs. Instead of the green and golden grass they had walked through all morning, weeds, charred ground, dust, and ash took its place. It was a shame, Sylas admired how beautiful the rolling hills were, and this section had its beauty taken away by the fire.

Before Sylas could ask the question, Geode grew furious. He cursed the name of Maelos, along with every one of the Fire mages that they had encountered several nights prior. "He corrupts *everything!* Geode spat. "He destroys all that is beautiful! All that is good!"

The destruction in the area was immense, covering nearly as far as Sylas could see. He imagined the raging fire, consuming everything in its wake, destroying any and all plant and animal life. He couldn't be sure how long ago the fire had taken place but imagined in his mind the rain that they had witnessed at the beginning of their journey putting out the fire, mother earth healing herself by stopping the damage from getting too out of hand.

They continued walking and eventually reached the edge of burned ground at the base of a large hill. After climbing the hill, the outer city walls of Gelendor finally came into view across the valley below them.

It looked like a *massive* jungle, slapped onto the landscape. It almost appeared out of place in the middle of the valley. It was as if the Gods themselves had planted a garden, growing the city with their divine powers. It was hard to tell from the distance, but the shape of a gargantuan tree seemed to stand at its center.

"There it is! We made it!" Torren exclaimed happily. "It's about *time*!"

"We will camp here tonight," Uthren said, dropping his pack to the ground. "We'll keep low, hopefully avoiding the chance of anyone finding us. We'll make our entrance in the darkness of tomorrow morning before the sun rises. Rest now, we'll go over tomorrow's plan for before the night falls."

Sylas plopped himself down upon the grassy hill, relishing in the thought that their travels would be *over* tomorrow. He brushed his hand through the grass a gentle breeze blowing through his hair. He gazed down the hill, across the valley at the magnificent city, surrounded by an immensely tall stone wall. His imagination ran wild. Even at a distance, he could tell that Gelendor was *nothing* like Shilvrst. Growing up he'd never heard too much about the surrounding cities. He'd been restricted from leaving Shilvrst basically his entire life. He knew his parents had been to other places, but they didn't talk about it much. It was probably to help him and his sister not be sad about never being able to see the world, but he wished they had been more open. He knew his mom was from somewhere far away, but he couldn't remember the name of the city that she'd let slip once or twice in conversation.

Torren and Samara sat down next to him after preparing their shelters for the night. Guesses about what the great city of Gelendor might look like filled the air around them as they waited for nightfall.

As the sun slowly approached the horizon, splashing red and orange across the cloud-filled sky, Uthren sat down next to them.

"Before we enter," Uthren started, "We'll need to make sure the path ahead is clear. If Maelos is planning an ambush, it would be right outside the walls of the city."

Geode joined the group, plopping himself down next to Sylas and slapping him on the knee.

"Geode and I have decided to rely on the eyes of two separate scout animals," Uthren continued. "One by air, and the other by ground. Once they return and report, we can then cautiously make our approach. Once directly outside the wall, we can use the Light to teleport inside the city. After entering, we will immediately seek out queen Nydria and relate to her the events that have transpired. Hopefully, she will then lend us her aid."

Uthren looked directly at Sylas, "Are you still wanting to attempt to speak to an animal? It will be difficult, it's not easy to convey complicated messages to simple creatures."

Sylas looked up at Geode who gave him a nod. He returned his vision to Uthren with a confident smile, "I won't let you down!"

"Very well. You've been improving immensely. I have faith in you."

Uthren pushed himself to his feet, "I'd like to have a short training session with both Samara and Torren. Geode will teach you what you need to know for tomorrow. May the Light be with you."

Waving to Samara and Torren, the three of them retreated, leaving Sylas alone with the powerful Nature mage.

Geode crossed his legs, moving his hands to his knees in a sort of meditative position.

"Are you ready?"

Sylas turned his body to face his master, reflecting his position with his own.

"Ready!"

"The first thing you need to know about speaking with animals, or plants for that matter, is how to first get them to *listen.* With plants, it's not so hard; they're bored sitting all day and night where they've been planted. Some species will talk your ears off. With small critters who are busy looking for food, a mate, or a hundred other things, it gets a bit more tricky. So, I like to cheat…"

Geode winked, placing his hand into an outer pocket of his battle mage robes. He pulled his hand out a second later, his palm filled with some dried nuts.

"When you talk to them, both plants and animals will be naturally curious, and slightly more trusting. But it still helps to give them a bit of incentive to listen. Keep calm, stay collected, and remain *still* as you call out to them. That will help give them the confidence and trust that they need to approach."

Geode placed the nuts on the ground in front of him, then made the symbol of Nature and opened his second mind. After the green glow appeared around his hands and in his eyes, Geode again picked up the nuts from the ground and placed them into his now extended hand.

"After opening your second mind, focus your senses on all the living things around you. Focus on the life energy of the grass, the trees, the bugs beneath the ground, and everything that contains the spark of life. Once you've found the creature that you want to speak to, narrow your focus down from all the things around you to just that one creature. Once you have it in focus, address the creature with a friendly salutation. My preference is a polite, 'hello there.' If the creature you have addressed has enough interest, it should respond, and you can go from there. The language that it speaks will be naturally translated into something that you will be able to understand, thanks to the power of the Nature Magick you're channeling. The more focused you remain, the clearer you will sound to whatever you're talking to, and the clearer it will sound to you."

Geode let out a breath of air and closed his eyes. After a few moments, he opened his eyes and looked around, a strange expression on his face.

"What's wrong?" Sylas asked.

Geode didn't reply but kept looking off into the distance, the same strange expression deepening on his face. Finally, he turned to Sylas and opened his mouth, but must have had a change of thought when he replied, "Never mind. Sorry to keep you waiting."

Geode again closed his eyes, but the expression never left his face as he continued his search for a nearby creature to grab the attention of. About a minute later, he smiled and reopened his eyes, then turned his head towards Sylas's left and gestured for him to look. Sylas slowly turned his head and saw a small chipmunk cautiously approaching them. It stopped moving upon seeing Sylas turn his head and sat back on its hind legs, ready to bolt the other way at any sign of oncoming danger.

Geode reached his hand with the nuts towards the chipmunk, and Sylas noticed the green aura around his hands and in his eyes flare slightly. The chipmunk dropped to all fours, twitching its nose as it slowly approached. The chipmunk dashed past Sylas before slowing its approach as it reached Geode's hand. It paused for a moment, then reached its front paws forward, grabbing a nut from his hand and stuffing it into its mouth. Geode continued to smile as the chipmunk proceeded to stuff fragments of nuts into its cheeks until they doubled in size. The chipmunk jumped into Geode's hand, curled itself into a comfortable sitting position, then continued stuffing nuts into its ever-growing cheeks.

"That's awesome!" Sylas whispered to Geode, trying not to disturb the chipmunk. "What did you say to him?"

"To her," Geode corrected. "I told her that I had some leftover food that she could have and that I meant no harm. I also told her that you would not try to harm her, and she could trust us. Remember, animals only have a couple of simple goals in life and making sure they have enough food is one of them, so coaxing them with food is usually not too difficult. Would you like to try?"

"Yes, please! What do I do?"

"First, connect your second mind to Nature. After that, extend your focus out amongst all of the living things around you, as I explained before. We'll start there."

Geode reached his other hand forward and stroked the top of the chipmunk's head, which it seemed to enjoy.

Sylas made the symbol of Nature with his hands and moved his inner life from his stomach into his head. His second mind opened, attaching itself to the influence and power of Nature. He was always a bit nervous about having another incident with unwanted visions intruding, but thankfully no such luck this time.

The Nature Magick flowing within him quickly agreed to the suggestion to connect with the living things around him. He was surprised to feel how much life was within an arm's reach. The grass sat still, motionless, careless to everything else that was surrounding it. Ants continued busily working, intent on finishing their endless list of tasks assigned to them by their queen.

The trees swayed gently in the breeze, docile, but ever watchful for danger, ready and eager to protect anything that needed its shelter. A slew of other plants and animals crossed his mind to which he simply observed in passive awe as they continued their activities in peace. One such event was not too peaceful, however. Sylas winced slightly as his mind crossed upon that of some warrior ants ruthlessly taking over a small beetle. They bit the beetle and climbed over it with overwhelming numbers, suffocating it beneath their combined weight until it finally succumbed to its awful fate. The ants then proceeded to carry the beetle carcass triumphantly back to their home, an offering to their queen, no doubt. *Some promotions are in order.* Sylas thought to himself.

Like he had been tossed into an icy lake, a powerful, cold feeling suddenly swept over him. The cold was radiating down upon him, as if the moon was producing its own coldness and was shining it down upon him like an icy sun. Sylas opened his eyes, startled at the strange feeling.

"You felt it too?" Geode asked, noting the expression on Sylas's face.

Sylas turned and looked behind where he was sitting. The hill that they sat upon was thick with trees and foliage. Whatever it was, he felt seemed to be coming from the grove of trees in the distance.

He peered into the shadows of the trees, trying to see if anything was watching them, but ultimately saw nothing.

"I… felt something. But I have no idea what it was."

"A cold feeling? Like the sun turned to ice?" Geode asked.

His description matching almost exactly what he felt, Sylas nodded. Geode again peered into the woods behind where Sylas sat for several moments before turning his attention back to him.

"Very curious…" Geode whispered.

"Try focusing back on the chipmunk, I don't believe that we are in any danger."

"You know what that feeling means?" Sylas asked.

"Maybe… but I'm not sure. It would be quite extraordinary, to say the least… Yet again…" Geode shook his head, "Never mind, let's continue with your training."

Sylas closed his eyes and again reached out to the living things around him. He strained momentarily back into the trees to see if he could find the strange cold feeling again, but it was now gone. He eventually gave up and returned his focus back to the chipmunk.

Focusing on the small animal in Geode's hand, he felt his conscience brush against the chipmunks. The chipmunk immediately reacted, raising its head up and looking straight at him.

Sylas felt the Magick flowing within his body, agreeing with his desires to communicate with the creature. Sylas focused his thoughts, then willed the words to weave themselves into the Magick.

"Good evening, Miss."

The chipmunk again intently focused upon Sylas until he felt a string of words enter into his thoughts.

"What you want?"

Sylas twisted his face slightly, *was there a hint of* annoyance *in that translation?* Trying to keep his demeanor kind and gentle, he continued, "How are those nuts? Are they nice and tasty?"

Sylas watched as the chipmunk scooped the remainder of the nuts out of Geode's hand and stuffed them into her mouth.

"Mine!"

"No, no. I don't want to take them from you. I was just wondering if you liked them. Which I guess is kind of obvious. I- umm…"

Sylas had never seen a confused look on a chipmunk before, but looking at the face that was staring back at him, he knew that the chipmunk had *no idea* where he was going with all of this.

Sensing the struggle between Sylas and the chipmunk, Geode reminded him that he needed to keep his queries simple and to the point and his questions and sentences short and polite, otherwise, she would just lose interest.

He thought for a moment, then reached into his pocket and pulled out a small coin. Extending it outward and allowing the light from the now almost setting sun to glint across its reflective face, he asked, "Do you like shiny things?"

The chipmunk perked its ears up slightly and leaned forward in Geode's hand, "Shiny?"

"Yes, shiny. I'll give this to you if you want it."

"I want shiny!"

"Okay, come over here and get it then. I won't hurt you."

Hesitating for a moment, the chipmunk turned to look at Geode for approval. Geode guessed what their conversation might be consisting of and gave a reassuring nod, then lowered his hand to the ground. She slowly crawled out of his hand and made her way closer to Sylas. Keeping her weight on her back feet just in case the need for a quick getaway arose, she continued to crawl closer and closer.

"It's alright, I won't hurt you," Sylas said, slowly lowering his hand to the ground and rotating the coin back and forth with his fingers. "Come and get the shiny."

She finally crossed the distance between them and cautiously reached her front paws out to grab the coin. Finishing the exchange, Sylas moved his hand towards her paws slightly, allowing her to grab the coin and skitter backward a couple of feet. She admired the coin, a sense of awe clearly visible as she copied Sylas, rotating the coin and causing light to gently reflect off the metal surface and into her dark, wide eyes.

With a jolt, the chipmunk opened its already stuffed mouth and put the coin in between its large front teeth and ran towards the nearest tree.

"Hey! Get back here!" Sylas called out with both his physical mouth as well as his second mind.

"Mine, mine, mine!" The words echoed in his mind as he watched the very first animal that he had ever communicated with climb up the tree, its robbery now complete.

Geode laughed out loud, leaning back into the laugh and falling on his back. Sylas must have missed something because having a chipmunk steal what little money he had was not very funny to him.

Wiping a tear from his eye, Geode calmed his laughter, rose back to a sitting position, and cleared his throat.

"That was a good first attempt." He choked on some residual laughter, then added, "As you can see, it's harder than it looks. Try it again."

Geode leaned over and handed Sylas a small handful of nuts from his bag. "You can try the same chipmunk if you want, but I doubt it will be willing to come back now that it's already gotten its prize."

"Stupid chipmunk…" Sylas mumbled under his breath.

Clearing his mind and focusing on the life around him, Sylas once again sent his focus towards the forest where the cold feeling came from before. The feeling had been so *mystical,* so mysterious. He searched amongst several birds, beetles, mice, and other creatures, but to no success.

Abandoning his search, he looked for anything close that might listen to him. A nearby crow piqued his interest, so he gave it a shot.

"Hello Mr. Crow, how are you this evening?"

The crow looked down at him, blinked once, then flapped its wings, taking flight.

"Shove off!" The words rang in his mind as the crow flew off into the sunset.

Sylas frowned, looking at Geode. "Hey, Geode? How *accurately* does Nature Magick translate?"

Geode pondered for a moment, "It's fairly accurate from what I have experienced, why? What did that crow say?"

Sylas frowned, "It told me to 'shove off'…"

Geode burst into laughter, rolling onto his back, pounding his fist into the grassy ground beneath him.

Sylas crossed his arms in frustration, *stupid crow. I didn't want to talk to you anyway.*

Geode, having far too much fun, once again encouraged Sylas to try again. Annoyed, Sylas continued his search for an animal to talk to. He was able to get two mice to come close to him, but each time he was only successful in giving the mouse a nut before it ran away triumphantly.

Frustrated, Sylas was about to give up when he felt the strange radiating cold feeling again. Refocusing, Sylas directed his flow of Magick towards the feeling, deep into the trees behind him. The cool presence grew colder and colder, as if he were slowly descending into a pool of icy water. Sylas refused to let the feeling escape, pursuing it with supreme focus. He closed his eyes, nearly able to *see* the energy in the darkness behind his eyelids.

"You're very interesting," a soft, feminine voice entered his mind.

Sylas flinched at the sudden voice in his head and opened his eyes, fully expecting there to be a young girl standing in front of him. He looked all around but only saw Geode sitting in front of him. A soft giggle rang in his head, its tone light and mysterious, yet playful and curious at the same time. Sylas closed his eyes again, willing the words to be directed towards the voice.

"Who are you?"

A mysterious whisper slithered through his mind, accompanied by continued high pitched giggling. He felt the presence move, growing slightly closer and stronger as it cautiously approached him.

"Yes, you're *very* strange. Much different from any human I've ever felt."

The voice was sly, and mysterious, like a shadow always out of sight, out of reach. Unlike any of the other animals he had connected with before, whatever this was felt *elusive* as though it were impossible to catch. His curiosity peaked, Sylas continued his attempts. Each time he felt that he was growing close to the cold, mysterious presence, it would vanish, popping up at a distance, a whispering giggle lingering at the very edges of his mind.

As quickly as the creature had appeared, it suddenly vanished. The cold presence no longer brushing against his outreaching energy.

"Sylas!" An excited whisper exclaimed. "Sylas Quick! Look behind you!"

Sylas opened his eyes. Geode sad directly in front of him, eyes extatically wide, a finger pressed to his lips.

"Turn around," he silently mouthed. "*Slowly.*"

As though a wild animal would pounce on him at any sudden movement, Sylas slowly turned his body towards where Geode was looking. Sweat began to form at the base of his neck, anticipating an angry bear or other dangerous animal to be staring at him.

The gaze of his second mind was the first to catch a glimpse of the creature, followed shortly by his physical eyes.

Lying low in the tall grass behind him, he saw what looked like a young fox. The fox's appearance was unlike any that he had ever seen before. Its fur was light purple, reminding him greatly of a toned-down version of the glow of Darkness Magick. White, glowing eyes shined brilliantly in the evening air, shining like two beautiful full moons in the night sky. White fur as pure and unstained as fresh, fallen snow ran from the bottom of its chin, down its belly, then made its way to the tip of its tail. Its paws were also white, along with white crescent moon shaped patches of fur around both of its wide, glowing eyes.

It was the most beautiful creature that Sylas had ever seen. A mystical, mysterious creature that had to be from an entirely different world. It stared at him from its crouched position, almost invisible despite the bright colors of its fur and the glowing within its eyes.

"I can't believe it-" Geode whispered, his voice barely audible.

"What is it?" Sylas whispered back, remaining as still as possible.

"It has to be- there's nothing else it could be…"

"What?" Sylas asked again, heart pounding in excitement.

"It's a moon fox…"

"Moon fox?" Sylas responded, watching as the creature lowered itself slightly in the grass.

"Yes… They're *extremely* rare. Legend says that they can disappear in an instant, making them nearly impossible to approach. Only the luckiest of travelers are ever able to catch a glimpse of one, and most likely will never come across another in their lifetime."

"It was that cold feeling," Sylas whispered in wonder. "That's what we were feeling."

"It makes sense now. Moon foxes are a type of *elemental* creature. Part of them is actually made of Darkness. I've heard stories about them, most of them I dismissed for tall tales, but now… seeing one in the flesh…"

Geode's voice grew slightly louder, rising with excitement. "They're said to be *extremely* intelligent, and along with having Darkness coursing through their veins, they possess the ability to *use* Darkness Magick!"

An animal that can use Darkness Magick? Sylas thought to himself. Almost as a response to his thought, the moon fox flicked its ears, tilting its head slightly above the grass, gazing at him with its intensely glowing eyes.

"You're like me," it said in its young, feminine voice. The words whispered through his mind, like a cold winters wind. "One with the shadows. I can *feel* it in you. What are you doing out in these woods?"

Not knowing what to say, Sylas simply responded with the truth, "We're on our way to Gelendor. We're looking for a stone… so we can bring peace to this land."

The moon fox tilted its head slightly, "And why would someone with so much potential in *Darkness* want to create peace? Could it be that you are lying to me?"

Sylas shook his head, the mysteries growing with every word that it spoke, "No! No, I wouldn't lie… We're the good guys. But… how- how do you know that I have potential for Darkness?"

The moon fox didn't answer. After a moment, it slowly rose to its feet, its mystical presence now fully visible above the grass. Step by step, the moon fox slowly started inching towards him. Sylas scooted backward slightly, but Geode sent him an assuring whisper that he was not in danger… at least, not yet. Gathering his courage, he watched with wonder as the creature cautiously approached him.

"A *pure-hearted* dark-souled human… *Very* strange... I didn't think it was possible."

Not knowing what to do, Sylas slowly reached his hand out towards the moon fox's head. It stopped moving at his initial approach, then gradually came closer. As it closed the distance between them, his fingers touched it on the top of its head.

Its soft fur passed through his fingers with ease. A softer material he'd never before had the pleasure of experiencing. As he stroked the top of its head, its glowing eyes stared intently into his own. After a few moments, the moon fox nudged itself forward and slowly put its front paws upon his lap.

Sylas ran his hand from its head down its back and across its large fluffy tail, which it seemed to enjoy. Curiosity poured from the creature's bright stare. Before he knew it, the moon fox had placed its paws against his chest, their noses nearly touching as they stared into each other's gaze. Sylas stared deeply into the moon fox's glowing eyes, feeling a strange tingling sensation beginning to spread throughout his body. His second mind almost seemed to reach out, as if it were forming a sort of mystical connection with the moon fox.

"You're very beautiful." He said, not knowing what else to say. "Maybe the most beautiful creature I've ever seen."

The moon fox continued to stare deeply into his eyes, as if it were judging the very intentions of his soul. "You said you're trying to bring peace? How exactly do you plan to do that?"

Sylas formed the thoughts in his mind, but then a strange feeling crawled over him. Acting upon the suggestion of the Nature Magick flowing through him, he instead allowed *images* from his mind to be sent to the moon fox. The images told the story of him and his friends finding the amulet. It recounted their travels and plans to go to Gelendor. He shared several parts of the visions he had seen, shared his knowledge about the Elemental Sones of Power, and revealed to the fox his deepest desires.

The process was surreal. It was as if he had unlocked a completely *new* way of communication, one where his literal feelings and memories could be conveyed with complete exactness.

Once his message was finished, a similar string of sounds and images began flooding into his mind. He saw a family of moon foxes playing in the night near a slow-moving stretch of river. Two older foxes that, when seen, Sylas instantly *knew* to be its parents, sat nearby watching. Sylas felt the love that was shared between this family of foxes, and also the extreme level of caution that they took when they were out and about.

Sylas instantly knew of the dangers that moon foxes faced every day. The knowledge that they were extremely valuable to hunters instantly becoming truth in his mind. He felt a false sense of security pricking at the edge of his mind, due to their ability to disappear into the shadows at a moment's notice using the Darkness Magick that lived within them.

Feelings of happiness and playfulness swam through his mind as the memory continued, but changed all of a sudden as new images flashed across his vision.

A band of men, not simple hunters this time, had surrounded them. Before they could react, a bubble of Darkness Magick formed around the area in which they were playing. As they had done many times before when confronted by man, the moon fox family tried to use their natural Magick abilities to disappear into the shadows. After disappearing, they scattered, each one of them attempting to escape. But it was no use, something about layer of Darkness Magick that surrounded them hindered them from passing through.

Sylas felt terror coursing through him as if it was his own. The panic of not being able to escape became real, as if he were living the moment right then and there. His heart raced, the frantic and primal urge to get away being denied. He watched as the layer of Magick that surrounded them began to close in, forcing them to move closer and closer to a center point. The men around the circle also walked inward, evil grins painted on their faces as their plans came to fruition.

The scene continued to get more dire, the intensity of fear more severe, until the circle became small enough that the entire family of foxes were all huddled together with no room to run and hide.

Sylas felt the comforting words of the mother and father moon fox, each telling the young ones that everything would be alright. Everything was *not* alright, though. A heart-wrenching sadness flooded his emotions. Sylas felt tears tearing at his eyes, to the point that he thought his heart was about to burst.

Unable to escape the scene, he watched as the men surrounding them stuck a strange metal tube through the Magick barrier and begin to blow sharp, pointed darts at what truly *felt* to be his family. The darts struck the father fox first, who was desperately attempting to protect his family with his own body.

Sylas watched with tears in his eyes as what seemed now to be *his* father, faded out of its invisible form that only he and the other foxes could see, into his regular purple and white form.

"Got 'em." He heard a gruff voice say. "One down, four more to go."

"No, you dimwit. There was only four of 'em," Another voice sounded.

"Nah, I seen five."

"You loon, you counted one of 'em twice is all. There's only four. Two big 'ens and two lit'le 'ens."

Sylas wasn't sure if the fox he was sharing this memory with knew what the men were saying, or if it was just because he himself spoke human that he was able to understand what the men said. Either way, the images, sounds, smells, and basically every sense that he was experiencing felt as though he were living it.

He watched as the men continued to fire darts into the circle until their deadly missiles would eventually strike another member of the moon fox family. It would then fade out of invisibility to the cheers of the men. After what seemed like hours of torment, four of the five members of the family had been shot by the darts, the one that Sylas was sharing the memory with being the only survivor.

"Shoot'a couple more in there. I know I seen five," one of the men said.

Sighing, the man with the metal tube shot several more darts into the ground, each barely missing its target.

"I told ya! Four of 'em's all there was."

The bubble of Darkness energy faded away as two of the other men lowered their hands into the area to scoop up their prizes.

As soon as the energy was gone, the last fox sprinted away into the trees, heart-pounding, sadness overbearing. She watched from the safety of the trees as her family was one by one picked up and placed into bags. Her heart broke as the evil men left the scene of the crime, laughing from their success.

The scene faded slightly, and in its place, images of lonely nights and heartbroken, sleepless days passed through his mind.

Just when Sylas thought it was over, that he wouldn't have to bear any more of the sadness being placed upon him by the memories of the moon fox, the images sprang back into view, now in a time that Sylas knew to be several months later.

She had searched long and hard to find her family, but to no avail. Luckily, she had found refuge with a kind group of regular red foxes and had been staying with them for some time now. At first, they were hesitant to allow her to join them, but had eventually softened their hearts.

Several weeks after joining her new family, while they were sleeping in the safety of a large tree, she heard the terrifying sound of men's voices upon the wind. A deep shudder filled her body as the voices slowly faded away. Not long after, another terrifying sound pricked her ears. This time, it was the sound of an immense, crackling fire. She dared a peak from the safety of the tree, her eyes falling upon deadly, hungering flames swiftly approaching.

Sylas again felt the pain and sadness of her memories as she watched the flames come closer and closer to the tree that she now called home. He felt her fear as her new family all huddled in the back of the hollowed-out trunk, awaiting imminent doom and the immeasurable pain of the flames as they slowly started to climb up the tree. The flames were relentless, devouring and destroying all that she held dear.

Sylas mentally received images in his mind of her bravely jumping from the high branch she had been on, through the thirsting flames and onto the ash-covered ground.

Pain entered into his feet as he felt her land hard on the ground from the long fall. A heart-wrenching sadness overcame him as he witnessed a new family, too scared to make the same jump. He pleaded with them in his own mind, calling to them with every fiber of his being to make the jump. His heart broke as the image of them was eventually consumed in flames.

The images slowly faded, the view of his surroundings and the moon fox once again returning.

"I'm so, so sorry…" He said, his voice choked. "You've been through so much."

"Twice, I've had my family torn away from me," She replied, a quivering in her voice as it was transmitted to him. "Both, by the evils of men."

Her eyes flashed as she looked at him, her thoughts now her own as they mysteriously swam within her.

"But you… are *different.* I felt you, several days ago as I was wandering. I got curious, so I followed with caution. Later, you connected with the Darkness, which was even more surprising."

The moon fox slowly pulled away, sitting down in the grass in front of him. Soft whimpers escaped her, her emotions obviously colliding in a massive mess.

Sylas brought his head up close to hers and rubbed his cheek against the side of her face. Tears again began to flow from his eyes as she returned the gesture, caressing her head with his. He wrapped his arms around her and brought her close to his chest. They embraced, man and beast, in an intimate and love-filled moment, one that would change Sylas's life forever.

Comforting each other, Sylas began to sob out loud as he tried to take the pain from her and place it upon himself. After allowing his emotions to be released, Sylas pulled away from the moon fox.

"That's why we're out here," he said softly. "We're here to *stop* people like that. I- I wonder… would you want to be a part of a new family?"

"A new family?"

"Yes. We'll take care of you. You can come with us on our journey, and *we'll* be your new family. You don't have to stay out here by yourself anymore, and we won't let evil men *ever* take anything else away from you!"

She looked at him, her eyes glowing in the darkness that was quickly starting to surround them.

"Yes. Yes, I think I would like that very much."

The tears again welled up in his eyes as his offer was accepted. A smile of pure joy, joy he had not felt in a *long* time crossed his face as a powerful, strange sense of Magick seemed to swirl within his body.

"Do you have a name?" Sylas asked.

"A name?" She responded, an edge of confusion in her voice.

"Yeah, something that I can call you. You can call me Sylas. That's *my* name."

"Sylas. That's interesting. I don't think I have a name. At least, not that I remember. I was very young when my family was taken from me. I'm still quite young in all reality..."

Sylas thought for a moment about an appropriate name for his new companion. Something feminine that fit an animal... As he pondered, Sylas looked up at the setting sun. It was just below the horizon now, beams of light splashing from behind a large cloud that was covering it. Golden rays passed through the clouds with beautiful, bright pink, purple, and orange hues filling the sky. Silhouettes of the mountains in the distance radiated a light blue, with pink light splashing behind them.

"How about Sky? Do you like that name?"

"Sky… Yes! I love it!"

Sylas smiled, "Welcome to the family, Sky. I'll have to introduce you to everyone else! You can trust them, they're all *good* people. They won't try to harm you in any way."

Sylas placed his hand behind one of Sky's purple ears. A strange sensation filled his mind, as though a powerful, unbreakable bond had been formed between himself and Sky, one that was infused with the very powers of Nature.

Sky's heart, once broken, now mended, beat in tempo with her new companion. She crawled into Sylas's lap, curled into a ball, and peacefully closed her bright, glowing eyes.

Sylas continued to pet the top of her head, a new feeling of *wholeness* filling his heart. Geode slowly stood, approaching them with his mouth wide open.

Sky made no sudden movements, fully trusting that a friend of Sylas was a friend of hers.

"Sylas… this is incredible. What happened?" Geode stammered, still flabbergasted at what he was witnessing.

Sylas wasn't sure *what* had happened. He explained the best he could how they had seemed to share memories with each other, and did his best to describe the strange, Magick sensation that still coursed through him.

"Sky…" Geode said as Sylas finished. "That's a beautiful name, fitting for a moon fox, too. I think, Sylas… I think you might have just used Nature to cast a *very* special spell. We still aren't sure exactly how it works… but basically what happens is that the Nature Magick within you actually causes a *bond* between two living sources. Once you have been bonded with your companion, you can share memories, sights, sounds, emotions, and senses with them, even over great distances. It's a very special spell that not many people have the privilege of enjoying. You should consider yourself *very* blessed."

Geode put his hands on his head, taking several steps backward, "I still can't believe it… Sylas, it's extremely rare to even *see* a moon fox in your lifetime, and you just *bonded* with one!"

His thoughts and feelings overwhelming, Sylas allowed the Nature Magick still flowing within him to be released. As the Magick faded, his connection with Sky seemed to remain, as though he had gained an extra sense. He sent some thoughts towards her, but no response came. Frowning, Sylas looked to Geode for answers.

"Do I have to have my second mind open every time I want to talk to her? Without the Nature, it seems like she can't hear me anymore."

Geode sighed. "Unfortunately, you *will* need to connect to Nature to communicate. She will always speak a language foreign to you, and you will always speak human. However, I do have good news for you. There's a way to enchant spells into items so you can sort of bypass that step. Most mages use this technique as an offensive or defensive tool for emergency situations, such as putting a shield spell into a ring or a fire blast spell into a staff or amulet. It comes in really handy, allowing you to cast a spell without needing to open your second mind. I don't personally know how to enchant items, but I know someone in Gelendor who does!"

"That would be great!" Sylas exclaimed. "Then we could talk whenever we wanted!"

Geode smiled, "You did good tonight. And I think we found a pretty good ground spy for our mission tomorrow…"

Sylas looked down at his new companion, a loving smile crossing his lips. "Yes, I believe we have."

CHAPTER 10
GELENDOR

Sylas slept exceptionally well that night. Sky accompanied him in his tent and slept curled up beside him as they helped to keep each other warm. It was a powerful connection that he had gained with Sky, something that he didn't know he was missing before but that now filled an obvious emotional hole.

Before going to bed that night, Sylas reopened his second mind and introduced her to the rest of the group. Torren and Samara were both flabbergasted that a creature like Sky even existed, and Uthren was just as much, if not *more* impressed that he had created a bond with such a legendary creature. Samara couldn't wipe the smile off her face at how cute the moon fox was and repeatedly told Sylas to make sure Sky knew how adorable Samara thought she was. He was glad that everyone accepted her as a part of their group, and they each committed to watch after her if danger ever came upon them again.

The cold morning air felt crisp in Sylas's lungs as he walked down the hill towards the massive stone walls of Gelendor. Sky walked by his side the dark, ready to turn invisible at any sign of trouble. Geode took the lead, a hungry bluebird perched upon his outstretched finger, negotiating a deal between an arial scouting mission and a couple of plump nightcrawlers.

It didn't take long to reach their intended destination, the morning sun still yet to peak up above the horizon. Whispering his last bit of instructions to the bluebird, Geode lifted his arm, releasing the bird into the barely lit sky.

Sylas pulled his hands into the symbol of Nature, opening his second mind and connecting his senses with Sky. Her mysterious presence brushed against his, eager to speak with him once again.

"I guess it's your turn now," Sylas said. "Keep safe. Tell me if you see *anything* that looks suspicious. Once you get to the wall, turn around and come back. We'll wait for you here."

"I'll do my best!" Sky said, eager to help her new family with their stealth mission. Her eyes shimmered in the darkness, and a moment later, Sylas watched with awe in his eyes as she faded into the shadows, becoming completely invisible.

"Sylas," Geode whispered, placing a hand on his shoulder. "There's one last thing that I forgot to tell you last night. This technique that connects you to Sky, there's a bit *more* to it that I forgot to mention. I told you that you are able to communicate over long distances because of the bond that you have made with her, but I forgot to mention that while you are within fairly close ranges of each other, you can actually use the connection to *replace* her senses with your own. You can see what she sees, feel what she feels."

"I can?!" Sylas exclaimed.

Geode nodded, "Why don't you try it now. Use the same feelings that you normally would to communicate, but instead of talking, concentrate on truly becoming *one* with her. Sense what she senses, see what she sees. Give it a try."

Excited, Sylas closed his eyes, pushing his consciousness towards his new companion. He felt his inner life flowing through his body as the Magick connected him with all of the nature around him. The feeling of freedom flooded over his body as he felt his thoughts flying upon the wind towards his companion. Finally, he focused purely on her, as she ran towards the walls of Gelendor.

He felt a tickle upon his legs as he ran through the tall grass, cold air rushing past his face. Brisk air swiftly entered and exited his lungs as he moved silently through the dark morning. Sky's vision slowly took over the vision of his second mind as he continued to will her senses to become one with his own. Opening his eyes, he could see what was in front of his physical body, but instead of the second perspective from his ghostly body, he now saw the vision of Sky, bounding through the grass as she ran.

Testing the telepathic portion of the spell, Sylas quietly asked, "Sky, can you hear me?"

Sylas watched through her eyes as she jumped off the ground and twisted backward in the air. He felt her heartbeat increase rapidly, her head spinning in all directions.

"Where are you? You scared me!"

"Oops, sorry. Pretty cool though, right? We can talk even when we're far away! And I can see what you're seeing!"

"Yeah, very cool. But how about next time you don't give me a heart attack?"

"Yeah, sorry. Have you seen any humans yet?"

"Not yet. Still looking."

Sky turned back towards Gelendor and continued running towards the city. Her head turned from side to side as she surveyed the area around her.

Sylas was surprised at how well she could see in the dark. It made sense, he didn't realize it before, but now that he had shared his thoughts with her and vise-versa, he had learned that *all* foxes were primarily nocturnal, not just moon foxes. On top of that, it was like Sky was *built* to be in the dark. Her bright glowing eyes made seeing in the dark a sinch. The colors of her fur helped her to easily blend in with the shadows of night, and with her ability to become invisible, it was no wonder moon foxes were only seen by the luckiest of the lucky.

Sylas watched for any signs of movement or signals that there was an ambush waiting for them. As far as he could tell, it looked as though the coast was clear. Sky made it to the massive stone wall and confirmed his thoughts.

"Nothing. So, I can come back then?"

"Yeah, I think so. We must have beat them here. Maybe take a slightly different path back, but I think we might be good to continue. I'll let the others know."

Sky agreed and Sylas pulled his senses away from her and felt them return back into the body of his second mind. Closing the connection with the Magick completely, a rush of energy filled him.

"Now *that* was cool!" He whispered to the others.

"Did you see anything?" Samara asked.

Sylas shook his head, "Nope. I think we're probably good, as long as Geode's bird says the same thing. I could see *super* well through Sky's eyes too. I'm almost positive there's nothing waiting for us up there."

"That's excellent news," Uthren said, letting out a sigh of relief. "Still, we should proceed with caution. Geode, how long do you think until the bird gets back?"

"Maybe just a few more minutes. She's quite fast because of her flight, but I don't share a connection with her like Sylas does with Sky, so I can only guess."

Silent as a shadow, Sky reappeared out of nothing standing directly in front of Sylas. He jumped slightly, the sight of her glowing eyes, purple fur, and oddly 'cute but dangerous' presence coming out of nowhere startling him. A swift thought of what an adult moon fox ready to pounce on him and tear him to pieces would look like flashed across his mind, sending a shiver up his back.

He made the symbol of Nature, opened his second mind, and connected himself to her. "See anything on the way back?"

"No, nothing out of the ordinary."

"Good, deal. Thanks for doing that."

"It was fun. I'm good at sneaking around."

Sylas didn't doubt it one bit.

They waited a few moments longer until Geode reached his hand into the air and caught the bluebird who had just returned to his finger. He stood, staring at the bird for several minutes, obviously having a conversation about what she had to report. Then reaching into the small bag he had placed the worms in, he pulled out two large nightcrawlers and placed them in the bird's open beak. She clamped down on the worms happily and took flight.

"She didn't see anything, either. She also told me that there's a clear spot we can teleport into just to the west of the main gate. There aren't many people up yet, so if we go soon, we won't have to worry about running into anyone."

"Let us hurry, then," Uthren said. "While the morning is still young. The sooner we are safe within the walls, the better."

The group walked cautiously and silently towards the city, watchful for any surprises lurking around the trees or in the darkness. Finally, the tenseness was brought to a halt when Uthren notified them that they were close enough to do the teleport.

Geode spent a couple of minutes describing to Uthren where they needed to teleport to. He had lived in Gelendor for a long time but needed the bird to be sure that things hadn't changed too much since he had been away so that they could land in a clear area.

The sun was now peeking just over the horizon, making the area around them visible enough to see a fair distance. Sylas was sure that the bright light that was going to engulf them during the teleport would still be able to be seen from a far distance but trusted that it would be alright.

After finishing his explanation, Uthren nodded then made the symbol of Light and opened his second mind. His eyes and hands glowed brightly, and he motioned for everyone to join hands. Sylas picked up Sky and placed her on his shoulder, then joined his hands in the group.

"Everyone ready? Remember, if anyone confronts us after we have entered the city, let Geode and I do the talking."

After seeing confirmed nods of compliance, Uthren focused the Light Magick and a bright pillar of Light descended from the heavens and engulfed them in Light. Half a second later, the Light disappeared with a flash, and they found themselves standing within the walls of the city.

As the Light dissipated, Sylas's eyes filled with wonder. The massive stone wall at his back was taller than any building he had ever seen. Looking towards the city, stone buildings that looked to have been *raised* directly from the ground, then mystically formed into their shapes were scattered about.

Bright green, flourishing plant life was *everywhere.* Luscious grass scattered across the ground. Brightly colored trees, bushes, and small plants brought the city to life, strange mystical looking orbs of green light swirling around most of them.

Further in the distance, the stone buildings gradually faded into what appeared to be a sort of 'organized' jungle. Trees ten times larger than he thought physically possible weaved their way through the city, wooden buildings that he could have sworn looked like they were *grown* straight from the trees scattered amongst their massive branches. Homes, shops, and other buildings held up by trunks and branches that were impossibly large striking his very soul with wonder.

Blinking his eyes, he realized that those trees were the *small* ones. The deeper into the city he looked, the larger and grander they became. Perfectly paved, stone walkways and streets led the way in front of him, towards what surely had to be the most magnificent place on earth.

"Welcome to Gelendor," Geode said with a smile.

Sylas looked at Samara and Torren, then gazed on silently, unable to put together any coherent string of words. Sylas took a quick glance at Geode, wondering how he could possibly be from such an amazing place. Surely, a people who lived in a place like this would look *vastly* different. A tree-dwelling race that had branches growing from their foreheads or something.

"Gelendor should be awakening soon," Uthren said, cutting off his train of thought. "We should head towards the center of the city. There we will find the Great Tree of Gelendor, and we can petition to talk to Nydria."

Geode led the way down a stone path towards the massive, jungle part of the city. As they walked, Sylas began to see people emerging from the stone homes on the outskirts. Some looked upon them with confusion, as if they had never seen people who looked like Sylas and the others before. Others gave them a kind wave, then went about their daily business. Against all logical thinking, the people that lived here really *were* human. Sylas realized, however, that it seemed that every person in Gelendor had hair that was as dark and black as night, as well as emerald-green eyes that sparkled in the light of the rising sun, just like Geode. Something else that stood out immediately, was the fact that Magick was a common *commodity* here, rather than an extreme rarity like back in Shilvrst. Even little children seemed to be using Magick, albeit simple.

Something else that was peculiar was the way that the people here dressed. It seemed as though everyone here was wearing almost the exact same thing. The men had dark green trousers and a lighter green shirt with varying lengths of sleeves, their boots also had a slight hue of green to them. The women wore dresses that matched the light green color of the men's shirts, many of which had long flowing sleeves with a white stripe that ran down them. Other women had the same type of dress, but they stopped further above the ankle and had shorter sleeves that hugged their arms instead of flowing freely. Sylas guessed that these dresses were more for working, while the others were for show.

As the sun slowly rose, shining its light upon the city, it brought more and more people out into the streets. Sylas continued to look around himself in awe until Torren tapped him on the shoulder.

"Sylas… Sylas l- look at that!"

Sylas turned his head to where Torren was pointing. His jaw dropped when his eyes caught sight of the spectacle. Behind the massive trees holding homes and other buildings. Beyond the vines and wooden bridges that were strewn between the trees, connecting the canopies to create what looked to be several layers of city stacked on top of each other. Above and beyond everything that screamed 'I was planted by the Gods themselves', stood an impossible, incomprehensible sight.

A gargantuan tree that completely dwarfed everything else around it towered above the canopies. Leaves the size of buildings rustled in a gentle breeze.

Geode led the group around a corner which opened up to a pathway that led directly towards the wonder. The colossal tree sat in the center of a massive fissure in the ground that seemed to separate one side of the city from the other. It stood upon massively tall roots that extended into the chasm of the fissure. A foggy mist caused by several waterfalls that fell from the base of the tree into the chasm rose gently into the air. In front of the tree stretched a large stone bridge with intricately designed railing and archways that connected the tree to the walkable land.

Surely, beyond a shadow of a doubt, *this* was the largest living thing on the entire planet. Its branches stretched upward into the sky, nearly scratching the heavens. Looking towards the base of the tree, Sylas noticed a massive wooden door that marked the entrance into the living shelter. Intricately designed wooden planks, along with naturally occurring branches and vines, curled themselves upward from the door, forming several balconies and rooftops. Large windows could also be seen, built into the trunk of the mighty tree, their glass covered with a constant fog from the roaring water and rising steam of the chasm beneath it.

It looked like a castle, a castle that had been built into the still-living tree. The dwarfed trees and other foliage that sat on the edges of the fissure seemed to lean in towards the massive tree, aspiring in vain to one day be as great as it was.

"It's not possible…" Samara said in amazement, echoing the very thoughts that were running through Sylas's head.

"This tree is even older than the knowledge of Magick itself," Geode responded, pride in his voice. "When Nymphara obtained the knowledge of Nature Magick, she and her followers gathered to this place, drawn towards the greatness of this tree. They poured their Magick into this already ancient tree, helping it to grow at a tremendous rate and shaping the land around it to make this kingdom. As she was the first to learn Nature Magick, Nymphara was the original King of Nature. This place became her palace, and from that day forward, her descendants have ruled the great kingdom of Gelendor. It is always the first-born daughter who inherits the throne. After that, the inheritance falls to any other daughter of the previous queen, and finally, if none else are suitable, to one of their sons. Gelendor is primarily a matriarchy, but if time calls for it, a man is able to take the throne for a time."

Geode gestured for them to follow him towards the massive gate that hung at the beginning of the long stone bridge as he continued.

"Magick is sung into the tree daily. It helps to provide the vast amount of nourishment that it needs to continue to live and flourish. The technique of singing Magick into living things to enhance their growth and life has been passed down from Nymphara through the royal family, and queen Nydria keeps the tradition going today."

Sylas continued to marvel at everything around him as they approached the stone bridge leading to the tree. Sky had turned invisible, but Sylas knew she was still there as she rubbed against his legs occasionally as they walked. He wanted to talk to her about the incredible sights they were seeing but decided against using Magick in the city for now.

"Do you have an appointment?" A woman clothed in nature battle mage robes asked as they approached the gate leading to the stone bridge. She had long black hair and bright green eyes that almost looked like she was constantly channeling Nature Magick. Her smile and kind demeanor didn't hide the obvious appearance of being able to handle herself in a fight, however.

"No, we don't." Geode said, approaching her, "But we have information that's vital for the queen to hear."

"Is that so?" She responded, raising an eyebrow. "Well, without an appointment I'm afraid you'll be out of luck. If you would like to make an appointment to see her, I can help you with that."

Geode looked to Sylas, nodding and holding out his hand. Sylas immediately knew what Geode was asking for. He reached down the front of his shirt and pulled out the amulet that was hiding behind it.

Pulling it off his neck, he handed the ancient artifact to Geode.

Geode stepped towards the woman, slowly handing the amulet to her.

Her smile faded away as the amulet was placed into her open palm. Purple light bounced off the terrified look of her face from the Stone of Darkness as she peered into the silver amulet.

"I think, you know what this is?" Geode asked softly.

"This can't be… How? Where did you get this?"

Her green, worry-filled eyes flicked up to Geode. After a moment, a slight look of recognition seemed to cross her face.

"Wait a minute. Do I know you?"

She scanned the faces of the party, her eyes seeming to only have a sense of recognition for Geode.

"Are you-"

"Please," Geode said, interrupting her. "We *really* need to talk to Queen Nydria. It's very important, as you can see. Can you help us?"

The woman rubbed her thumb over the Stone of Darkness, and a cold sense of fear crossed over her face. She shook herself, as if trying to rid the dark thoughts that had just come over her, then hurriedly handed the amulet back to Geode.

"Right then, I'll bring you to her. Please, follow me."

She made the symbol of Nature, and her eyes and hands began to glow. Waiving her hands, several roots that were wrapped around the large gate began to unravel, and the gate slowly swung open with a loud creak. Sylas felt Sky rub against his leg, signifying that she was still there as he followed Geode across the large stone bridge.

Sylas felt his blood grow cold as he walked across the massive stone bridge. He tried not to look down, but his natural, morbid curiosity unfortunately got the better of him. The chasm seemed unending, infinite. Its depths looked to descend even past the horrible underworld that kids would always tease each other about.

It took nearly everything that he had to continue walking across the bridge, praying that their additional weight wouldn't cause the bridge to fail, as ridiculous as the thought seemed. As they grew closer to the tree, the roaring of the waterfalls that fell behind it became so loud that he could hardly hear himself think. The rumbling of the massive amounts of water seemed to vibrate through his body, reverberating within his chest like the pounding of a massive drum.

Arriving at the huge, wooden door that led into the tree, several guards standing at the door raised their hands to greet them. The woman leading them gave the guards a nod, causing the guards to step aside. Grabbing the large metal handles of the door, they pulled it open, revealing the inside of the tree's trunk.

Sylas stepped through the doors, grateful to no longer be suspended above an endless pit. He found himself inside a long, polished wooden tunnel. Green glowing orbs of Magick energy floated at evenly spaced distances within the tunnel, lighting it with a somewhat eerie green glow. Endless dark colored rings of wood spiraled through the tunnel, showing how ancient the tree really was.

Exiting the long wooden tunnel, the tree opened up into a massive central room. His mind spun at how impossible it was that he was still *inside* of a tree as he gazed at his surroundings. The room was several stories high, flights of spiraling staircases that led to different parts of the tree swirling in each of the corners of the room. Hallways that led into what had to be hundreds of different sections of the palace were connected by small wooden tunnels throughout the tree.

He felt like an ant exploring through a great oak as they were led through tunnels, climbed staircases, and crossed wooden bridges all contained within the tree.

Eventually, they came to a stop at the end of a particularly long tunnel that led to a large wooden door. The door appeared almost as ancient as the wood that surrounded it, the same symbol of the tree that was on Geode's battle robes etched into the top of its dark wooden trimming. The woman placed her hand on the door and knocked three times. A couple of moments later, the door opened slightly and a large man with the male version of nature battle mage robes walked out.

"What is it?" he asked in a deep burly voice.

"These people have requested to talk to queen Nydria, and I believe that their reasoning is sound."

"I don't have any appointments on my schedule. What's this about?"

"It's really an urgent matter, I can-"

"I'll be the judge as to whether or not it's important enough to request visitation with the queen without an appointment!"

The guard had deep green eyes and night black hair that fell over his eyes slightly. He stepped out of the door and closed it behind him. He had muscles that looked like he could yank a tree out of the ground with his bare hands. He looked straight at Geode, curiously studying his nature battle mage robes that were of a slightly different design than his own.

"Those robes are of an old design… I think I recognize them, though. You got them from here in Gelendor, didn't you?"

"I did indeed," Geode responded. "I used to be in the military group known as RiverWalkers. We were in charge of protecting the outer wall, as well as helping neighboring cities when necessary."

"I've heard of it," The guard said. "It was a bit before my time, though."

Geode nodded. "Ten years ago, I was sent to Shilvrst when the Dark Mage Maelos attacked. We were unsuccessful, as you know, but I decided to take residence there and try to help out the people that lived there as much as I could without being too noticeable."

"Hmm." The man said, continuing to study Geode. "Well, go on then. I can respect someone that used to be a RiverWalker. What's this you need to tell queen Nydria about?"

Geode stretched forth his hand and presented the amulet to the man. "Do you recognize this?"

Grabbing it by its silver chain, he lifted it out of Geode's hand and studied it. The Stone of Darkness was still sitting in the center of the amulet, glowing with its eerie, wispy purple light amidst the sea of darkness within.

The guard took a step back, his eyes wide. "The stories are true?" His eyes lingered on the Stone of Darkness, then slowly made their way back to Geode, "Where did you find this?"

"That's what we've come to discuss with queen Nydria. We need to make plans for what to do with it. We want to make sure it doesn't fall into Maelos's hands."

The man stood wide-eyed at the information that was presented to him. He hardened his expression as he scanned the group of strangers in front of him.

"Nydria will be anxious to hear what you have to say, follow me."

Handing the amulet back to Geode, the guard turned and opened the large wooden door behind him and extended his arm, gesturing for them to enter. Geode handed the amulet to Sylas, which he placed around his neck and tucked under his shirt. The metal amulet felt cold against his skin, colder than it should have felt, like it had been sitting in an icy stream all morning long.

Sylas checked once more for Sky by shuffling his feet to the side until he felt her bump into his leg again. *I have to find a better way of knowing when she's around while she's invisible,* he thought. He followed Geode and Uthren through the door and into a large room with high vaulted ceilings.

Vines from the massive tree climbed up the edges of the room and wrapped themselves along the many carvings and symbols that were engraved into the walls. At the back of the room, two guards stood at the ready next to a large wooden throne. The guards were wearing battle mage robes, but they looked slightly different from the other robes that Sylas had seen. The robes had golden trim that swirled around the tree symbol in the middle of their chest, and the colors of the robes were slightly brighter, signifying probably the high ranks that they needed in order to guard the queen directly. The guards held large spears and round wooden bucklers. Just by looking at them, Sylas knew that the guards would be just as dangerous with Magick as they would be with their weapons.

Behind the throne were several large stone statues of mostly women, atop of all their heads were metal crowns signifying their royalty. A woman, whom Sylas guessed to be Nydria, sat on the throne watching as they entered the room.

She was much younger than Sylas had pictured in his mind, he guessed that she might even be just a few years older than himself. She had the same, almost copper toned skin as Geode, and his same dark black hair, flowing over her shoulders down to about her mid torso. A metallic crown with a bright green emerald sat atop her head. Her robes were bright green with gold trim around the edges. A bright silver trim ran down her sleeves and swirled across her chest, finally meeting at the belt area.

“My greetings, friends. How may I be of service to you today?” Nydria asked.

Geode took a step forward, then knelt on one knee, bowing himself before her. Uthren did the same, causing Samara, Torren, and Sylas to quickly follow their example to show their respects.

"Greetings, queen Nydria. My name is Geode, and these are my companions and friends. We have traveled here from Shilvrst, seeking your counsel and wisdom. We have some grave news concerning Maelos and wish to ask for your help and guidance."

Raising her hand in the air, she gestured for them to stand up, "Please arise. What news do you have concerning Maelos, and how does it concern the people of the kingdom of Gelendor?"

Geode and the rest of the group stood up and he continued, "My queen, I was once a part of this great city and served under your mother as a RiverWalker before Maelos attacked. I knew your great mother personally and know from conversations with her that as direct descendants of the great Nymphara, you and your family possess a great deal of knowledge concerning the Vault of Kings and the Elemental Stones of Power."

Nydria again raised her hand, cutting him off. She looked over at the woman that had been their guide as well as the guard that let them through the door and with a smile, asked if they would leave them to discuss the matter alone. With disappointed looks, they both agreed and left the room. Sylas imagined them pressing their ears against the other side of the now-closed door in hopes of catching pieces of the secret conversation, like he had done so many times at his parents' door.

"Please continue, Geode."

"Yes, my queen. As you may or may not know, there was a dark mage by the name of Aracorn, who associated closely with Maelos for some time. He gained great strength in Darkness Magick and built a crypt just outside of the town of Shilvrst."

He stretched his hand out towards Uthren and continued, "We don't know exactly what he was doing down there, but eventually Uthren and others from the Council of Light from Sindmyr felt a dark presence and decided to investigate. Upon finding the crypt, they did further investigation and ultimately were forced to slay Aracorn. They believed that they had destroyed all of the evil that he had conjured down there, but it was not so. Many years past and these young folks were exploring the ruins of the Ancient Crypt and accidentally discovered something."

Geode turned to Sylas, "Sylas, would you kindly show queen Nydria what you found?"

Sylas reached his hands up to the back of his head, grabbed the amulet by its silver chain, and removed it from his neck. The artificial light that was created by the orbs hanging in the room glinted off the amulet as he held it in the air. The Stone of Darkness sat in the center, staring at Nydria with its cold, dark, wispy aura.

Nydria leaned forward in her throne and stared back at the stone with a worried look. She then raised a hand and spoke to Sylas, "Can you please bring that to me, I would like to have a closer look."

Sylas nodded and walked towards Nydria, keeping the amulet held out in front of him. Upon arriving at the throne, he placed the amulet into the outstretched hand of Nydria, then took a couple of steps backward. Nydria held the amulet by its chain and examined it for some time. She then grabbed its metal surface and brought it close to her face so that she could stare into the depths of dark color the stone emanated. Without breaking her concentration on the stone, she asked, “What is your name?”

“My name is Sylas, queen Nydria.”

“Sylas, this is quite the mess you’ve gotten yourself into…”

She ran a finger over the stone, her eyes reflecting deep contemplation as she studied the ancient artifact and the powerful stone embedded in its center. Eventually, she stretched her hand forward, placing the amulet back into his hand.

“So, Geode, what is it that you want to know from me? I’m interested in hearing your plans as to what you intend to do with this discovery, but I would like to know what you want to ask me first.”

“I was hoping you would be able to tell us more about the Vault of Kings. Being at the rank I was, I was entitled to little more than the rumored information that floated amongst those who were curious enough to receive it. I know that many details about it are well-kept secrets amongst the royal families. I wondered if you would be able to shed some light on the subject.”

Nydria sat back in her throne and put a hand on her chin, “Very well, I’m willing to talk about some of what I know. How far back do I need to go? I assume that all of you know who the original Kings were?”

"We've taught them some of the history of Magick and told them about the Original Kings and how they obtained their power, but have not given them much information beyond that," Geode said gesturing to Torren, Samara, and Sylas.

"Very well then, we can start from there. The original six mages are also known as the first 'Kings'. Nymphara, my ancient ancestor, was one of these Kings, she being the first to master the power of Nature. The Kings gained much power and influence from the gift that the Gods gave them, yet still they desired more. Legend tells that the six Kings came together and climbed the Kandarin mountains to see if they could receive more power and knowledge from the Gods. They heard a voice of warning descend from the heavens, telling them that if they sought out too much power, they would become corrupted and ultimately consumed by that lust for power. They did not heed the voice, however, and continued to pray to the gods for additional knowledge. An angelic creature descended from the heavens and granted them their request."

Nydria shifted in her throne, "The description of what he looked like that has passed down from my family, described him as having dark black wings, wearing nothing on his torso, and dark black robes from the waist down. His name was Erebus, God of Darkness. It was said he had seven orbs hovering around him, orbiting slowly as if he was the center of his own universe. They described him as terrifying, and at the same time, awe-inspiring. He told them about the history of the heavens and more about each of the elements that they already possessed. He taught them about the hierarchy of the heavens, about each of the Gods that ruled over the different elements, and divulged to them many other secrets. Sadly, the majority of those details have been lost through time. I don't think that they were lost because they weren't important, though… I think they were lost because they were *too* important, too great for mortals to know and were probably forgotten on purpose."

Nydria looked toward the amulet, "The angel, or God, pulled six of the seven orbs from around him and using his godly powers transformed them into the six elemental stones that we know of today, one of which you have in your possession. As you may or may not already know, the elemental stones give the person that possesses them additional power and an advantage to learning new techniques when using Magick of that element. When you are in possession of one of the stones, you are able to achieve feats with that element in a short amount of time that would rival that of a master who has studied that element for a lifetime."

Sylas looked down at the amulet, peering into the Stone of Darkness in its center. "The angelic being also gave unto them a secret, which proved his warning to be true about the possibility of corruption and lust for power. The Kings regretted their decision to plead for more knowledge, wishing they had heeded the warning of the Gods. All six Kings decided that the secret was too great for man to know; if it fell into the wrong hands, it would spell doom for all. They asked the angelic being to forge for them a key and build for them a vault that could only be unlocked with that key. They desired that the key should be able to contain all six of the elemental stones, so that the only way that the vault could be opened was if all six of the original Kings, or their predecessors, came together in unison and harmony to unlock the vault. They hoped to try and prevent anyone from coming and stealing the secret without consent from everyone else, or one tribe taking dominance over the others, by requiring that each stone be placed into the key for it to work on the vault."

Nydria looked Sylas in the eye, "The knowledge of whatever is contained within the vault was lost when the last of the original Kings died. The stones were eventually hidden in safe places or lost due to the corruption of man and their lust for power. No one truly knows what is contained within the Vault of Kings. All I know is that whatever it is, it will give the wielder immense power, and a knowledge of something that the original Kings thought should not be known to the world."

Standing up from her throne, Nydria approached Sylas with an outstretched hand, "I was told that the Kings voted to give the key to the first mage, Zephyr. I was taught that he vowed to keep it secure, so that it wouldn't fall into the hands of someone who would try to collect all of the stones and use whatever was inside the vault to assert dominance over the land."

Sylas placed the amulet in her hand and watched as she examined it again, slowly turning it around in her hands and feeling the Stone of Darkness with her fingers.

"Over the years, its existence turned into a myth, which in my opinion is safer for the world anyway... Somehow, it must have been stolen or traded away and forgotten to end up in Aracorn's possession. It's nothing short of miraculous to be holding it my hands."

Nydria eyed each of them, studying their intents. "I would like to know what your intentions with this amulet are…"

It was Uthren who spoke up this time as he slowly walked closer to Nydria and Sylas. "The reason we have come to you is for both guidance and help. As you know, Maelos has almost all of Evendreil under his strict rule, and the cities that he rules are slowly dying. Only Gelendor, Sindmyr, and Winjjrith were able to withstand his first wave of attacks ten years ago. I'm sure that he's preparing for another attack as we speak, and this time he won't stop until he gains control of everything."

"We have thwarted Maelos and his attempts at taking over our great city, and we will do it again. Have you seen any evidence of him preparing to attack?"

"Not exactly, but we do have great reason to believe that he has plans to attack again. We also worry because we believe he has gained much more power since the last time he attacked. What do you know about Darkness Magick?"

Nydria handed the amulet back to Sylas and looked into Uthren's eyes. "I know that it's evil, despite what others may say to try and defend it. I also know that it's very powerful and resourceful and can be very dangerous. You should think the same as

I do Light mage, you know very well that Darkness is not an element that can be trusted."

"You should know then of some of the capabilities that it has when it's used by a master as capable as Maelos," Uthren responded. "I've been studying a very ancient book that one of my instructors gave me long ago. It was a book on advanced Darkness techniques and theories as to what might be able to be accomplished if someone were to gain enough power. I have evidence to believe that Maelos has unlocked some of these ancient, dark secrets. Aaracorn worked with Maelos extensively on something very dark, and I believe that he succeeded before the Council of Light and I were able to stop him."

Uthren looked at Sylas, his eyes full of fear and concern. "One of those techniques I believe he mastered is called *Living Darkness*. It is an ancient, evil art that is only mentioned in the most obscure texts. If what I have studied is true, then it is a way to take a part of your soul and bind it to an object, thus allowing you to, if your body dies, have someone remove your soul from that object into another body, and you will live once again in that new body. I believe that Maelos and Aracorn must have figured out how to do this, and a part of Maelos is *bound* to the Stone of Darkness."

"Uthren-" Geode said, his eyes falling upon Sylas, as if he didn't want Sylas to be hearing where this conversation was going.

Uthren continued, casting his eyes away from Geode. "I believe that when Sylas touched the stone, something might have gone wrong with the spell… I believe that the power of Living Darkness that was meant to remain within the Stone of Darkness, was somehow transferred into Sylas…"

Sylas's eyes grew wide, the realization of what Uthren was saying starting to sink into him.

"Along with this and many other problems, I have reason to believe that Maelos is building an army of skeletons brought back to life with an ancient form of Darkness Magick to once again try his hand at conquering the cities that he was not able to overthrow the first time."

Nydria walked back to her throne and sat down. Her eyes didn't leave Sylas, as if she now saw a stain that corrupted his very soul. Obviously troubled, she put on a facade of confidence.

"So, what's your plan then? Find a way to rid this Living Darkness from inside of Sylas? Find all of the stones and combine them with the amulet? Gain the knowledge inside of the Vault of Kings to try and stop him before his plans can be fulfilled? I hope you realize that I will *not* endorse a mission to go directly *against* the wishes of my ancestor, and all of the original Kings to gather the stones together and seek out the Vault."

Geode bowed his head slightly as he spoke, "My queen, you must realize that it's only a matter of time before Maelos is able to enforce his rule over not only Gelendor but other strong cities as well. He won't stop until he's the supreme ruler over everything! We can't let him gain enough power to do that. He's hunting us down right this very moment because he knows that we have the Stone of Darkness in our possession. He most likely knows that we are here in Gelendor, he could be at your doorstep any day now. We have the amulet, so that can be to our advantage! Aracorn must have found it at some point and hid it away to one day use it as leverage against Maelos if he ever felt that he was not getting the recognition he felt he deserved, or some other dark purpose. If Maelos were to get the amulet… he would stop at *nothing* to find the remainder of the stones and open the vault himself. We need something to give us the power to defeat him and rid the land of his presence before any of that can happen! Whatever is in that vault might be the key to *ending* this war!"

"My ancestors and the rest of the Kings kept whatever is in the vault a secret to protect us!" She responded sharply. "They knew in their *wisdom* that it was not right for it to be known to the world, so they hid it away. I will not entertain this conversation any longer!"

Queen Nydria slammed her fist on her throne, causing her two guards to shift slightly in the defensive.

"However," she added, "you bring up a good point about not wanting the amulet or the stone to fall into his hands… So, I will be taking that from you now."

Nydria reached her hand out towards Sylas and petitioned him to hand it over. Sylas looked to Geode and Uthren for guidance, but the guards at her side quickly stepped forward, forcing him to comply. Reluctantly, Sylas placed the amulet into her hand, which she promptly placed around her neck.

"Rest assured, the amulet will be safe here with me. You are all welcome to stay in Gelendor until you feel it's safe to leave, but I expect *none* of this conversation to be mentioned outside these walls. Is that understood?"

Geode and Uthren looked at each other for a moment, then with a sad countenance, agreed to her demands.

Nydria nodded and sat back in her throne. "Very good. Well then, if there's nothing else, I will thank you for your concern, assure you that we are safe within the walls of our great city, and bid you a good day. Guards, will you please kindly escort our friends out of the Great Tree?"

"Yes, my queen." The guards both said in unison as they slipped their spears and bucklers onto their backs.

Without giving them the chance to argue, the guards escorted them through the many tunnels and staircases of the Great Tree until they were at the large wooden door in front of the stone bridge. They then told them to enjoy their stay in Gelendor before opening the doors and ushering them out onto the bridge.

Sylas and the others slowly walked across the bridge, their heads hanging lower than usual.

"So, what now?" Torren finally said, breaking the silence. "Does this mean we just go home and back to our old lives?

Uthren sighed. "I'm so surprised… I thought for sure, she would want to help… As it is, it looks as if our journey has been cut short."

“It’s not all bad news,” Geode said, trying to lift their spirits. “You kids won’t be exposed to any more danger, and I’m sure that your parents will be happy to see you back sooner than anticipated.”

Uthren shook his head, “I fear that it’s just a matter of time until things go from bad to worse…”

Geode smiled and changing his tone of voice slightly put his hand on Sylas’s shoulder.

“Not all hope is lost. As Nydria said, Gelendor is a strong city. As long as the amulet and the Stone of Darkness are here, it means that Maelos won’t have access to it. We should be proud, our mission is complete! It’s not what we had thought it would be, but nevertheless, we did our job in making sure that it wouldn’t fall into Maelos’s hands. Well done, to all of us!”

Uthren sighed, his countenance growing slightly. “Thank you, Geode. You’re always able to lighten the mood.”

Geode smiled, “Now, we can enjoy ourselves! This doesn’t mean that we have to go home empty-handed. We will stay here in the city for a while to try and get Maelos off our trail. In the meantime, we should look for something to bring home to your families. The stone will be in good hands here and I don’t think there’s anything else we can do to change Queen Nydria’s mind, so we might as well make the best of our stay in Gelendor.”

Sylas half smiled, then remembered his previous conversation with Geode. “Can we find someone to enchant something for me so that I can talk to Sky more easily? I’d really like to be able to do that before we return to Shilvrst.”

"That sounds like an excellent idea," Uthren replied, trying to match the energy of Geode. "We should try and find something for all of you to bring back. We worked hard to get here, and I think we deserve a bit of a break."

"Geode, do you know of any good places to eat around here? I'm starving!" Torren said, trying to help cheer up the rest of the group. The sound of a nice hot meal made Sylas's stomach growl.

"Yes! That's what I vote we do first, too!" Samara added.

"As a matter of fact, I *do* know of a place." Geode replied. "It's also a place where we can stay for the night in a warm bed rather than on the ground. To the Flowing Treeline Tavern, it is!"

The thought of sleeping in a bed almost sounded better than a hot meal to Sylas. He picked up the pace to keep up with the others who were now almost jogging to get across the bridge.

It's not all bad, he thought, *now we can go home, and I won't have to worry about getting killed every minute of the day. I won't have the weight of needing to find all the stones on my shoulders anymore, and I'll get to see my family again. It's not all bad news. This is probably the way things needed to happen anyway. Better for everyone...*

CHAPTER 11
ENCHANTMENTS

Sylas awoke to the sound of exotic birds chirping outside his window. A wide smile stretched across his face as his eyes cracked open. He sat up in his bed, stretching his arms and breathing in the crisp, refreshing air of Gelendor. The remembrance of what today was to bring filled his mind with excitement. The past three days in the Capital of Nature had been incredible, but today was sure to be the best day yet.

Climbing out of his bed, he grabbed one of his pillows and walked over to where Torren was sleeping. With a smile of deviousness, he raised the pillow high above his head and brought it down hard on Torren's blanket-covered torso. Torren awoke with a *Hoouf!* The air he had been so peacefully breathing in suddenly being forced out of him.

"Wake up, Torren! Today's the day! That enchanter guy is going to finish that ring for me!"

"That's what you said yesterday, but do you have the ring he promised? Nope!" He sleepily replied, pulling the blankets over his head and curling himself into a ball.

"That's because he was behind on one of his other projects, but he said it would be done today for sure!" Sylas ripped Torren's blanket off him and threw it on the ground.

"C'mon! Get up! Plus, that girl at the bakery next to his shop might be there again…"

Torren opened his eyes, unsuccessfully trying to suppress a smile. He coolly sat up in his bed and stretched his arms. At the end of the stretch, he brought his arms into a flexing position and stared at his right bicep.

"Yeah, your right. We wouldn't want her to miss out."

Sylas shook his head, slipping his boots on. "I'll meet you downstairs. His shop opens early, remember? I want to get there as soon as we can so that I can figure out how the ring works and use it today with Sky."

He finished lacing up his boots then walked over to the small dresser that he and Torren shared. Sky was sleeping in a soft bed that Geode had weaved together for her with Nature Magick from some long, exotic grass and flowers he had picked.

Sylas gently patted her on the head, "Soon, it will be a lot easier for me to talk to you, then I'll *really* be able to get to know you."

Turning towards the door, he reminded Torren to hurry up, then headed towards the stairs.

The Flowing Treeline tavern was a nice place built into the massive trunk of a beautiful, leafy tree. Rooms that were held high above the ground, nestled within the leaves of mighty branches, overlooked a beautiful section of the outer parts of the city. They were treated to a room and two hot meals a day for a price that Uthren called 'agreeable'.

Sylas wondered if Geode had house somewhere in the city, perhaps a family too… but decided to let Geode bring that subject up in his own time.

Reaching the bottom of the stairs, Sylas found a seat at an empty table and waited for Torren to meet him.

"How ya doin' hun? Can I get anything for ya this mornin'?"

Sylas turned his gaze towards the owner of the tavern, patting his stomach gently. "No thanks Rosalee. I had that roast of yours last night and I'm *still* full."

Rosalee was a heavyset woman with a big heart and an even bigger attitude when someone did something disrespectful in her tavern. Like everyone else in Gelendor, she wore the signature green robes, but her sleeves had been cut off near the top of her arm and she always wore a large white apron.

"Well, I'm glad to hear ya liked it. If ya change your mind, then just let me know hun. Y'all've been such good visitors, not causin' trouble or makin' a scene. It's been nice havin' you."

"It's been nice being here! Man, if my family could see this place… They wouldn't believe it! I think they'd really like it here in Gelendor."

"You should bring 'em down sometime. Y'all'd be more than welcome to stay here at my tavern."

"If I ever get the chance, your tavern would be the first place we'd visit. I think my father would really like your cooking."

"Honey, *everyone* likes my cookin', because it's the best cookin' in town." She said, sending him a wink.

Sylas watched with a smile as Rosalee retreated from the table, helping others as they began descending the twisting, wooden staircases into the tavern's mess hall. After a few minutes, Torren finally showed up, sitting at the table with a sigh.

"What took you so long? I've been waiting forever!"

Torren ran a hand through his long hair and shrugged, "You can't rush beauty, Sylas. It takes time for one to look *this* good."

He gave Sylas a toothy smile and raised one eyebrow, "I'm going to ask her what her name is today, so I thought I'd spend a couple of minutes to make sure I look my best. I probably didn't need to, but you know how it is."

Sylas let a loud snort escape his nostrils as he stood up from his chair. "Whatever, just come on. His store is probably open by now."

Sylas and Torren walked the stone paths that winded their way through the city. Large deer-like creatures with massive antlers pulled carts filled with both people and goods along the twisting paths. Incredible plant and animal life that made Sylas feel like he was still inside of an entirely different world surrounded him. The majority of the buildings in this section of the city were still made from stone that looked to have been raised from the ground and shaped using Magick, but the occasional residency or complex of shops built into towering trees dotted in between the stone structures.

Sylas picked up the pace as one of his favorite parts of the city came into view. A large, circular fountain with intricate streams of water shooting into the air marked the place where the city started becoming truly incredible.

More than half of the city was high above the ground. Immensely large trees with wooden staircases carved into their sides acted as entry points to what the people here called 'the upper levels'.

Long vines and ropes hung from branches large enough to light an eternal fire, creating bridges that connected the upper canopies of the trees. Within the jungle of limbs and leaves, stood general stores, places for fine dining, specialty markets, and lavish houses for those who were particularly wealthy. The higher the levels that you ascended to, the more expensive- and *awesome*- things became.

Sylas and Torren swayed back and forth along the suspended vine and wooden bridges, enjoying the quick rush that came from looking down at the ground far below.

Eventually, the irresistible smell of a specialty bread store marked that they were in the right location. A medium-sized building nestled between large, twisting branches held a rustic wooden sign above the door that read, 'Fiskee's Fabulous Enchantments'.

Sylas pushed open the wooden door and heard a *ding, ding* from the bell above his head. The enchanter he was looking for was rummaging around with some boxes near the front counter of the store, apparently looking for something.

"Hey Fiskee, you looking for something?" Torren asked, shutting the door behind him.

"Looking? No, no. I'm *searching*. Searching for my *blasted* spectacles! I know I left them around here somewhere… I need to examine a pile of rare, exotic Icefire gemstones before Lognor arrives. They're clear from the icy mines of Azul, if you can believe it! I told him I would have them inspected before he got here today, and I can't do that without those confounded spectacles!"

Fiskee usually looked a bit frazzled, the long unkempt hair that stood nearly a foot above his head helped with that, but the short, slender man looked even more frazzled than usual today.

"I don't know if I know what spectacles are… but could those be them on your head?" Sylas asked, pointing to an object sitting on top of Fiskee's head.

"On my-" Fiskee looked at the ceiling as if to see the top of his own head, then reached his hands up and pulled the metal wire framed glass off his head.

"Moss of the Great Tree! I say, boy, thank you! I'd have searched all day for them if not for you! Sometimes I wonder if I'm going crazy! Mr. Rubybuster will get his gems inspected after all! Sylas, was it? Right, Sylas! I never forget a name. It's all up here, filed away, neat and tidy!" Fiskee tapped the side of his head with his finger.

"What can I do for you today? And how is that moon fox of yours? Wait… don't tell me, S… Skoo… Smmee… Sky! Sky, ha! You see? It's all up here, all I have to do is dig it out! Don't worry, I haven't told anyone that you have a moon fox, although I'm still waiting for you to bring her in here so that I can meet her!"

Sylas and Torren looked at each other with muffled grins. They liked Fiskee. Even though they were sure he was just moments away from insanity, he was fun to be around.

"Sky's doing great," He responded. "She was sleeping when I left her this morning, or I would have brought her in. She seems to be getting lazy now that she doesn't have to look for food every day."

"Animals will do that, you know," Fiskee said, plunging his hands nearly shoulder deep into a box filled with strange looking tools. "It's not in their nature to not have to work hard to get their necessities every day. They turn into piles of lazy bones once they are charmed by some mage wanting a companion. Why, my cousin Rita charmed a tiger rabbit once and just a couple of years after she got it the silly thing got so fat and lazy, he wouldn't even get up to walk to his bowl of food! She had to carry it over to him! Can you believe that?"

"A what?" Torren asked. "Did you say a tiger rabbit?"

Fiskee popped up from the box, pulling a small metallic object near his eye. He dropped the spectacles down over his eyes, which made them look like they grew nearly twice their size from

Torren and Sylas's point of view, then gazed into the object with a slight scowl.

"Oh, yes. Sorry, I forgot that you are from the northwestern part of Evendreil. Shilvrst, did you say it was? Honestly, it surprises me how in-the-dark those smaller towns can sometimes be. Before Maelos attacked, the ports around Evendreil were actually used for more than just sending goods wherever Maelos commanded. If I recall, Shilvrst was a magnificent place to go if one wanted to charter a ship to the Scorched Lands. Who in their right mind would want to go to that desert wasteland is beyond me, but there are crazier folk in the world. Ahh, the days when one could actually get out and explore the world… Such dark times we live in… You do know about the geography outside of Evendreil, do you not?"

"A little-" Sylas started.

"Excellent!" Fiskee cut him off. "Yes, good, good, good. Well! I'll tell you boys something… There are creatures that live in this world that are beyond your imagination! There are some that live on the other continents that are quite fearsome, too! The Scorched Lands with the legends of their dragons and other fiery creatures. Northrinde, and the deadly, living ice that chills the blood of even the bravest of adventurers. Oh! Here in Evendreil, the mystical fey and wonderful, whimsical creatures near Lake Crystalmere. And the creatures of Darkness within the mysterious valley of the Whispering Hills…"

Fiskee exaggeratedly shivered, pausing for a moment and taking the spectacles off his face, then placed them back on the top of his head.

Sylas smiled, thinking about whether or not he would lose them there again anytime soon.

"A tiger rabbit is kind of like a regular rabbit that you would see here, but about three or four times larger. The stories say that they live mostly in the tropical lands of TrindJhim, but I've heard tale of them being seen here in Evendreil as well! Instead of eating purely vegetables or green leafy things, they are carnivorous and hunt small prey. You could almost compare them to a coyote or small wolf, but with long rabbit-like ears and fur that has a striped design like that of a tiger, thus we called them… tiger rabbits! Quite imaginative, wouldn't you say?"

It was hard to tell whether or not Fiskee was trying to be facetious or if he really meant what he said sometimes, so Sylas did the safe thing and just nodded in response.

"I never knew the world was so… creative?"

"Spectacular, I think you mean to say!"

"Right, yeah that. I was wondering though… Were you able to finish enchanting that ring for me yet?"

Fiskee jumped backward, slamming into a pile of boxes. "Dear me! Yes, I have! I was so caught up in our conversation that I completely forgot the reason why you would be here in the first place!"

Fiskee shoved several boxes aside, sending one crashing to the floor and spilling its contents everywhere. He rummaged in a messy pile for a moment, then opened a small wooden box and produced a silver ring with a small emerald fastened in the center face.

"Here it is! I think it turned out rather incredible, if I do say so myself."

Fiskee walked over to Sylas and held the ring out in front of him, "Go on, take a look!"

His heart skipped a beat as he reached forward and plucked the ring from Fiskee's open hand. The emerald in the center shone brightly against the silver contrast of the band in which it was set. Curious as to why it looked as if the emerald was giving off some of its own light, Sylas asked, "The emerald looks like its glowing… Am I just crazy? or…"

"You're not crazy! That's how you can tell that it has charges of the spell in it still! Nature Magick has been infused into the gemstone, giving it the marvelous green glow. As you use the ring, it will gradually get dimmer and dimmer until the stone looks like a normal emerald, that's when you will know that it's time to charge it back up again."

The cool metal band snuggly wrapped around his skin as Sylas excitedly placed the ring on his finger. "This is so incredible Fiskee. Thank you so much! Can you tell me how to use it?"

"Not only that, but *you* are going to help finish the enchantment! I've done all the complicated work, but now you get to help me finish it! For the enchantment to be complete, you will need to open your second mind using the symbol of which the enchantment is originated, in this case, that would be Nature."

A grin spread across his face at the thought of being able to be a part of the enchantment process. Sylas excitedly made the symbol of Nature and focused his thoughts toward the pool of inner life that dwelt within him. As he brought that energy into his head and opened his second mind, his hands and eyes began to glow with the same color of light that the emerald produced.

"Now, all you need to do is touch the emerald with your ethereal body's finger. That will complete the enchantment. When items are enchanted, they are imbued with a specific spell, or in some cases, a range of spells that they can perform. For the item to have the ability to cast the spell, it needs inner life bound to it. Once you have finished the enchantment, the ring will act sort of like your second mind does. As long as you are wearing it, all you have to do is simply *will* the request to the object that has been enchanted, and it will be done using the energy that has been stored within the object instead of your own energy."

Fiskee shuffled himself to Sylas's side, pushing Torren excitedly, "Torren, you will need to stand behind Sylas in case he needs you to catch him. Depending on how much energy you want in the ring, this might leave you a little light-headed and weak. And be ready, it goes fast!"

With Torren standing behind him, Sylas reached his ghostly hand towards the ring on his physical finger and touched it. The ring flashed bright green as the energy within his body began to decrease rapidly. It felt like someone had just opened a floodgate within his body as his energy was sucked out of him and placed into the ring. Not knowing how much energy he needed to sacrifice, he tried to hold on as long as he could but eventually was forced to remove his ghostly hand from the ring and closed his second mind.

Sylas saw stars glittering in the corners of his vision as he fell backward into Torren's arms. He attempted to pull himself to his feet so that he would not fall unconscious but was stopped by Fiskee.

"I told you it would go fast! Neat, isn't it! Just set him down in that chair, Torren, and let him rest for a second."

Torren placed Sylas in a wooden armchair in the corner of the room as Fiskee fetched a bottle of water to give to Sylas.

"Here, drink this," Fiskee said, handing the bottle to Sylas. "It slipped my mind to tell you that you needed to take your finger off as soon as you had put a sufficient amount of energy for your needs into the ring. Good thing you let go before you passed out! The good news is now you will have plenty of energy to cast the spell many times before you will need to refill it, right?"

Still dazed from allowing the emerald on his finger to basically suck the life out of him, Sylas just weakly chuckled, "Yeah, good news…"

After Fiskee explained the actual process of how to use the ring, now that it had been charged, Sylas and Torren listened to him go on and on about other subjects and issues completely unrelated to anything that either of them cared about.

After several minutes, Sylas felt his energy slowly return to him. At reaching a point where he felt that he could successfully walk back to the tavern, he and Torren thanked Fiskee for his help and gave him the gold coins that Geode had given them for payment.

"Please come again! And tell everyone else how great of an enchantment you got on your ring, it will help with business! See you soon!"

After retreating far away from Fiskee's shop, Torren asked, "Do you think if you use Magick too much it goes to your head and makes you crazy? I mean, Fiskee sure knows his stuff if he can do things that even Geode can't do, and his job involves using Magick a lot… You think it's gone to his head?"

Sylas and Torren stopped walking, grins gradually growing on their faces until each of them burst into laughter.

"Maybe… But I think there's a little more going on upstairs with him. I like him though, and I'm glad he was so willing to help. This ring is going to make talking to Sky *so* much easier."

On the way back to the tavern they tried to decide if they believed what Fiskee had said about all the strange creatures that lived on the other continents. They came to the conclusion that they believed that there were other animals that they might never have seen before, but that they would be way less exotic than what Fiskee had made them out to be.

Sylas pushed the door of the tavern open, and his eyes immediately fell upon the image of Samara sitting at a table in the middle of the mess hall. A silver and green decorative pin poked out of her hair that she had pulled up into a bun. Green battle mage robes clung to her body, showing off several of the curves that made the other girls her age in Shilvrst so jealous. She lifted her head, and her eyes met his. The robes she wore complimented her eyes fantastically, making her look even more beautiful than she usually did.

"Hey guys, where have you been this morning?"

Sylas tried to talk, but the words choked in his throat. Torren graciously saved him, "We went off to a guy named Fiskee's so that Sylas could get a ring enchanted. Now he can talk to Sky without having to do the whole Magick thing every time."

He elbowed Sylas in the ribs, signaling that he was looking like a fool just staring at Samara. "Isn't that right, Sylas? Show her your fancy new ring."

Sylas mentally shook himself and took the ring off his finger. "Yeah, it's really cool. Here, take a look." As he placed the ring in her hand, his fingers brushed against hers, sending a flush of heat straight to his head. Trying to recover, he quickly added, "I really like the new outfit by the way, and the way you did your hair. It's pretty."

Samara smiled, making his head even hotter as she thanked him for the compliment. "Geode bought them for me. He said that every aspiring mage needs a set of battle robes. Although I think I'll be sticking to Light for now, I do really like the color. It matches my eyes, and I think it suits me well."

She moved the ring back and forth in her hands, admiring the soft glow of green light that emanated from the emerald that sat in its center.

"This is really cool. It looks like the emerald has Nature Magick inside of it… I'm guessing that's why it's glowing?"

"Yeah," Sylas responded. "Fiskee had me dump a bunch of my inner life energy into the ring while I had my second mind opened. That's how you charge it back up once it has run out."

"'Bout knocked him silly when he did it too, you should have seen it," Torren added in, surely trying to embarrass him. He slapped Sylas on the back and gave him a large toothy grin. "He put a little bit too much juice in there, but he's doing all right now."

Samara looked at the ring for a moment longer before handing it back to Sylas. "You know, the truth is I'm pretty sad about our adventure ending so soon."

Samara looked down at the floor, her voice growing soft, "Sure, I miss my family. And it's scary having to run for your life away from Maelos and his minions… But I've really enjoyed being out here with you guys. I've fallen in love with learning more about Magick, seeing new sights, meeting new people. I feel like I'm finding out who I *really am* out here."

Sylas pulled up a chair and sat next to her. "Just because we have to go home doesn't mean that the adventure has to end. We can still learn more about Magick and maybe even use it to get out of Shilvrst again! As long as we don't get caught, I bet we could even make it back to Gelendor."

"Yeah!" Torren added. "I bet you anything that there are other cool cities like this that aren't too far away from Shilvrst. I'd have to look at my dad's old map. Maybe once our parents see that we can be out here on our own just fine, they will let us travel with some of the merchants or something so that we can see more of what Evendreil has to offer than just our boring town. I mean just look at this place! Gelendor is so amazing! There's got to be other places that-" Torren stiffened suddenly and slapped his palm to his forehead.

"No! Aww, man!"

Confused, Sylas looked toward Samara for answers. Unfortunately, she was just as confused as he was.

"What? What's the matter?" Sylas asked.

Pulling his hand off his forehead, he grabbed Sylas by the shoulders. Torren looked his best friend right in the eyes, his voice filled with devastation, "The bakery! We forgot to go to the bakery!"

It took a couple of moments for that sentence to register in his brain, but then the remembrance of a certain pretty girl at the bakery next to Fiskee's flowed into his mind. The confusion he had was instantly washed away, like a wave of water washing sand off a smooth rock, and Sylas burst into laughter.

Samara still had no idea what was happening, but she laughed along with Sylas at the obviously hysterical moment of sorrow that Torren was forced to pass through.

After visiting with Torren and Samara for a while longer, Sylas excused himself and headed up to his room. His heart pounded with excitement as he stared into the light green glow of his new ring. Opening the door to his room, he found Sky still lying on her new bed, sleeping the day away.

Fiskee was right, she is getting lazy, he thought to himself with a smile. She was cute when she was lazy though, so Sylas didn't mind at all. He patted her on the head softly, and Sky opened her eyes. She yawned, stretching herself out on the bed and arching her back. Her glowing white eyes stared into his as she finished her stretch, swishing her tail back and forth happily. Sylas thought about the ring on his finger, trying his best to *will* the desire to talk to Sky. The emerald on the ring flared with a slightly brighter green glow, and the words in his mind echoed slightly as he thought them.

"Sky, can you hear me?"

Sky shifted to her hind legs, scratching her back paw behind her ear. "Yes, I can hear you."

"Awesome!" He replied. "I'm not using Magick at all. I'm using the ring I was telling you all about. It's doing all of it for me!"

She stopped scratching her ear, her white eyes glowing slightly brighter.

"Really? That's exciting news!"

"Yeah, check this out!" Sylas lifted his hand with the ring up so that she could see it glowing.

"*Finally*. Now I won't have to walk in silence and constantly bump into you so that you know I'm there. How long does it last?"

"Fiskee said that it should last a long time. I accidentally dumped more energy into the emerald than I should have, so we shouldn't have any issues for a while. When it does run out though, he said I'll know because the emerald will stop glowing. When that happens, I can just add more energy, and we can use it again."

An idea suddenly popped into his mind. "Hey, would you like to go out and see the city today? You haven't really been out of this room much since we got here."

"No. There are too many humans."

"You can just stay invisible though, plus if you want, I could empty my bag and you could get inside and I'll carry you around. You're small enough to fit in there if I take all my stuff out. You could just poke your head out of the top and look around while staying invisible."

Sky thought for a moment, turning her head towards the window. Finally, she agreed but insisted that he keep a couple of things in the bag so it didn't look as suspicious. Sylas grinned ear to ear as he emptied his bag of everything but a blanket and a few other soft items. He picked her up, placing her gently in the main pocket of the pack.

"See? Nice and soft even. This will be fun! I want to show you some of the buildings in the trees, you're going to love it!"

****

Torren ran his fingers through his hair one last time, trying to catch his reflection while looking at the store window. *Come on, what's the big deal? She's just a girl... the girls all fall for you, right? What's there not to like?*

Torren didn't usually have to sike himself up to talk to a girl, but for some reason this just felt *different.* He didn't know what to say and was somehow nervous that he would make a fool out of himself. Tightening his muscles, he took several deep breaths, then turned and walked into the bakery's front door.

The scents that penetrated his nose were delightful. He could make out the scent of biscuits, pastries, pies, and other delicious goods, but the most dominant of them all was the smell of freshly baked bread. It reminded him of better times when things were not so dreary, and his family could actually afford bread. Distant memories of his mother baking bread and his father coming home *happy* from duty with the king's guard calmed his nerves.

Of all the senses that were being triggered, the one that was the most pleasing was that of *sight* after his eyes laid upon the girl standing behind the counter in front of him. Her long black hair draped over her shoulders, glistening from the light that peered down from the sunroof above her head. Her dark brown eyes met his, exotic when it came to Gelendor. It seemed that everyone in this city shared the same dark black hair and bright green eyes. Seeing the beautiful, woody brown that stared back at him was like peering into the eyes of an angel.

With the smoothness of a highly trained professional, Torren approached the counter, placed one hand on its smooth, glassy top, then waved his other hand in front of his face in a whiffing motion.

"Oh man, it smells good in here! What'cha got cookin'?"

A faint smile crossed the angel's lips. "Well, it's really *baking* more than cooking… but mostly bread right now. Would you like to try a free sample?"

Torren mentally took his hand and slapped it across his face for saying *cooking* instead of *baking*.

"Yeah! I'd love to."

"Which kind would you like to try? We have woody wheat bread, some bread with apple and cinnamon, or our newest recipe, a special herb and cheese that you can only find here in Gelendor."

"Only here, hu? How'd you know I was a visitor from a mysterious, far away land? Let's do that one!"

Her faint smile turned into a full-on smile at Torren's enthusiasm. She even let out a small giggle, which gave Torren a massive confidence boost. *Yeah... I got this...*

"One slice of Nuu've Herb and Cheese bread coming up!" She turned, her perfect black hair falling around her shoulders as she headed towards the back of the store. She returned a few moments later with a small slice of bread on a flat silver plate. As she handed the plate to Torren, he made sure to brush his fingers against hers as he grabbed the plate from her hands, a move he had used *many* times before. She blushed, looking at the floor after handing him the plate, "I hope you like it."

Inexplicably, her shyness made her look like an absolute goddess. Torren sent her his best devilish smile, then placed the piece of bread in his mouth.

His taste buds instantly rejoiced, as if the heavens had opened and sent all their goodness straight into his mouth. The warm cheese melted on his tongue, sending pure happiness into his brain. The strange, almost woody tasting herbs gave the bread a slight bitter tinge that complimented the cheese beautifully. The bread was soft and chewy and a delight to consume. Torren stared at her as he chewed the food until he gladly swallowed it, easily the most fantastic thing he had ever eaten.

"That was... incredible..." He said softly. "That was so *good*!" Louder this time. "Did you make that yourself? It's so amazing! You have to tell me how you did it!"

She smiled brushing her hair behind her ear as she spoke. "Thank you. It's my father's bakery so he usually makes all the recipes. But yeah, this is actually my special creation. I'm glad you liked it."

"Liked it? I loved it! It's probably the best thing I've ever eaten!" He paused for a moment, waiting for her eyes to glance back towards his.

As her dark brown eyes met his, he continued in a slightly softer tone. "So hey, what time do you guys usually close up shop? Maybe after you're done working you could show me around the city a bit? I'm new here, and I'd love to see more of Gelendor before we have to leave, what do you say?"

She bit her bottom lip, her cheeks turning bright red as she spoke. "We close about an hour before sunset usually. I don't know if we would have very much time to see the city."

A bit of a fight, hu? Torren thought to himself smugly. *Good. I like it when I have to work for it.*

"Hmmm…" He said thoughtfully. "What if you were able to get off a bit early?

"I don't know." She replied, her cheeks still blushing. "I've never asked to get off early before… My father might not like the idea."

"What if you told him you were doing a great *service* to a guy that was desperately wanting to see more of the great city of Gelendor before he had to leave? You could tell him that you are just doing it to be nice and that it would really mean a lot to him."

She thought for a moment, then looked at the floor as she pulled her hair behind her ear again. "I guess

I could ask him… We weren't very busy last night, so he might let me leave a little early."

Now to set the hook, he thought. "If you can't, then it's fine, I guess. I could ask around if you're going to be too busy. I just don't know how much longer I'm going to be here."

"No, it's okay," she quickly responded, looking up from the floor. "I think he'll be fine with it, actually. I would love to show you around."

Torren grinned, "Awesome, that sounds great. So, what time should I meet you? And where?"

She paused for a moment, "Have you seen the fountain that's next to the tree that leads to this part of the second level?"

Torren thought about the tree with the stairs that he had climbed to get here. He didn't give it too much attention but definitely remembered seeing a fountain nearby.

"Yeah, I think so. It has streams of water spraying out of the top right?"

"Yeah! The fountain sprays one additional stream of water into the air for each hour that has passed since sunrise, starting at one and going up to six when it's midday. As soon as it has been spraying all six for one hour, it goes back down, one at each hour, until there are none spraying anymore."

"Oh, hey that's cool! So, when the sun rises, the fountain sprays one stream. Then after each hour, an additional one starts spraying?"

"Yep. Then as soon as they're all full, it will go backward until there aren't any spraying anymore."

"How does the fountain know when the sun has come up?" He asked, genuinely curious.

She paused, "I'm not sure actually... It has something to do with Magick, but I'm one of the few around here that doesn't know much about using Magick. I just know that it was built a long time ago and that's what the city has gone by for basically forever. It's a way we keep track of time and when shops need to be opened and closed. They are placed at many different key points of the city so that people can easily see them."

"Hu? I would've never guessed. Alright, so, meet by the fountain then?"

"Yes. Meet me by that fountain when there are only two streams of water left spraying, that should be about four hours from now."

"Perfect, sounds like a date," he said, giving her another warm smile.

She blushed again, tucking her hair once more behind her ear. "Is there anything else I can get for you today?"

"I think I'm good for now. Just one thing… I don't know your name."

"Ahrina, but you can call me Ahri if you want."

"Ahri, that's a pretty name. My name is Torren," he said, sticking out his hand. She placed her hand in his which he raised up to his lips, giving her a soft kiss on the back of the hand. Her hand was soft and warm to the touch, like most girls' hands were, but hers was *different*. Sparks were sent into his head as he kissed her hand, making his heart beat faster than normal.

"It was nice to meet you, Ahri. I look forward to our date tonight."

"Nice to meet you too, Torren. I also look forward to it."

He let go of her hand and walked towards the door of the bakery. He turned back one last time and gave a kind wave which she happily returned.

Stepping out of the door and away from the bakery, Torren pumped his fist and let out a whispered but enthusiastic, "Yes!"

****

Sylas and Samara both gave Torren a hard time when they all returned to the tavern that night. Samara had been out exploring the waterfalls around the Great Tree they had talked to Nydria in, and Sylas had spent most of the day with Sky on the second and third levels of the city. He mentioned it looked like there were some spots he saw that even went to a fourth level, but he couldn't find any way to get up there.

Torren spent the remainder of his day pacing back and forth, taking walks to the fountain he was going to meet Ahri at, and looking at himself in the mirror. After looking in the mirror for about the hundredth time, he came to the unfortunate conclusion that he didn't look as *amazing* as he always thought he did.

Something about this girl was different than any other girl that he had been out with before; it made him nervous, made him lose his cool. Every girl in Shilvrst looked at him with love in their eyes, he hardly had to try back home. The only one that had ever escaped his charm before was Samara, and that was fine with him because she was one of his best friends and it would just be weird.

Ahri seemed to like him, at least that's what he thought and hoped the signals showed when he was in the bakery. Still, something about her made him nervous. *Was it just how pretty she was? Was it that fantastic bread she'd made? Was there a love spell in the bread? Can Magick make you fall in love?* Questions continued to swim through his head as he stood up out of his chair.

"Torren, you really need to calm down, she's going to see how nervous you are and she won't want to go out with you again," Samara said, taking a bite of stew.

Geode and Uthren had joined the three of them for dinner at the tavern. And although the stew smelled delicious, Torren just couldn't get his stomach to cooperate with him. He hadn't eaten hardly any of the delicious looking meal.

"You don't strike me as a boy who gets this nervous about going on a date," Uthren said, placing a spoonful of stew into his mouth. "She must really be something else to get you so nervous."

"I'm not like this, ever! It's making me go *crazy*! I don't know what's wrong with me. Something is up… Geode!" Torren pointed a finger towards him as if accusing him of something. "Is there such thing as Magick that makes someone fall in love with you? I think she could have put some in the bread… or maybe she did it before then, and I just didn't notice... Well? Is there!?"

Geode took another bite of stew then placed his spoon on the table. "Even if there *were* such a spell,

I doubt that you would be able to enchant it into a slice of *bread*. Magick needs more precious and durable items to be bound in. Bread just wouldn't cut it."

Torren sat back down in his chair and took in a deep breath. He looked out the window and noticed that the position of the sun had dropped some since he last looked. "I think it's about time," he said, standing up again. "I'd better get going. Sylas, how do I look?"

"Besides the massive stain on your shirt, you look fine."

Torren gasped and looked down at his shirt. He didn't see anything there and looked back at Sylas for help, only to find him choking in laughter on a piece of meat he had just placed in his mouth."

Torren scowled. "Don't die, buddy. You wouldn't want to go out on a note like that." He patted Sylas on the back a bit harder than he needed to then straightened his shirt.

"Whatever. I'm going. I'll be fine, I just need to be cool, smooth, just be me."

He headed towards the door with a nervous energy in his step. He heard Samara say something but mentally blocked out the words, he knew that she was just saying something stupid to make him more nervous.

****

Torren took in several deep breaths as he walked towards the fountain. He placed a sweaty palm over his rapidly beating heart and focused on inhaling and exhaling. His heart began to slow down as he cleared his mind and focused on the breathing exercise.

He turned around a corner and noticed a large flowerpot full of yellow and purple flowers that twisted together in a mystical pattern. Assuring himself that the owner wouldn't mind if he had just one of them, Torren picked one of the larger flowers and held it to his nose. It smelled sweet and reminded him of the flowers that his father used to bring home for his mother when times were good, which always sat on the dining room table as they ate.

He continued walking until the fountain came into view. Two streams of water flowed upwards into the air before gravity pulled them back into an arching waterfall into a lower basin. A third, smaller stream of water that just barely had enough pressure to push it about a handbreadth into the air before it fell, signifying he was just a touch early. Sitting down at the edge of the fountain, he watched as the third stream of water got smaller and smaller until it was just a trickle of water.

"Hi, Torren," A voice said softly behind him.

He spun around excitedly, his eyes landing upon her beautiful figure. Her black dress flowed gently across her body, making her appear even more delicate and beautiful than before. Her dark black shoes shined slightly in the lowering sun. A silver bracelet sparkled above her nervously intertwined hands as she looked down towards Torren's feet.

Her long black hair had been put up into a bun, similar to the way that Samara had hers, with the same silver, emerald encrusted pin poking out of it.

Torren's heart jumped as his eyes surveyed the very personage of beauty in front of him.

"You look *incredible*!" He said in a slightly stunned tone. "I don't have any fancy clothes here… so this is the best I've got."

Smiling, she looked up at him, "I think you look great just as you are."

Torren looked at the flower in his hand, then back into her eyes, "Here, this is for you."

She took the flower from his hand and placed it next to her nose. Closing her eyes and taking in a slow breath she smiled, "It smells lovely, thank you."

Torren stuck out his arm, gesturing for her to grab it, his usual confidence slowly returning to him. "Well then, my lady, shall we be off? I'm excited to see whatever it is you have planned to show me tonight."

She looped her arm inside of his and placed her hand on his forearm. Then matching his exaggerated formality responded, "We shall. Let us be off."

****

It was the best night of Torren's life. Ahri led him, hand in hand, through the winding streets of the city. Mystical, glowing green bugs that he'd somehow never noticed seemed to dance in the air around them as she expertly explained to him the different sections of the city. After the tour, she took him to a small, yet beautiful lake that nestled in the center of a massive ring of trees that housed more places to eat than Torren thought he'd ever be able to visit.

At the lake, Ahri paid for them to ride in a small boat for two. Torren rowed with a twinkle in his eyes as Ahri really started to open up, her shyness fading away with the light of day. She revealed a wild, adventurous side that nearly melted Torren in his small wooden seat. At one point she almost tipped the boat over, just to prove to him that she was surely a faster swimmer than he was.

Ending the boat ride, they finished the night off by stopping at Ahri's favorite dessert place across the lake. Torren had the pleasure of consuming what had to be the most delectable thing that had ever entered into his mouth, a sort of cake with an extremely tart fruit topping much more exotic than he'd ever seen before.

Even with the dessert gone, they continued to sit across from each other, staring into each other's eyes, talking the night away until the owner of the establishment had to kick them out at closing time.

The pinnacle of the night came when Torren took her back to her house. She lived on the ground floor of the city, not too far away from the fountain where they'd met. Even so, her house was larger and more beautiful than even most of the massive houses that he'd seen, even on the second level of the city. It was constructed of dark, polished stone that had been beautifully shaped to match the landscape around it.

Torren could tell at an instant that Ahri's father made more money in a day than his parents would see in several years. He put together that it must have been due to their bakery on the second level of the city. It was unique and special, just like her.

They sat on her front porch for a long time, neither of them wanting the night to end. They swung back and forth gently on a bench suspended by chains, looking into the night and attempting to count the stars. Eventually, the time came when he knew he needed to let her go.

"Tonight, was *incredible*, Ahri," he said, opening her front door for her. "Thank you for showing me the city. You live in such an amazing place. I hope that maybe we can do this again sometime? I know I already said it, but I'll *literally* die if I never get to eat that weird fruit stuff again."

She laughed and touched his hand, "Well we can't have that! If you died, who would I resume counting the stars with?"

Her dark brown eyes blinked slowly, her teeth biting her bottom lip gently. "Yes, I'd love to go out again sometime. I had a wonderful time."

As the moment of truth approached, Torren's heart thumped in his chest so hard that he worried Ahri might see it bouncing in his shirt. He decided that he would play it cool though and embraced her in a hug. He felt her heartbeat against his as their bodies met. Like a synchronized drum, their hearts pounded quickly, matching beat for beat.

They embraced for several minutes, neither one of them willing to let go. Torren finally pulled away slowly, allowing his cheek to brush against hers. She looked up at him with her dark brown eyes only halfway opened and leaned in towards him, placing her lips upon his.

****

Torren floated back to the Tavern. His head felt so light that it seemed to carry him back as if he were weightless. He didn't even remember taking any of the turns or passing the landmarks he used to get back to the tavern. His body traveled there purely by instinct while his mind danced with the memories of his newfound love.

He opened the door to his and Sylas's room and was surprised to see Sylas still awake, sitting up in his bed waiting for his return.

"So, how did it go?" He asked.

Torren ignored his friend and plopped himself down on his bed, letting out a sigh.

"That good huh? Well, good thing I stayed up so late so that I could hear all about it..."

Without lifting his head, Torren responded in a tone that Sylas had never heard before, "I think I'm in love, Sylas… Ahri is so… I think she might be the *one*."

Sylas leaned over his bed, raising an eyebrow as he looked at his best friend. "Don't you think it's a bit early to tell? I mean, you've only been with her for one night."

Torren sat up in his bed and gave Sylas a twitterpated smile, "Maybe you'll understand when you're older. Sometimes you can just *tell* when you've found the one. Ahri is… she's *really* special. I can't stop thinking about her. It's different than how I've ever felt about anyone."

Sylas's face went flat, "You realize you're only a year older than me, right? Not even a year if we're being honest. But hey, if you feel like she might be the one, then I hope things continue to work out."

He almost brought up the fact that they would be leaving for Shilvrst soon but decided that he probably shouldn't break his friend's heart on his best night ever.

"Thanks, buddy," Torren sighed. "I hope so too."

CHAPTER 12
ARMY OF THE DEAD

"I will ask you once more, Aracorn, did you find it?"

"No, my lord. Even with the guidance of the stone its whereabouts remain a mystery. I did as you commanded and have hidden the stone within the Darkness for now. It's near the place you made your grand discovery, I thought it would be a rather appropriate location."

Maelos nodded, "At least you aren't *completely* useless. I agree with your judgement for its new hiding place. I will need it to be safe, where only you or I can retrieve it when the time is right."

Maelos turned his back and peered at the map hanging on the wall in front of him. Several sharp pins with ribbons wrapped around their heads poked out of the parchment where several cities were depicted.

"Thanks to the power of the stone, I was able to unlock the secret of the fabled Living Darkness. Its secret will live with me and me alone for the eternities. My quest is almost complete, Aracorn. Soon *all* will bow down before me in fear. However, I'm still missing a *key* piece to assure my victory and immortality. A piece that *you* have been assigned to take care of and have continued to disappoint me with!"

"Perhaps it really is a myth, my lord. A story that was constructed by the original Kings to distract one who wanted to gain power over the world?"

A dark aura flowed around Maelos as he turned around, his hands radiating artificial Darkness. An inescapable fear gripped at Aracorn as he peered into the void of darkness that had replaced the once humanoid eyes in front of him. Aracorn fell to his knees as Darkness swirled around him, terrifying whispers forcing themselves into his ears and tormenting his mind.

"I *know* it exists, Aracorn. And for your sake, you had better find it and bring it to me before my window has passed. Otherwise, I will gladly find a use for your corpse in the front line…"

****

Sylas shot up in his bed, sweat dripping from his body as he tried to orient himself. Fear gripped at his confused mind. His heart was beating rapidly, an almost deafening ringing in his ears. Ringing? No, not ringing, it sounded more like a bell… several large bells all chiming at once. Amidst the confusion, another sound slowly became clear within the chaos.

"Sylas! Can't you hear me? Get up! Something's going on out there!"

Sylas shook his head, rubbing his face with his hands. Forcing his mind to come up to speed, he saw Torren scrambling to put on his trousers.

"Torren, what's going-"

Uthren crashed through the door to their room, cutting him off. "Get your things, now! Gelendor is under attack!"

The ringing of the bells grew louder as his mind continued to wake up. The screams of women and children coupled with the war cries and panicked instructions of their fathers and husbands growing ever louder.

Sylas tore the blankets off his body and almost fell to his knees as he hit the floor. The adrenaline in his body immediately kicked in to help stabilize him before collapsing. He searched amidst the dim candlelight of his room for Sky before remembering his ring. Using its Magick, he called out to her, "Sky? Where are you?"

She faded out of the shadows, standing in front of him on the bed. "I was hiding. What's going on?"

Sylas frantically searched the ground until he found his bag lying at the foot of his bed. Hoisting it into the air, he began throwing his essential traveling gear inside.

"Gelendor is under attack! Stay invisible and stay close. If I ever get too far away, call out to me so that you don't get lost!"

Sylas grabbed whatever possessions were easily accessible and shoved them into his bag, then finding his clothes got himself dressed as fast as he could.

"It *has* to be Maelos. I think he found us!" Torren said, throwing his bag onto his back. "Hurry, Sylas, we need to get down there and help!"

Sylas's fingers trembled as he finished lacing up his boots. He and Torren sprinted together down the hall towards Samara's room, Sky following invisibly behind. Just before reaching the door, she and Uthren swung the door open in front of them.

"Quick, everyone downstairs and stay together! Keep an eye on the front lines and stay *back!* I don't want any of you near the battle lines, understood? Pray that the armies of Gelendor can defend against this attack. Meet back at this tavern when the chaos is over, understood?"

After seeing them all nod, Uthren continued, "I'm going to try and find Geode. He's probably at the front of the attack already, but I'll let him know of our meeting place if I see him. Now go! Keep each other safe!"

Uthren made the symbol of Light with his hands and with a battle cry, ran through the hallway, down the stairs, and into the ensuing chaos.

Torren took charge as leader of their small band, hoisting his sword out of his sheath and gritting his teeth in anger, "They will *pay* for any damage they cause to this city! Turn on your Magick and follow me! We'll see what's going on and if we can help, then I'll decide what we do from there."

Samara and Sylas looked at each other, fear enveloping them as the thought of more combat sank deep within. "Uthren said we needed to stay away-"

"You're going to just sit by and watch when we might be able to help!?" Torren yelled, cutting Samara off.

"Listen, we'll stay safe. We'll just help from a distance if we can. But I *refuse* to let Maelos take over this city!"

Samara's eyes started to grow wet with fear, but she shook her head, banishing the tears. "You're right. We *have* to help if we can!"

She made the symbol of Light, after which her hands and eyes began to glow. Sylas shakily brought his hands together at his chest and did the same. The power of the Light radiating through him gave him confidence, and a *deep* desire to protect the land that he had fallen in love with.

"Follow me!" Torren exclaimed, running towards the stairs.

As they exited the front door of the tavern, the dark reality of the situation began to set in. All the guard towers that were set atop of the high barrier wall had their emergency beacons lit. The light that they cast down onto the battlefield showed a scene straight from a nightmare.

Rubble from a large section of the destroyed outer wall lay scattered across the ground. Thousands of animated skeletons with deep purple glowing orbs for eyes crawled over the rubble, like ants ready to conquer a rival colony. The skeletons wielded swords and bucklers, some with longbows and arrows, firing deadly shots into the lines of the defending army of Gelendor.

"The Skeletons from my vision…" Sylas whispered, a chill running up his spine. He looked to

Torren for guidance, but an unearthly roar turned his blood to ice. Every hair on his body stood on end as the deathly roar echoed across the battlefield. The bravery that the Light gave to him the only thing allowing him to turn towards the sound, Sylas's eyes caught sight of a scene more terrifying than he could imagine.

A creature pulled directly out of legend stepped through the gaping hole in the wall. It's large, powerful head tipped upward into the sky, toothy maw open wide as it released a second roar into the air. It's long, serpent-like body crawled through the wall, a massively long tail swishing back and forth. Wings that stretched nearly the length of its body unfolded slightly as it slowly made its way across the rubble.

A mage with dark robes sat upon the terrifying beast, his eyes and hands glowing with a sinister purple glow.

"A d- dragon?" Torren choked.

"No, no it can't be! The dragons are all gone! Plus, look at it! It's… It's…"

"It's dead…" Sylas finished for Samara.

That was the only way he could describe the creature. This was *surely* one of the dragons from the legends of old, but instead of beautiful scales and brightly colored hides, this dragon was nothing but bone.

A deep purple glow exited from the dragon's sunken eyes, more Darkness Magick filling its empty rib cage and glowing powerfully where the thinner fibers of its wings should have been. The creature waved its long, boney tail back and forth as it crossed the last pieces of rubble, the mage upon its completely exposed spine pointing his arm in the direction of the warriors of Gelendor.

A bright flash of light and a booming crackle of thunder came from the darkness of the city. A lightning bolt shot towards the skeletons, striking several of them and bouncing from one to another. More than a dozen dropped to the ground, whatever had given them life leaving as their bones turned to ash.

The quick flash of light revealed Uthren, his eyes and hands glowing a crackling light blue color from combining Light and Fire Magick to make Lightning. A host of other mages and warriors of Gelendor stood by his side, ready to face the undead invaders.

The mage riding the skeletal dragon lifted his hand and pointed towards the group of defenders. His hand flared the same purple and black color which swirled in the eye sockets of the dragon and undead army that he commanded, and the skeletons began to charge.

Torren took in several sharp breaths of air. He dropped his pack on the ground, hoisting his sword in front of him, “You can’t have this city!” With the bravery of a true warrior, Torren tore off towards the oncoming skeletons.

“Torren don’t!” Samara screamed.

“Samara!” Sylas yelled, the power of the Light *demanding* that he help protect the city. “You stick with Torren and make sure he stays safe. Shield him from a distance and watch his back. I’ll loop around on the right side and see if I can get into a good flanking position."

Samara twisted her head back and forth between her two best friends. Eventually she nodded, dropping her pack and taking off after Torren. Small orbs of Light formed around her hands as she prepared for battle.

Sylas turned his attention back to where Uthren and the others were. Powerful green glows from the masses of Nature Mages filled the air. Lightning once again crackled in the distance as Uthren led the charge towards the skeletons.

Sylas watched Uthren pull his hands over his head and with a mighty throw, cast another Lightning bolt at the skeletons. It struck a skeleton with a spear right in the chest then proceeded to bounce to four other nearby enemies. The bolt of Lightning rippled through their animated bodies for a short moment before they crumpled to the ground.

Almost in perfect unison, several Nature mages behind Uthren pointed their hands in the same direction, sending beams of Nature Magick through the air towards a grove of large trees. The beams of light struck the trees, sending a ripple of green light pulsating up their trunks and down each branch and leaf.

A couple of seconds later, the trees began to shake and glow brightly. Roots began bursting forth from the ground underneath the glowing trees, upheaving rocks and dirt violently as they pulled themselves out of the earth. The trunks of the trees split near their base, forming two separate columns of wood that acted as legs as they continued to pull themselves out of the ground and move towards the advancing skeletons.

Sylas quickly pulled his attention back to the mages that had conjured the Magick and noticed that they were moving in the exact same pattern as the trees were. Looking back at the trees, he realized that the trees were *duplicating* the actions of the mages that were controlling them.

The movement of the trees got smoother and quicker as they uprooted from the ground and eventually started walking towards the skeletons. They swung their large branches like natural clubs, crushing and throwing the animated bodies through the air as they joined the fight.

An arrow whistled through the air and stuck into the ground just inches from Sylas's foot as he watched the trees. Turning towards the direction that the arrow came, he saw two skeletons with bucklers and short swords rapidly approaching him, as well as a skeleton archer nocking another arrow to fire at him. Sylas took his pack off and tossed it to the side. Focusing his energy on his ring, he called out a warning to Sky.

"Stay here! I'll come back for you!"

"Stay safe," she replied. "I'll be waiting."

Sylas commanded the Light flowing through him to create a shield around his left arm. The shield of Light grew, lighting the area around him with a warm yellow glow.

The skeletal archer pulled back the string of his bow and loosed another arrow. The deadly point whistled through the night sky. Sylas raised his arm, blocking the arrow and sending it end over end before landing on the ground. His shield of Light rippled with energy, as if it were proud that it had just protected its master.

Pulling his sword from its sheath, he charged towards the skeleton, the Light within him demanding holy justice to be served.

The nearest skeleton raised its sword over its head and brought it down towards Sylas. He parried the blade with his shield, then swung in an arching motion with his sword at the skeletons head.

The skeleton brought its buckler up, blocking the blow. The second skeleton warrior arrived moments later and took a jab at Sylas's chest with the tip of its blade. Sylas twisted his shield, barely able to knock aside the skeleton's blow before being skewered.

Taking advantage of the double vision that his second mind gave him, he saw the first skeleton raise its sword high above its head and swing it down towards him again.

He raised his Light shield up and again forced the blade to bounce off it, this time adding in a burst of energy to the shield to push the sword away with additional force.

The sword flew from the skeletons hand and stuck into the ground several feet away, just as another arrow was loosed from the archer. Sylas jumped backward as the arrow flew past his face, the wind that it carried, creating an audible whistle through the air.

Realizing that he was quickly becoming overwhelmed, Sylas turned more towards the offensive. He brought his shield arm in towards his body, then throwing it outward in an arch, sent his shield forward as a projectile of Light. The Light sliced through the air towards the skeleton warriors in front of him.

The slashing beam of Light caught the skeleton on his right just below the chin, and sent it flying backward. The one on the left got hit directly in the chest, the Light singeing its bones then rippling through its body.

The skeleton took a weak step towards him then crumpled to the ground, the purple light that filled its sunken eye sockets flaring for just a moment before disappearing completely. The skeleton that had been hit under the chin began to slowly raise up off the ground, its head sitting slightly crooked on its neck.

Sylas focused a ball of energy into his left hand, pointing it towards the skeleton. Releasing the energy, he sent a beam of Light straight into its torso.

The Light slammed into the skeleton's body, sending bones scattering into the early morning air. Its skull landed on its side, the light in its eye sockets fading into oblivion.

Two down.

Taking a quick glance at the battle around him, Sylas quickly saw the severity of the situation. Although the warriors and mages of Gelendor were much more powerful and skilled than the skeletal army that was upon them, the sheer *number* of enemies that were flooding through the walls of the city were starting to overwhelm them.

Animated Tree Giants fell to the ground, swords and arrows tearing their bark and limbs to pieces. Other Tree Giants swung their branches at the horde, smashing their foes under their incredible strength, desperately trying to keep their ground amongst the seemingly endless waves of enemies.

The sound of metal on metal rang through the air as swords clashed against each other. Flashes of green light, mixed with the occasional crackle of thunder and lightning from Uthren sparked through the air as the mages of Gelendor defended their home with powerful Magick.

Sylas caught a glimpse of Torren, surrounded by sword-wielding skeletons. His body glowed with Light Magick as Samara stood behind him, protecting him with her shields while casting the occasional beam of Light at approaching enemies.

Sylas turned his attention back at the skeleton archer in front of him. It had already nocked another arrow and was aiming its bow straight at him.

Allowing the element of Light to give him suggestions, he called to remembrance the feeling of moving through space at blinding speed when being teleported by Uthren. Sylas then cocked his sword into a jabbing position just as the arrow was shot in his direction.

Moments before the arrow reached his location, he allowed the Light Magick flowing within him to flood over his body, as a pillar of Light descended from the sky and engulfed him. Less than a second later, the Light dissipated, and he found himself standing behind the archer.

Thrusting his sword forward, he pierced the skeleton through the back of its rib cage and pulled his sword through its spine, separating the skeleton into two halves. The bones fell to the ground in a heap, the wispy purple light that gave it life fading into the darkness.

Sylas smiled at his success, taking in a deep breath of the cold night air. His moment of victory was cut short, however, as another terrifying roar rippled through the air.

The skeletal dragon had left the ground and was now flying towards the army of Gelendor, its bony jaws open wide as it produced a dark purple, almost black jet of flame from its maw.

The flames set a group of Gelendor defendants ablaze, burning their bodies to a crisp in an instant. After their bodies fell to the ground, Sylas saw the dark mage who was riding the undead dragon hold out a lantern in front of him.

The lantern glowed an eeire purplish green color, the light fleeing from glass panes connected by a metal outer rim. A long, metal chain linked the tip of the lantern to a small saddle that the mage was sitting in.

He held his hand in the air, palm facing towards the sky as a dark purple and green orb appeared in his hand. Then, to Sylas's horror, each of the warriors and mages who had been struck by the black flame of the dragon had a wispy white light exit their crumpled bodies and fly slowly through the air. Upon reaching the lantern, the lights were violently sucked into its dark glass one by one, each making the lantern glow slightly brighter as they entered.

Frozen in terror, Sylas watched as the dragon carrying the dark mage jumped into the sky and circled towards another group of warriors. It once again opened its jaws and spewed a dark flame upon them. The mysterious lantern glowed in delight as additional souls were sucked into its eerie frame.

Sylas nearly dropped his sword in shock, his vision catching the sight of skeletons pouring through the gaping hole in the outer walls of the city.

His heart fell into his stomach as he watched the city he had grown to love being destroyed right in front of him. A chill ran up his spine as he suddenly recognized the scene from the vision he'd had in the crypt.

It wasn't Shilvrst I saw in my vision… It was Gelendor!

Several of the stone ground floor buildings began to crumble as the heat of the dark flames consumed their foundations, the crumbling sound being muffled by the war cries of the ensuing battle.

Suddenly, a sharp pain flared in Sylas's leg as he watched a building fall. He looked down at his leg and to his horror, saw an arrow protruding from his calf.

Spinning around, he watched as two more skeletons with bows walked slowly towards him, each nocking another arrow. Sylas winced as he shifted his weight off his injured leg and quickly conjured a shield of Light around his left arm and held it out in front of him. The skeletons shot their arrows, which struck his shield of Light and bounced off landing several feet to the side.

Gathering his courage, Sylas reached down and grabbed the arrow by the shaft. Taking in several deep breaths, he pulled on the arrow as hard as he could. The arrow came out partially, but its head was still embedded in his leg, the wound now much larger than it had been before.

Screaming, he dropped down to one knee in pain. As his concentration on the shield of Light broke, the glow it produced faded away into the night. He looked back up towards the archers, terror filling his eyes as he watched them nock additional arrows to fire at him. Two more skeletons with swords and shields that had heard his cry began running towards him, evil dripping from their eyes.

Sylas tried once more to pull the arrow from his leg, but once again only succeeded in causing himself more pain and making the wound worse.

His vision started to get starry as pain coursed up his leg and throughout his body. *This is how it ends...* he thought to himself, as he gave one final effort to pull the arrow free. He wrapped his hands around the shaft as close to his leg as possible and with all of his strength, pulled outward. The arrow slid out of his leg with a sickening *Thwuck*, blood spurting out of his leg onto the grass.

About to faint from pain and exhaustion, Sylas ignored the fact that he was about to be struck by oncoming skeletons and poured healing energy into his hand, then placed it on his wound. An instant relief replaced the pain in his leg as the Magick mended and stitched his muscle and skin back together.

Exhausted from all that had happened, his eyes and hands stopped glowing as his second mind was forced closed.

"Sylas! Watch out!"

Sylas turned his head to see Samara running towards him, her hands outstretched. The two skeleton warriors fell upon him with their swords raised high, then slashed them down at his head.

He raised his hand to attempt to block the blows, but to his relief, an orb of Light appeared around him, bouncing the swords aside. Sylas watched as the shield then changed shapes around him and shot outward as four separate beams, each one striking a different attacking skeleton in the chest. The Light made a loud *bang* and flashed brightly as it hit, sending piles of bones flying through the air.

Samara kneeled on the ground next to Sylas. "Are you alright? I heard you scream and got here as fast as I could. What happened?"

Pushing himself to his feet, Sylas shook his head in an attempt to clear the stars from his vision.

"I'm alright. I got shot in the leg with an arrow and tried to pull it out. It drained my energy pretty bad. Where's Torren? Is he alright?"

"A bunch of skeletons ran past us and started running through the city. Torren took off after them. Sylas… it- it looked like they were *searching* for something…"

Sylas's eyes grew wide, the hair on his neck standing on end. "The amulet… Samara, we can't let them get it!"

"Torren told me to find you. He said he was going to go into the city and would try to lead the people away from the skeletons and keep them safe. Sylas, what should we do?"

"We have to find Nydria. We need to get the amulet from her and go before it's too late!"

Animated trees fell, blasts of dark purple, almost black flames consumed everything in its wake. Gelendor was falling…

Samara nodded, tears in her eyes as she took Sylas by the hand. She was about to start running towards the Great Tree to find Nydria when something caught her eye.

"Geode!"

Sylas spun around to see where she was looking. Geode was standing in front of the dragon with his hands held high above his head. His eyes and hands were glowing with the power of Nature Magick as he brought both arms down towards his side.

Several bright circles of white light appeared in the sky, like glowing orbs of moonlight. With a bright flash, beams of moonlight descended from the circles, carrying orbs of energy down with them. The moonbeams killed a dozen skeletons that were surrounding him, a much larger beam striking the dragon in the head. The dragon reared back in pain, sending a jet of dark flames towards Geode.

The green glow disappeared from Geode, and in a motion almost too quick to see, Geode brought his hands to his chest and made two symbols in quick succession. Sylas thought that one of them he might have recognized, but the other he'd never seen before. A light brown, sandy color filled Geode's hands and eyes, and he twisted his body with a corkscrew motion, sinking into the earth and disappearing into the ground.

Moments later, two pillars of what looked like rock shot up from the ground, one under the dragon striking it in the chest and throwing it up into the air, the other shooting Geode high into the air.

The brown glow faded, and Geode once again brought his hands together in the symbol of Nature. As the green glow met his hands and eyes, he brought his hands up above his head and sent another large moonbeam down towards the dragon.

The dark mage riding the dragon jumped off as the moonbeam struck. The dragon roared as the powerful blast sent the undead beast slamming into the ground. A burst of moonlight boomed across the battlefield. Sylas could feel the power of the blast even from where he was standing.

The boney dragon let one last muffled roar escape its throat as the purple light in its eyes slowly faded away. Geode and the dragon's rider stood across from each other, the powerful glow of different Magicks flowing around their bodies.

The dark mage looked at his now dead dragon for a moment, then back to Geode. He walked over to the dragon and raised a glowing purple hand in the air. A large wispy white orb exited the crumpled dragon and was forced into the thirsting lantern, making it glow brightly. He then pulled his hood off his head and let it fall back on his shoulders. His eyes glowed with the purple color of Darkness Magick as he raised his hands in preparation to fight.

Geode brought his hands out in front of him, making the symbol of Fire as his eyes turned from green to red. He flexed his biceps, screaming into the air as his muscles grew exponentially. His powerful legs pushed off the ground as he charged towards his enemy.

The dark mage threw his hands out in front of him, several shadowy figures appearing around Geode. In unison, each of the shadows pointed a finger towards Geode and shot beams of Darkness Magick towards him.

Geode crossed his arms in front of his chest and a sphere of red flames appeared around him. The beams of Darkness struck the flaming sphere, growing dark before dissipating. Geode then threw his arms outward, exploding the shield with a fiery vengeance towards his enemy.

Pulling his hands back into a symbol that Sylas didn't recognize, his eyes faded from red to sandy brown once more. Geode once again twisted his arms and sunk into the earth.

A second later, Geode exploded from the ground, a fist that looked to have chunks of hardened sand surrounding it flying at the dark mage's face.

The dark mage disappeared from his original position, leaving a shadowy figure in its place as his body traded places with one of his previous shadows, dodging both the fiery explosion, as well as the deadly fist of Geode.

The dark mage waved his hands in front of him, conjuring what looked to be a dark, spectral door. Grabbing the door by the handle, he opened it, revealing a dark dimension room like the one that Sylas had been transported to while in the crypt. He closed the door behind him, disappearing from view.

Geode waited, his eyes and hands still glowing sandy brown. Finally, a new door opened up behind him. Stepping out of the door, the dark mage was now holding a two-handed sword with a dark, black blade. Geode slammed the ground with his foot, and a large chunk of earth floated up behind him. Taking two short steps forward, then punching towards the dark mage, the rock and earth flew at the mage's location.

The dark mage again flared his arms outward, creating shadowy images of himself and teleported to one of them, allowing the rock to fly through a shadow instead of himself.

Geode and the dark mage continued exchanging blow after blow of advanced Magick, both of them seeming to be on the same level of expertise. Geode continued showing mastery of several elements, even combining them into colors and effects that Sylas had never seen before, while the dark mage used purely Darkness Magick.

"He'll be fine, Sylas, we need to go!" Samara said, grabbing his hand.

Sylas struggled to pull his eyes away from his mentor, but finally agreed and let Samara take him by the hand as they ran towards the center of the city.

The battle raged on as they ran, the sound of swords clanking, warriors screaming, and thunder crackling filled the air. The crashing of living trees swinging their large branches at their enemies echoed with the cries of war and fear from both those who were fighting and those who were fleeing, sending chaos throughout the night. The warning bells in the city continued to chime loudly, adding to the chaos.

Several groups of skeletons had made it into the inner parts of the city now, running through houses and climbing up the towering trees to the higher levels of the city in search of their objective. Sylas hated to run past them instead of stopping to help, but he knew that it was *essential* that he find the amulet first.

The sun began to poke up from the horizon as he and Samara ran for the Great Tree, signifying that it was much later into the night than he had initially thought. Its warm orange glow splashed against the cloudy horizon, spreading its light onto the city.

The long stone bridge came into view as Sylas and Samara rounded a street corner. Several rows of warriors stood with spears and shields raised at the ready, a line of men and women in battle mage robes standing behind them.

Nydria sat upon a large brown horse at the very back, her eyes and hands glowing green with Magick. Upon seeing Samara and Sylas, Nydria kicked at her horse and closed the distance between them.

"I knew you would come here. Where are the others?" She asked.

"Geode and Uthren are fighting in the front lines," Sylas responded. "Torren is somewhere in the city trying to fend off the skeletons that have broken off from the main army."

Nydria quickly removed the amulet from around her neck and held it out towards Sylas. "You need to take this and *leave*. Get your friend and your mentors and go before anything happens to you. From what my guards tell me, it doesn't look good for our city. You must continue your quest and obtain all of the stones so that you can defeat Maelos! We will keep the armies of the dead occupied as long as we can so that you can make your escape, but you must go now!"

Sylas grabbed the amulet from Nydria, hesitating for a moment. "Nydria, we-"

"That's an order, Sylas! If Maelos gets ahold of that amulet, there's no telling what evil and destruction he will be able to amass upon Evendreil. With it, we have a *chance*. I'm sorry that I did not listen to you when you first approached me. That is a mistake that I must take responsibility for. But you must not let my mistake cost us our one chance at victory!"

Sylas held the amulet in front of him, staring into the cold purple light of the Stone of Darkness in its center. "Come on. Let's find Torren then get Uthren and Geode and go!"

"Before you go," Nydria said, letting the glow of Magick fade from her eyes. "The Stone of Nature… It's *here* in Gelendor. You won't have time to retrieve it now, but I pray that by the grace of the Great Tree and the Gods above we will be able to fend off this attack so that you can come back one day and obtain it. If I'm not here when that day arrives, I need you to know where it is."

Nydria jumped off her horse and approached Sylas. Placing her lips next to his ear, she proceeded to whisper to him the location of the stone.

"Keep that a well-guarded secret, Sylas. That knowledge is meant for the royal family of Gelendor alone. I ask that you only share it if it becomes *absolutely* necessary, and if so, only to those whom you trust completely. Can I count on you?"

Sylas nodded, "You can count on me! We'll come back some day and get the Nature Stone. I won't let you down!"

"Thank you, Sylas," Nydria said, returning to her horse. "Now go. Find your party and leave. As for me, I ride into battle. I won't let Gelendor be overtaken so easily!"

Her eyes and hands flared green as she made the symbol of Nature and kicked at her horse. Her guards ran to her side, then they all took off towards the main battle.

Sylas placed the amulet around his neck, tucking it under his shirt. "Right. Torren first, then Uthren and Geode. Then we get our things and leave."

Without any warning, Samara threw her arms around Sylas.

"I'm scared, Sylas! I don't want to die!"

Sylas held her for a moment before pulling away, "I *won't* let you die. I swear it! We need to go now, though, before it gets too late. The sun is already starting to rise, we'll need as much cover as we can get if we are going to escape without being seen."

****

They ran from house to house, searching for Torren with no success. *Where could he be!?* Sylas thought to himself as he ran into another house, finding it empty. Just as he exited the abandoned home, he heard Samara scream, "Sylas! Sylas help!"

He ran towards Samara's voice, pumping all of his energy into his legs. *Please be okay, Torren. Please be okay!*

He ripped around a corner and jumped over several skeleton bodies. His eyes fell on Samara kneeling on the ground next to someone, several others standing in a semi-circle around them.

"No!" Sylas cried out in agony as he slid on his knees next to Samara. It wasn't until then that he noticed that her eyes and hands were glowing with Light Magick. Several dozen dismembered skeletons lay strewn across the ground around Torren, who had a giant wooden spear protruding from the right side of his chest. He was still breathing, but it was in small, sharp breaths.

"He-y bud-dy," Torren said, coughing out the words.

"Torren, I said, be quiet! Don't Talk!" Samara said, tears running down her face as she continued to pour healing Magick into Torren's chest.

"Sylas, hurry! We need to get this spear out of him. I- I need your help! I can't do it on my own!"

Choking back the tears, Sylas made the symbol of Light and opened his second mind. "Don't even *think* about it, Torren!"

Torren let out a choking laugh, wincing at the pain. "Th-ink a-bout wh-at?"

"Can you save him?" A girl standing next to him asked, her voice just as distraught as Samara's.

Sylas placed his hands on the shaft of the spear, ignoring her completely. Just as he was about to pull up on the spear, a man standing next to the girl he had ignored stopped him. "Wait! Let me pull it out, then you can be ready to heal him as fast as possible."

The man was large and burly, definitely much stronger than Sylas was. He remembered the incident where he tried to pull the arrow out of his calf with several unsuccessful attempts and decided that might be the best idea. Sylas nodded and allowed the man to kneel down next to him.

"Alright, on three, then," the man said, wrapping his hands around the shaft of the spear. "This is going to hurt, my boy. One. Two. Three!"

The man pulled up hard on the spear, which exited Torren's chest with a sickening *Slunk.* Torren screamed, then instantly fell unconscious as the spear left his chest. Sylas and Samara quickly placed their hands on the wound, trying to stop the blood from exiting as they poured their Light Magick into him.

Sylas focused intently on aligning his desires with his second mind to heal Torren. *He's a protector of the innocent... He's a good and just person... He's my best friend, he* deserves *to be healed!*

He repeated the words over and over again in his mind as he poured his energy into the wound. It took much longer than any other injury that he had healed, but eventually, with the help of Samara, the muscles and skin around the wound started to glow with a soft yellow light and slowly started to weave themselves together.

After a few minutes, the blood stopped pouring from the wound and a large scar formed as his skin finished pulling itself together. Sylas and Samara removed their hands from Torren and let the Light Magick fade away. The man placed his hand behind Torren's head and lifted him up slightly. The girl standing nearby kneeled down next to him and with tears streaming down her face called out to him.

"Torren?"

Torren cracked an eye open and gave a faint smile, “Hey guys.”

Tears filled her eyes, and a cry left her lips as she wrapped her arms around the large man next to her. The large man looked at both Samara and Sylas with admiration and thanks.

“How do you know Torren?” Sylas asked, still confused as to why these random people were acting so emotionally towards Torren’s near death.

Wiping away her tears, the girl stopped embracing the man and explained. “Sorry, my name is Ahri. Torren and I went out together last night. You must be Sylas and Samara, he told me so much about both of you. And this is my father, Jhort.”

“Torren saved our lives,” Jhort said, still looking at Sylas. “We would have been dead for sure if it weren’t for him. I may look big, but I’m not a fighter. We owe our lives to him.”

His eyes bounced back and forth between Ahri and Jhort, it was no wonder that Torren was so nervous to go out with her… she was easily on par with Samara in beauty.

Sylas shook his head, “Torren, Nydria gave us the amulet and told us we need to leave. We need to find Uthren and Geode and go! Can you walk?”

He sat up slightly, looking at Sylas intensely, “Isn’t there a stone here? That’s the whole reason we came here. We can’t leave without getting it.”

“Yeah, it’s here. Nydria told me where it was, but we don’t have time to get it. We’ll have to come back for it later.”

Torren shook his head, "How do you plan on coming back if the city is overthrown? That's going to be a bit hard, don't you think?"

Sylas pondered the question. Torren was right… If the city was overthrown, how would they get back in? It was hard enough getting in and out of Shilvrst with Maelos guarding the place, Gelendor would be an entirely different story.

"Well, what do you suggest we do then!?"

Torren looked at Ahri, then his eyes met Sylas's, "My father taught me about war, about what happens when a city is first taken over. In this case, they're definitely here looking for something specific. When they aren't able to find it, Maelos is going to be ticked. Things will get really bad, like *Shilvrst* bad or even worse. But because *we* know where it is, we'll have hope that we can bring to the people. The people here will *need* that hope Sylas. They'll need to know that help is coming, that they still have a chance. Otherwise… this place is going to turn out like Shilvrst… and I can't let that happen. Not here. I'm going to stay."

Samara and Sylas both protested, but Torren raised his hand in defiance.

"Listen to me! I can help the people here survive through all of this. I can strike up a rebellion or something so that we have a way to fight from the *inside*. Let me stay here. Let me help this city by letting them know that there's a *plan* and that there's someone out there who's collecting the stones and is going to defeat Maelos someday. They'll *need* that reassurance, or this town will turn into what Shilvrst has become, a place of broken people struggling to survive and unwilling to fight back. Uthren will know what to do, and if you're going to have to come back for the Nature Stone, you're going to need one of us on the inside to help with that."

Sylas listened to his best friend speak, knowing that he was right but not wanting to agree. He kicked a skeleton's dismembered arm in frustration, "You're right… I hate to admit it, but I think that you should stay."

"Sylas, no! We can't leave Torren here!" Samara cried. "He could die! We just saw him *almost* die! What would've happened if we weren't here?"

"We can tell Geode to stay as well," Sylas replied. "We'll go back to the battlefield, grab our things, and tell Uthren and Geode the plan. Geode can stay here with Torren, and Uthren will come with us. That way he'll have someone else here to help protect him."

Samara glared between her two friends before throwing her arms around Torren. She cried on his shoulder for a moment and told him repeatedly that he had better not be *stupid* and make sure he stays safe. Torren returned the hug and assured her that he would be fine. Sylas tried to not let the tears welling up in his eyes escape, but they defiantly broke free and rolled down his cheeks. Torren held out his hand towards his best friend, which Sylas clasped. They brought themselves together and embraced as friends and as brothers.

"I'll be alright, Sylas. You watch out for yourself, too. I feel like I'm actually the one taking the safe road by staying here. I've lived under Maelos's bondage almost my whole life. Who knows what trouble you're going to run into out there? Now go, you'd better hurry and leave before it's too late."

Sylas released the embrace, wiping the tears from his face. "Right, let's go."

Sylas and Samara gave one last goodbye as they ran from their friend back towards the battlefield.

****

Skeletons crawled through the outer buildings of the city in waves. The armies of Gelendor were being driven back, the endless swarm of the undead army too much for them to handle.

Sylas jumped over fallen townsfolk, then caught sight of Uthren running through the streets.

"Uthren! Over here!"

Uthren turned from his original trajectory and ran towards Sylas. Sylas could tell that something was wrong as he approached them.

"Sylas, Samara, where's Torren? We need to leave the city! Nydria told me that she gave you the amulet. We need to go before we're caught!"

"We know, we were looking for you. But Torren… he- isn't coming…"

Uthren looked worriedly at Sylas, "What do you mean he isn't coming?"

Sylas quickly explained their situation and what Torren had told them. He also added that they were going to ask Geode to stay with him and that he had Ahri and Jhort watching out for him as well.

"That's a mighty foolish decision to make on your own," Uthren responded angrily. "But I agree that it could be to our advantage to do it this way. Very well, you two get your things. I'll find Geode and let him know. Meet me at the place where we first teleported into the city, it isn't far from the west gate where we can make our escape."

Uthren ran towards the heat of the battle, as Sylas and Samara ran towards where they had begun the fight, to find their packs.

The sun was now mostly in the sky, shedding its light upon the city. Buildings were vacant and broken, many of them ablaze with a dark flame conjured by the now dead bone dragon. Bodies lay strewn across the ground, some of them ordinary townsfolk trying to escape the madness, others those who were brave enough to try and defend their homes. Bones from countless slain skeletons covered the ground in stinking heaps.

Before reaching his pack, Sylas used his ring to call out to Sky, "Sky, are you still safe? Are you still where I left you?"

A moment of silence proceeded, but the tension was finally broken by a timid, "Yes, I'm still safe. I'm scared."

"I'm coming. Are you still near my bag where I left you?"

"Yes." She responded.

"Hold on. I'll be there soon!"

They arrived at their packs just as a loud crash sounded in the distance. Sylas picked up his bag and told Sky to make herself visible.

"It's crazy out here right now, no one is going to notice you with us, it will be easier for me to keep track of you if I can see you."

Sky faded into view as Sylas spoke, shaking with fear as she walked towards him. He gently patted her head to try to comfort her, then looked towards the sound of the crash. A giant pillar of ice had slammed into one of the vacant buildings in the distance.

Geode stood atop the roof of a different building just behind the pillar of ice, his eyes and hands emitting a blue glow. Sylas assumed from the colors and from the giant icicle embedded in the building that he must be in a state of using some sort of Water Magick.

"How many elements does he know?" Sylas said out loud. He remembered that Geode had said that he was proficient with all the elements, Darkness being the one he was the worst at, but he didn't think that meant that he was good enough use all of them when it came to life and death!

Sylas watched as Geode changed elements once again, his eyes and hands glowing bright red. He jumped from the top of the roof where he was standing and slid down the icicle towards the dark mage.

Sylas couldn't believe how long the battle between these two masters had gone on. He thought for sure that Geode would have overtaken him by now, especially with the dragon no longer being in the fight.

The dark mage was still holding his massive black sword. Glowing white runes were now visible, running down the wide part of the blade. He raised his hands up and conjured a shadow clone just off to Geode's right. Sylas had seen him do this many times throughout the beginning parts of their battle and assumed that shortly after, he would see the dark mage teleport to the new position to try and get off a quick sneak attack.

Geode must have anticipated it as well, as he turned his body towards the shadowy clone, predicting the teleport that the mage would do moments before it happened.

"He's got him!" Sylas yelled out to Samara.

Timing his attack so that it would hit just as the dark mage made his teleport, Geode raised a fiery fist and threw it at the face of the shadow clone. The fist flew forward with powerful vengeance… then passed through the shadow harmlessly…

Behind him, another shadow appeared, which was quickly replaced by the dark mage himself. Geode was slightly off balance from throwing his fist through the shadowy image and stumbled slightly to retain his footing. He was slow to turn and defend himself from the awkward positioning.

A dark, menacing black blade shot through the air with blinding speed, striking Geode in the chest. The blade exited his back with a spray of blood.

"NO!" Sylas screamed in horror. He watched in terror as the dark mage twisted the blade with a vicious hatred, then yanked the sword out of Geode's chest. Geode struggled to stay on his feet, the red glow around his hands and in his eyes fading rapidly. The dark mage raised his leg and kicked Geode in the stomach, sending him to the ground.

"Geode!" Sylas screamed again, trying to run towards his mentor.

Samara quickly grappled him and held him at bay. "Sylas, no! We can't help him. He's gone," she said in a choked voice. "There's nothing we can do. We have to leave!"

Sylas struggled for a moment longer against Samara but eventually stopped as he watched the scene continue to unfold in agony.

The dark mage retreated a short distance to where his fallen dragon lay and swung his sword at the chain connecting the lantern to its saddle. Hoisting the lantern into the air, he slowly walked towards Geode's fallen body. Tears ripped themselves from Sylas's eyes as he watched Geode struggle to raise his head up off the ground.

Upon reaching him, the dark mage ruthlessly placed his foot upon the gaping hole in Geode's chest, then lifting his sword into the air, stabbed it down into Geode's stomach and removed his foot from his chest.

Geode gave one last heroic effort to rise from the ground but was stopped by a quick kick to the face. A dark sphere formed in the evil man's hand as Geode's body gave up and slumped to the ground.

The dark mage pulled his hand downward, then slowly lifted it into the air. A white, wispy object floated slowly up out of Geode's corpse, glowing brightly in the morning light. The white light floated towards the lantern, then was violently sucked into its evil frame. The lantern glowed in delight as another soul was added to its dark collection.

Sylas fell to his knees, tears continuing to stream down his face. Samara knelt down beside him, her breath choking in her lungs. They watched together as the dark mage pulled his sword out of Geode's lifeless body and walked further into the city.

"Sylas," she squeaked. "Sylas, I'm so, so sorry… but we need to go. We need to get out of here before we're all killed."

She helped him to his feet, taking him by the hand and leading him towards the wall to meet Uthren. They didn't have to wait long for him to show up.

"Where were you!?" Sylas exclaimed angrily as Uthren arrived. "You were supposed to find Geode! You could have helped him! We watched him die, and you weren't even there!"

Uthren spoke in a soft tone, trying to calm Sylas. "I was headed that way when I saw Torren charging towards the battle. I stopped him and gave him further instructions for staying in the city. He was going to run into the battle, so I had to convince him that it was already lost, and he needed to hide until the mayhem was over."

Uthren's voice began to quiver, the usually strong man now looking as frail as Sylas had ever seen him. "I- I didn't reach Geode until it was already too late…"

A single tear fell from the old man's eye as he looked at Sylas. "I saw him fall… I could have, should have been there for him… I let my friend down tonight, and I let the darkness win…"

From an unknown source, Uthren seemed to gain additional strength, "I won't let anything happen to you though. We'll mourn our losses later, but now we have to move!"

Sylas breathed heavily through his tears, his anger and sadness peaking. Following Uthren, the three of them took off together through the western gates of the city, across the grassy valley, and into the surrounding forest.

CHAPTER 13
SINDMYR

Sylas's eyes stung from the salt of his tears. His heart ached and his lungs burned as he ran away from Gelendor, descending deeper and deeper into the surrounding forest. The sounds of war slowly faded away with the distance that he put between him and the city as they ran.

The image of the black blade of the dark mage's sword piercing his friend and mentor Geode played relentlessly in his mind over, and over, and over again. Part of him couldn't believe it, he hadn't *actually* seen what he saw... Surely, Geode and Torren would appear behind them shortly, running into the forest for safety.

Chills ran up his back as he recalled the dark mage pulling what seemed to be Geode's soul from his body and trapping it inside of that awful lantern. Thoughts of Torren crossed his mind as well, now coming to terms with the fact that his best friend was trapped inside of a falling city, with no Geode to protect him. Uthren had assured him that he had given Torren ample instructions for staying safe until the city finally surrendered. Still, he worried about the possibility of the evil attackers not taking prisoners and just killing everyone in the city.

They turned towards the south and continued to run through the trees for the better part of the morning, slowing to a walking speed to catch their breath, then picking the pace back up to a jog.

Finally, Uthren signaled that they had put a good amount of distance between them and Gelendor and that they could stop and rest.

Sylas dropped his bag on the ground, collapsing near a large rock. His mind spun; his heart ached. His breathing wouldn't calm down, even after he'd stopped moving. Sky sensed his sorrow and curled herself into a ball in his lap for comfort. Her presence brough instant relief. As he stroked her head and back, he saw a faint glow emanate from his ring as she spoke to him.

"I'm so sorry for your loss… I know what it feels like to lose someone like family. Geode seemed like a good man."

"He was a good man. He was a *great* man," he responded in a choked voice. "He didn't deserve to die, *especially* not like that. And Torren… He's still stuck in Gelendor. Who knows what his fate will be..."

She stood up in his lap and placed her front paws on his chest, putting her face right next to his just like the time they first met. Sylas stared into her bright shining eyes and felt a wave of comfort rush over him as she spoke."

"You helped me when all seemed lost, and now, it's my turn to help you. Are you going to be alright?"

Sylas breathed in sharply at the question. He knew that *eventually* he would be okay, but right now, he didn't see how that day would come. Geode was more than just a mentor and a friend. The time that they had spent together almost made him feel like family. He was like an uncle to him or something of the sort. It made it even worse that he had to witness the horrible way that he died. He'd never been super active in the religion he'd been taught growing up, but he did know about the afterlife. *Would Geode's soul be able to make it to the heavens? Or would it be stuck forever in that awful lantern?* The thought made him sick to his stomach, so he dismissed it.

"I'll be okay eventually. Thanks, Sky. At least we still have each other, right?"

Sky licked his face with her dark black tongue. "Right, and we still have Uthren and Samara. Torren is a smart boy, I have no doubt that you will still have him too, and that you will be reunited someday."

Sylas was truly appreciative of the bond that Magick had helped him create with Sky. He looked through his tears over at Uthren, "Uthren, did you see what that dark mage was doing with that lantern?"

Uthren sat on the ground several yards off to his right, his head bent forward and his face in the palms of his hands. He looked up and over at Sylas, wiping the tears from his face as he spoke.

"I did. It was an abomination! A truly evil, dark, abhorrent…" His words cut off as he placed his face back into his palms.

Sylas stood up and walked over towards Uthren, carrying Sky in his arms. He sat down on the ground next to him and placed Sky gently on the grass.

"I'm sorry for getting angry at you this morning," Sylas said, picking at the grass in front of him. "It hurt me a lot to see Geode die, and I wished that I could have helped him somehow. I know that you would have done anything you could to save him if you knew that was going to happen. I shouldn't have blamed you. It probably hurts you even more than me… I know how close you and Geode were. I'm sorry."

Uthren took in a deep breath and let it out slowly before responding. "Thank you, Sylas. I worry about Geode's eternal soul… I hope to the Light that there will be a way to release him into the afterlife. I'm angry at myself that I did not make it to him in time…"

His voice changed slightly as he picked his head up from his hands, "I also worry that we had to leave Torren in the city without Geode there to help protect him. I do hope that the boy will be alright."

Samara walked over and joined them on the ground. She put a hand on Uthren's shoulder as she sat down, "So what's the plan now? Where do we go from here?"

It took him a moment to respond, the weight of sadness still bearing heavily upon his emotions. "I think that our next course of action is to head towards Sindmyr, the capital of Light."

His voice quivered as he spoke, "Not only is it the next closest major city that has not been taken over by Maelos, but it's also where I believe the Stone of

Light is located according to Sylas's latest vision. You said that there was a glowing stone inside of the large maul in the statue you saw, correct?"

Sylas nodded. "Yeah, it was inside of the head of the maul."

"I wouldn't have guessed it to be in such plain sight. Perhaps that it why it is there. The statue is of the original Light mage, Freyr. I'm sure that the high-ranking officials in the Council of Light long ago decided that it would be a safe place for the stone. It will be a long journey to the capital of Light, but we have experience in long journeys now, don't we? I would refrain from training in Magick for a while, Sylas. We don't want any mishaps while we are traveling that would let Maelos know the direction that we are going. The longer it takes for them to realize that the Stone of Darkness is not in Gelendor, the better chance we have of making it to Sindmyr without incident."

"Before we go…" Sylas said, standing up, "I want to have a service for Geode. I don't want to go on without first acknowledging his death and paying him respect."

Uthren rose to his feet and placed a hand on Sylas's shoulder. "Thank you, Sylas. I wouldn't have it any other way. I'll construct a small shrine in his remembrance, and we can do the service before we continue onward. You two can go searching for flowers or other items that you would like to place on the shrine. Take some time to contemplate the words you will say. I don't think we need to be worried about being in too much of a hurry right now. Take your time, do some meditation if you need, and try to find peace. Meet back here in an hour. We will then do the service, say our goodbyes, and continue our journey."

Sylas retreated from where they had stopped and headed towards a large hill as he searched for a quiet place to be alone and think. Memories of the many hilltops that he had climbed with Geode by his side ran through his head as he started up a nearby hill.

After reaching the top of the hill, Sylas looked back towards the city of Gelendor. He could see smoke rising up from the city and could still barely make out the spot in the outer wall that the enemies had broken through as their point of entry. "Stay safe, Torren," he said out loud. "I couldn't bear to lose you too."

He put a fist on his chest and with determination in his voice continued, "I swear, I'll do everything I can to avenge your death, Geode. Maelos will *pay* for the countless lives that he's taken, for the families he's ripped apart, the dreams and hopes that he's torn from the innocent. I'll continue my training until I'm a master like you were. I won't stop until I've mastered all the elements! I never quit until we've collected all the stones! I'll open the Vault of Kings and use whatever is inside to stop Maelos once and for all!"

Sylas sat down on the grass next to a small bush as he let himself release his emotions. He let his tears carry the sadness and despair from his eyes, screamed out his anger and hatred for Maelos and his henchmen, and heavily breathed out his fear and anxiety. Physically and emotionally drained, he laid down on the grass and closed his eyes. Sleep quickly overtook his exhausted body, and his mind entered the world of dreams.

****

Sylas cracked his eyes open, the sound of lapping water gently reaching his ears. He found himself lying on a beach, the sky darkened with thick gray and black clouds that covered the entire sky. A vast ocean stretched out before him, waves gently swaying back and forth at his feet. The sun was low in the sky, just above the horizon, yet its light was considerably dimmed by the endless waves of clouds.

The sun shone a dim white behind the dark clouds, casting a strange, silvery light across the land, giving everything in sight a silver hue. Massive black pillars of rocks protruded from the ocean in front of him arching in twisted, chaotic patterns, creating otherworldly formations.

Sylas looked around him and noted that it wasn't just the sun that appeared silver; *everything* around him appeared to be set on a grayscale, as if the entire world had lost all color except for gray, white, silver, and black.

Extremely disoriented, Sylas tried to remember what had happened just before seeing this scene in front of him. *How did I get here? Where was I before this? What was I doing previously?* All these questions went unanswered in his mind, but their importance seemed completely irrelevant. The only thing that seemed to matter was that he was here, and it seemed as if it was where he was meant to be.

He shrugged his shoulders and walked along the beach, exploring his new surroundings. The silvery glow from the sun along the waters was beautiful to behold. Even though everything was dark and somewhat eerie, this world had a very strange beauty to it. The gentle lapping of the water against the sandy shore reached his ears, and he realized how quiet everything was. Besides the water and the soft sounds of his feet hitting the sand, there was no sound at all. Typically, a scene like this would have been terrifying, but this was different… this was calm, peaceful, and beautiful in its own way.

Sylas continued walking along the beach, admiring the jagged rock formations that spewed forth from the water and surrounding shoreline, until he saw a man off in the distance. He was lying face down in the sand, not moving at all.

The man had long unkempt gray hair that flowed down to his shoulders. He was skinny and frail and appeared to not have eaten anything for days. He wore old rags that were dirty and torn.

Sylas knelt, turning the man over onto his back. Wrinkles covered his face and around his eyes, showing his old age.

The man opened his eyes and looked up at Sylas. He lifted one hand towards him, grabbing him by the shoulder in a surprisingly strong grip, "Please, help me."

Sylas looked around for anyone nearby that could help, but there was no one. "What happened? Are you alright?"

As if the man hadn't heard his question, he again responded in a dry raspy tone, "Please, help."

Sylas suddenly had a remembrance of Light Magick flow into his mind. He brought his hands to his chest, but before he could complete the symbol of Light, he heard a powerful voice behind him.

"Sylas..."

The voice was deep and booming, it was as the voice of thunder, or of the great crashing of a waterfall. He spun around and saw a majestic figure looming behind him.

The figure had dark black wings that were outstretched as he floated in the air. He wore dark black robes from the waist down, with nothing on his torso, which revealed a muscular chest, arms, and abdomen. Seven small orbs were orbiting him slowly, glowing in different colors. His eyes glowed with a dark black and purple aura, sending fear straight into Sylas's soul. Sylas felt paralyzed in his terrifying presence, yet he gazed upon the figure with amazement and wonder.

"Sylas, this man in front of you is named Slovik. He is the father of Terrim, who is the one that killed your mentor, Geode."

A surge of rage and hatred coursed through Sylas as he turned from the angelic being in front of him back down to the cowering old man that laid at his feet. A remembrance of what had happened to Geode flooded back to his mind, sending anger and sadness flowing through him.

"Please." He said with a weak voice, "I mean no harm. I haven't done anything wrong!"

Sylas gritted his teeth in anger towards the man. "Your son killed my friend. He attacked an innocent city and killed women, and children, fathers and brothers. I watched helplessly as he took their very souls and trapped them inside an evil lantern!"

"Spare me! I beg you!"

"Sylas..."

The angelic voice boomed behind him again. Sylas turned towards the angel and saw that he had floated down from the air and was now standing next to him. The angel was tall and powerful, several feet taller than any mortal man could ever achieve. His arms looked strong enough that they could have ripped a tree right out of the ground without effort. A dark aura of light pulsed from him as he reached out a hand towards Sylas. Out of thin air, a dagger with a silver hilt and a dark black blade appeared in front of him, floating in the air at eye level.

"I am the Angel Erebus, God of Darkness. I rule over darkness, death, shadows, and this Realm of Darkness in which you now stand. I have brought you here to enact your vengeance."

Sylas looked at the dagger floating in front of him in the air and imagined plunging it into the chest of the man who laid before him. He wasn't directly responsible for Geode's death… but maybe his death would cause the one who *was* responsible the same grief that Sylas himself felt. Or perhaps the act would at least help him to feel justice for avenging Geode's death.

Anger continued to flow through him as he called to memory the sight of the man's son stabbing Geode with his dark bladed sword and then pulling his soul into the evil lantern that he held.

Sylas reached out and plucked the dagger from the air. The metal hilt felt cold in his hand as he rotated it back and forth, the silvery light of the sun glinting off the dark blade.

"Enact your vengeance upon this man, whose son has caused yourself and others so much suffering. Assert your power and dominance over him."

The words of the angel entered with great force, tempting him to lash out in anger and release the sadness that was built up inside of him. Sylas turned towards the old man lying on the ground. He had his hands held above his head, a look of utter terror covering his face as he pleaded again.

"Please, spare me!"

Sylas breathed heavily, his emotions running wild. Memories of the past continued to flow into his mind, the stupor of thought caused by this strange place slowly fading away as his thoughts cleared, and his memory returned. A moment of clarity caused Sylas to hesitate, his heart now feeling slightly softer than before.

"Darkness is *power*, Sylas," the angel continued. "Power over those who are weak, and those who *deserve* to die. This man's son killed your friend, will you not answer by enacting vengeance upon him? Let your hatred for what he has done fuel your strength."

Dark thoughts flowed through his mind again, egging him on to extinguish the light that still lived within Slovik. *A life for a life…* It would feel so *good* to know that justice had been delivered, that the one who took Geode's life would suffer as he had suffered. He stared into the man's cowering eyes as he lifted the dagger above his head.

"No, please!" The man screamed. "Spare me!"

Sylas gritted his teeth, he felt energized as Darkness Magick seemed to flow through his body and mind, egging him on to proceed with the action. It taunted him and justified his actions, whispering sweet lies into his very soul. Sylas yelled and brought the dagger down towards Slovik.

"No!" Slovik screamed, his final moments flashing before his eyes. But to his dismay, the dagger stopped inches from his chest. Tears formed in Sylas's eyes as peered into the terror-filled eyes of the man. Sylas let out a choked breath of air as he threw the dagger to the side.

His conflicting emotions swam through his mind in chaotic patterns, but ultimately his conscience got the best of them. "No. It's not right. I won't do it."

Slovik breathed rapidly as he looked up at Sylas, a dim spark of hope in his eyes that his life would be spared.

"I'm sorry…" Sylas said, extending his hand to Slovik.

Confused but relieved that his life was not ending, he took Sylas's hand and was pulled to his feet. Sylas then turned towards the angel standing behind him.

"I won't kill him," he said, fear trembling in his voice at defying a God. "I don't need vengeance. Geode taught me that Darkness is not evil by nature, it's only evil when its *user* corrupts it, and uses it for evil purposes. I won't let myself become the same as Terrim, or Maelos. If I'm going to learn how to use Darkness to defeat evil, then I need to learn how to first resist the urge to use it for evil, or I'll become exactly what I want to defeat…"

Erebus stood motionless for several moments, his dark eyes piercing into Sylas as if he were enacting judgment upon him. Finally, the dark angel smiled and waved his hand towards Slovik, whose image faded away into nothingness.

"Well done, Sylas."

Erebus floated towards him and placed his hands on his head. A surge of energy flowed through Sylas as he spoke, "Light cannot exist without Darkness, neither can good exist without evil. There must be *opposition* in all things; however, each element can be used for both their good *and* evil purposes. May you continue to discover the hidden *good* that comes from the shadows."

Sylas felt as his second mind was being opened by the God of Darkness. A small, seemingly corrupted piece of him that he had not noticed before, but now was clearly visible, was slowly being pulled from his second mind. Like removing a thorn from your finger, the piece of him that the angel removed granted him instant relief, a relief that he did not know he needed. Then his vision faded away into nothingness.

****

Sylas awoke with a start. He was lying atop a green hill, the grass beneath him tickling his face. He sat up quickly and tried to focus his thoughts on what had just occurred. *Was that just a strange dream? Or did that really just happen?* The question repeated in his mind several times as he tried to collect his thoughts. Not knowing how much time had passed since he fell asleep and remembering that Uthren told them to meet back in one hour, Sylas pushed himself to his feet and headed back towards their original stopping point.

Uthren and Samara both sat with each other next to a large stone obelisk, Sky was sitting in Samara's lap, munching on some kind of treat that Samara had found.

"We've been waiting, Sylas," Uthren said, standing up. "Did you find the peace that you were looking for?"

Sylas hesitated for a moment before responding, "I think I might have had another vision…"

A look of alarm crossed both Uthren and Samara's faces, but before they could respond, Sylas quickly continued. "It's okay. This one felt, *different.* I don't think it came from the same place. In fact, it almost feels like… like maybe whatever was connecting me to Maelos might be *gone* now…"

Sylas could tell by the expressions on their faces that neither of them knew what he was talking about, so he went into more detail about what had happened in his dream. He told them about how it seemed like the God of Darkness was testing him, and how it seemed like he had passed the test. He concluded with the God of Darkness placing his hands on his head and seemingly taking out whatever it was that had entered him in the Ancient Crypt.

"I can't really explain it," he continued. "But if what you were saying is true, Uthren, that part of Maelos that was bound to me when I first touched the Stone of Darkness, I think it's gone. It *feel's* like it's gone. I think Erebus took it away. It almost seemed like he wanted to *help* me, to see if I was up to the task of finding all the stones and opening the vault. I almost wonder if all my visions have had parts in them that were not from Maelos, but from *him*, trying to give me hints to things…"

Uthren sat pondering for several minutes, trying to make sense of what Sylas had just told him.

"To be honest, Sylas, I have no idea what's going on with you and your visions. I didn't think that anything like this was even possible. Man hasn't directly communicated with the Gods since the time of the original Kings. If what you say is true, something miraculous is happening indeed. I guess we'll just have to see and let time tell what's truly happening. You are *sure* though that Maelos didn't see where you were during this last vision?"

Sylas nodded, "It's hard to explain how I know, but yes, I'm sure."

A look of relief crossed both Uthren and Samara's face. "Good, then let us have a moment to remember our friend, Geode."

Sylas watched as Uthren turned towards the stone obelisk that he had constructed. He picked up several flowers that he had collected from the valley and placed them at the base of the structure. The obelisk was made of a smooth, shiny type of stone and had a large square base that connected to a large, precisely cut, rectangular prism that extended several feet in the air. At the top of the prism, the four sides slanted inward until reaching a point at the top, creating a pyramid shape. The obelisk was about as tall as Sylas was, and by looking at it, you could tell that it was made with Nature Magick. On the front-facing side of the rectangular prism, glowing green letters shone, displaying the words: "Geode, the sun shined brighter because he was here."

"It's beautiful, Uthren," Sylas said as Samara followed Uthren's example and placed several flowers that she had collected at the base of the obelisk. "Is it alright if I say a few words?"

"Please do." He said, taking a few steps back away from the obelisk.

Sylas stepped forward and placed his hand on the face of the obelisk. Its surface was cold and smooth, the edges and curves of the stone cut to absolute perfection by the Magick that was used to build it.

"You taught me so many things, Geode… You taught me how important it is to give everyone the benefit of the doubt, and that good can be found in everything. You were a great example to me and a wonderful teacher. I promise that I won't let your sacrifice be in vain. I'll do everything in my power to bring light back to Evendreil and stop the darkness from spreading."

The words weren't coming as easily as he had hoped they would through his heightened emotions, so he decided to end it there and took a couple of steps backward towards Samara. Sky rubbed against his leg as he approached. He picked her up, receiving comfort from her presence.

Samara went next, placing her hand on the obelisk as she spoke. "Geode, I didn't know you for long, but for the time that I did know you, I knew that you had a kind and loving heart. You were big and strong on the outside, but on the inside, you were kind and loving and gentle. You helped me to feel safe while we were traveling. After that night when we were attacked, you would sit with me in my tent until I fell asleep, just to assure me that everything would be alright." Tears welled in her eyes as she talked. "You don't know how much that meant to me. Because of you, I knew I would always be safe… I knew I could depend on you to save us if we ran into trouble. May the afterworld be as kind to you as you were kind to this world. Farewell."

Samara wiped the tears from her eyes as she stepped away from the obelisk and back to Sylas's side. She wrapped her arms around his and pulled him in close for comfort. Sylas welcomed the gesture and added what little emotional strength he had to hers as he, Sky, and Samara all comforted one another.

Uthren then took his turn and placed his hand on the obelisk. "Geode, my friend. We've been through many things together. I was always sure that I would be the first one to go and that you would be the one saying words for me instead of I for you. You were always there for me. You always believed me even when others didn't, and supported me in my decisions, even when they were wrong. I'm sorry that when you needed me the most… I was not there for you."

Uthren pulled his hand from the obelisk and placed it over his face as he began to sob. He shrunk down to his knees and leaned his head against the obelisk for support. Sylas and Samara both knelt down beside him, wrapping their arms around him. Together, they all cried for their friend who was now gone.

Sylas wished that Torren could have been there to honor Geode with them. He knew how much Torren loved and respected him, and it made him sick to his stomach to know that Torren was still in danger back in Gelendor. *Why did he stay?* He continued to repeat the thought over and over as he, Samara, Sky, and Uthren sat huddled together under the physical representation of Geode's legacy.

After the service was over and emotions had settled down, Sylas and the others shouldered their packs in preparation for their journey towards Sindmyr. Sylas took the amulet out from under his shirt and stared into the black and purple stone that sat in its center. He couldn't put his finger on it, but somehow it looked different than it had before. Something about it seemed less dark and evil, and he seemed to understand its potential for good.

"Do you think we can do it?" Samara asked, walking up beside him. "Do you think we can find the rest of the stones and defeat Maelos?"

Sylas moved his finger along the amulet, feeling each of the indents where the other stones would fit, imagining himself placing a different glowing stone into each slot. He looked up at the horizon in the distance in front of him, knowing that the journey to Sindmyr would be just as treacherous and difficult, if not even more so, than the one that they had embarked on for Gelendor. He let the amulet fall back to his chest, this time allowing it to hang on the outside of his shirt so that it was no longer hidden, no longer a secret to the world.

"Not only are we going to find the rest of the stones, we're going to bring *hope* to Evendreil. A hope that even though we have been shrouded in darkness for the past ten years, assures everyone that the light is soon to come. We will be that light in the darkness, the light that tells everyone that we have the power that we need to stop him. Then, while that light spreads, we will collect all of the stones, open the Vault of Kings, and use whatever is inside to defeat Maelos. We weren't successful in Gelendor, but I won't let that happen again. Next time, we will bring the fight to Maelos, starting with Sindmyr…"

THE STORY CONTINUES IN…
THE VAULT OF KINGS: ALLIANCE

Authors Note:
Thank you so much for reading! I hope that you enjoyed jumping into the world of the Vault of Kings as much as I did writing it! If you liked the story, please consider giving it a review on Amazon. I am self-published, so everything you see here is all done by me. I don't have a marketing team, or a publishing company or anything like that to help get the word out about my story, so the only way for more people to get the chance to jump into my world is by word of mouth and seeing awesome reviews on Amazon. It helps out more than you'd think! Also, consider mentioning it to your friends!

If you want more from me, check out my website at MattTaylorBooks.com, and feel free to email me at MattTaylorBooks@gmail.com. I also have a YouTube channel linked on my website where I record myself reading my books and using AI to generate awesome images of the world of The Vault of Kings. Hope to see you in the next book! They just get better and better from here!

If you want to support me in my dream of becoming a full time author, one of the best ways is by checking out my Patreon at https://www.patreon.com/TheVaultofKings for exclusive access to secret stories and other awesome goodies.

ABOUT THE AUTHOR

Matt Taylor was born in 1992 in Southeast Idaho. As a child Matt always enjoyed telling stories and creating new games for his family and friends to play. His favorite books growing up were the Eragon series by Christopher Paolini and the Goosebumps series by R.L. Stine.

From May of 2011 – 2013 Matt Served an LDS mission for the Church of Jesus Christ of Latter-day Saints in the Florida, Orlando mission, speaking Spanish. In 2016 Matt graduated from Brigham Young University-Idaho with a bachelor's degree in computer information technology.

Matt began writing as a dream that he had always wanted to fulfill. In hopes of sharing his wild imagination and love for characters and stories with the world, he wrote The Vault of Kings, hoping that it would reach the hearts and creative minds of anyone who was willing to listen, and anyone who was ready to embark on the adventures of his mind.

For questions or feedback feel free to email MattTaylorBooks@gmail.com

www.ingramcontent.com/pod-product-compliance
Ingram Content Group UK Ltd.
Pitfield, Milton Keynes, MK11 3LW, UK
UKHW041953190726
13854UKWH00005B/1945

9 798349 246661